The Fall of America

OPERATION INSTANT FURY

Book 9

WR BENTON

LOOSE CANNON ENTERPRISES
Auburn, CA

ISBN 978-1-944476-91-5
Ingram Spark edition

Cover image by: Used with Permission
Author photos © Copyright 2008 Melanie D. Calvert-Benton
Edited by Bobbie La Cour and Daniel Williams
Logo fonts [*Shortcut, Dirty Ego*] by Eduardo Recife,
misprintedtype.com

www.loose-cannon.com

DEDICATIONS

To my friend, Robert Woods; Renowned actor, movie personality, and just an all around good man.

To my grandson, Levi Hollis, you're a special gift from God, son. Always remember you are loved and warmly welcomed into our family.

BOOK 9

OPERATION INSTANT FURY

CHAPTER 1

The explosion was loud and destructive. Bodies, parts of bodies, and various pieces of the building flew through the air, just missing two Russian soldiers. One of the soldiers saw a big truck, filled with cargo in the back, thrown high into the air. It landed upside down with an earsplitting crash and then erupted into flames. The contents of the vehicle was scattered all over the road. Then other debris began to fall, and with it a rain of ruddy blood splattered on the white sidewalk, with some striking the two frightened young Russians. A foot, still laced up in a dress shoe, fell and rolled toward the men. One of them turned his head and puked. Screams were heard, but the blast had been so loud that many could not hear at all as blood ran from their damaged ear drums. Smoke, dark black, filled the sky overhead and many fires on the street were burning out of control.

"W . . . what happened, Lev?"

"I think a bomb placed by the partisans just exploded or some fool caused this, maybe. Are you injured, my friend? I smelled nothing before the explosion, did you? By smell, I mean gas of any kind that a leak might give off."

"I am fine and have no injuries. No, I smelled nothing and I can't believe we were just eating in there and now, now, it's blown to hell and on fire! How many died in the mess, Captain? Huh? Why all the killing?"

The Captain knew his new friend was not experienced and this was his first time tasting combat of any sort. In a month, just thirty days, he'd change. Death and mutilations were common in this war with America. Lieutenant Vlalic Lavr was brand new and just off the plane earlier this morning. He was about six feet tall, auburn hair, pencil line reddish mustache; his intense and intelligent green eyes clashed with his bright white teeth. His dress and behavior was typical of all Russian officers; his uniform, now stained with faint drops of blood, was spotless before the blast.

"You are an infantry Lieutenant and you know how partisans operate. They kill when and how they can do the job."

The sounds of the siren indicated the base was under attack, but both Russian soldiers knew it was because of the explosion. First responders were heard nearing, their sirens clashing with the base defense sirens, and both were loud enough to hurt their ears. The two young Russians looked, but they saw no one in the mess alive or even moving. All around them was death, destruction, and flames.

A Senior Sergeant neared, saluted and asked, "Are the two of you injured?"

He was fully armed and had four grenades that were seen, a bayonet on his old AK-47, and his steel pot was on his head tightly. The two officers wore their 9 mm service pistols under the tails of their uniform coats, where they were not easily seen.

They returned the salute and Lieutenant Vlacic Lavr said, "No, Senior Sergeant, we are fine. I do not think you will find any survivors in the officers mess. It is shocking, because we left the place and two minutes earlier, as soon as we crossed the street, boom, the explosion went off."

An ambulance, firetruck, and emergency situations command post recreational vehicle (RV) parked and the crew quickly left the RV. A Captain began yelling orders and the men began setting up their mobile command post. The EMT personnel quickly moved to the rubble that was not in flames and began looking for survivors or bodies.

"Are you with Security, Senior Sergeant?" Captain Lev Tolya asked.

"Yes, sir. I am the senior enlisted man on Colonel Ludomir Yurievich's staff, sir."

"Has the Colonel been notified?" Captain Tolya asked, as he pulled out a small notebook and began taking notes.

"Yes, sir. I called him from the Non-Commissioned Officers (NCO) Open Mess and then ran here. It is about a block down the street, toward the base center, and he is on his way."

As they made small talk, a staff car showed up a few minutes later and a tall, muscular Colonel, near 55 years old, walked from the car to the mobile command post where he informed the Captain he was now at the location. After some useless chatter with the younger officer, Yurievich walked to his senior NCO.

All three saluted the Colonel, who more or less waved a salute in return. He looked the facility over and slowly shook his head.

"Bomb, huh? Do they have any idea how it was stored or how much explosives were used, Petr?" the Colonel asked.

"Nothing yet, sir. I think once they have the fires out and the experts have arrived, they will know all we will need to know to brief the Wing Commander in the morning, sir." It was common in the Russian army for a superior to call a lower ranking individual by his first name. However, it was not an invite for the lower ranking person to call the Colonel by his or her first name.

"I suspect you are correct, as usual, Sergeant, but Colonel Lazarev needs to know what is going on so he can answer any questions Moscow may have."

"Oh, I agree, sir. Colonel, this is Captain Lev Tolya and Lieutenant Vlalic Lavr. The Lieutenant is new and just arrived today. Captain Tolya is with the...?" the Sergeant said and then looked at Tolya.

"Airborne Infantry, sir. I am a platoon leader under Lieutenant Colonel Orya Shura."

"One hell of a violent welcome, Lieutenant." the Colonel said, as he pushed the smoking foot in the shoe off the curb. He looked at Tolya and said, "Your commander is a very brave soldier and she started out in this war many years ago as a simple sniper. After 540 something confirmed dead Americans she was promoted instantly to Captain. She then attended the necessary schools and has had a very successful career. She is a very good Commander."

The Senior Sergeant immediately thought, *Did I hear some jealousy in my commander's voice?* He then asked, "What are your orders, sir?"

"Senior Sergeant Vova, I need you to return to the office and keep things running smoothly until we get done here. I am expecting Junior Sergeant Antoliy in my office at sixteen hundred hours, so we can promote him to Senior Sergeant. If I am not back by then, I need to have you and Lieutenant Pickovic to place the new tabs on his shirt. Tell him I will present him with his medal for valor tomorrow and I want to shake his hand. He is one tough young man."

Saluting, the Sergeant said, "Yes, sir, he is a tough soldier. I will see things in the office are done properly, sir." Once his salute was returned by the Colonel, he did an about face movement and then walked toward his office.

Senior Sergeant Vova was an ex farm boy who could not afford to attend college, so he went into the military so he'd have the educational benefits and would have his service behind him. However, he discovered he liked the rigid discipline and had advanced rapidly. He currently had a line number for Master Sergeant and that was as high as he could go. If all went well and he wasn't killed, he'd put his new stripe on in about ten days. In any army though, death could come at any time.

Vova was a big man, six feet six inches, 250 pounds, and all of it was muscle. His sandy blonde hair was cropped short with maybe a quarter of an inch showing on top. The sides were what the American army called "high and tight." His blue eyes reflected his deep intelligence and his teeth were white and even. He was not a man to give a hard time, because he was known to use his fists if needed, and more than one trooper had arrived at morning formation with a black eye. He wore a thin pencil mustache and it was always neatly trimmed, just as his face was. He could have been a model for a Russian enlistment poster, but he had little time for nonsense and was all business.

When he entered his building, someone yelled, "Master Sergeant in the building!"

He was well aware they were warning others, so anyone goofing off could regain their composure and the Sergeant would never know what had been going on. He'd done the same as a young Private or Corporal.

"Emergency classified message from Moscow in the message safe on the Colonel's desk."

"Is it marked for his eyes only, Private Jora?"

"No, Sergeant, but it is classified Top Secret and none of us have a high enough clearance to open it. The carrier brought it in, told us what it was, and then dropped it into the slit in the safe. We do not have the combination or need to know, so we did nothing."

"I suspect, Private Jora, you are very good at doing nothing. Are you not?"

Confused, the young man answered, "Yes, Sergeant. The army has taught me how to do nothing very well." He then gave his words some thought and added, "Only, I was polishing my boots and I need to return to my job. I was doing something, but not all the others were."

"Turning stool pigeon, Private?"

"Uh, no Sergeant, but I am not real sure what you mean?" His face turned red and he lowered his head.

"A stool pigeon is someone who tells on others, friends or not. I hope that is not you, is it?"

"On no, not me, Sergeant. I simply meant I had no idea what the others were doing while you were gone, that is all." He grew nervous and anxious.

"Go back to your boots, while I read our emergency message." Senior Sergeant Vova said as he moved to the safe and began turning the tumbler using the combination. On the last number, the door popped open.

Classified marking covered the envelope when he picked it up. He opened it and began reading.

"*Headquarters Moscow, Lieutenant General Krovavich, 21 May 2036, 2030 hours, Classified Top Secret, Eyes Only.*" He knew the 'Eyes Only' meant Commanders and Senior NCOs with the need to know.

"*Beginning on 24 May, 2036, two hours before dawn, all airborne units will be operational and airborne at that time. They will be dropped near the three largest partisan bases in Texas. One base is near Dallas/Fort Worth, another near San Antonio, and the last is near Lubbock. Of the three bases, Lubbock is the most remote and is considered historically and geographically as the Llano Estacado. The remote town is part of the southern end of the High Plains. For Lubbock and San Antonio, much fresh potable water will be needed. The areas were primarily desert, with the southern base being the hottest and driest. Dallas/Fort Worth is in a busy city which will supply the needs of any Russian forces. Expect bloody resistance at all three locations.*"

Senior Sergeant Vova stopped reading; he'd read enough, and glanced at his watch. It was late on the 21st of May, so he had three days to be ready on the 24th. His was an airborne unit and most had jumped in training within the last six months, but in America, with this war, few airborne units jumped and even fewer jumped into combat. *Spetsnaz* and other special operations units did as they wished, so they jumped when they wanted. The Sergeant thought the Russian army messed up when they assigned airborne troops to work as conventional troops and failed to use them wisely. But, as any career man or woman in the army knows, in any army in the world, the army makes all the big decisions.

"Private Rostislavovich, get your butt in here and now! Bring Junior Sergeant Antoliy with you!" the Senior Sergeant yelled.

A couple of minutes later there was a knock on the Colonel's door and the Sergeant said, "Enter and report."

The two men entered and walked to the Colonel's desk, where the Senior Sergeant was sitting, and Junior Sergeant Antoliy said, "Sergeant, Junior Sergeant Antoliy and Private Rostislavovich reporting as ordered."

"Antoliy, you are a Senior Sergeant as of this minute. The Colonel said he is sorry, but the explosion at the officers open mess caused him to send me instead of him to promote you. At this time, he is investigating the explosion. He will be here to give you your medal in the morning at Stand Up and said he looks forward to presenting the medal to you. I can tell you, he thinks you are a very efficient soldier, and is proud of you."

"Thank you, Sergeant, and that is fine with me. I look forward mostly to my pay increase. As a young married man, every ruble helps, and my wife is excited."

"It is not everyday a Russian soldier is promoted a year ahead of being eligible for promotion to Senior Sergeant. Your medal is no small one either. Now, here," He handed a cloth with the rank of Sergeant sewed on to Rostislavovich and added, "If you will get his left shoulder, I will do the right."

In a minute or less his old rank was gone, and Senior Sergeant Antoliy stood with a big smile.

"Son, you look professional now and you are finally starting to get into some good money. Not as much as an officer makes, but you will do well in a combat zone. Now if you will wait a minute, I have something in the Colonel's desk for Private Rostislavovich." he open the top drawer, pulled out the cloth stripes of a Corporal and tossed them to the man.

"Your promotion is automatic, Corporal, so no pinning on your rank. That is only done with combat promotions and in an officer's office. Your two years are up, but you extended another year to come to this hell hole. Would you mind telling an old Senior Sergeant why?"

"I need more benefits and as you know, the amount we get for benefits all depends on the number of years we serve. With three years under my belt, I can go to a university, then be placed in a good paying job, and even my wife can go to school. I also will get free burial and with a ceremony if I serve three years."

"Wait a minute, what wife?"

"Oh, I do not have one yet, Senior Sergeant, but I have a woman I will ask once I return home."

"Remember son, you will not ask any woman if you are killed in this place. America has a habit of eating young Russian Corporals for breakfast."

Unsure what to say, the young man bowed his head and remained quiet. His great grandpa had been in the Great War against the Nazis and he told the young man that more died than survived in a war. He also told the young man to continue to pray to God that he'd survive, because the Lord had saved his Grandpa's life numerous times. Of course, he said none of this to the Sergeant.

"Now, Antoliy, you will take over the second squad from Volavich and tell her to report to me. I have another assignment for her. Now, I expect both of you to celebrate tonight, but do so in moderation. For the next three days, you will all be in intense parachute training, only on the ground."

Silence.

"Now go, and congratulations to both of you on your promotions. Antoliy, you be at Stand Up at 0700 hours on the dot and be prepared for Colonel Lazarev to congratulate you, once Colonel Yurievich pins the medal on you. Look sharp too, because you represent all Airborne soldiers. Dismissed."

The two young men turned and walked from the room. The time for talking was over and they were sent back to work.

At 0700 the next morning, the conference room was filled, mostly due to the eyes only message from Headquarters Moscow. Some of the men were excited to be jumping into combat, some were greatly concerned, while others were terrified. When the unit dropped, every man and woman, except those in the hospital, would drop as well. Equipment had to be triple checked, ammo and munitions handed out, and parachutes made ready, along with wills and next of kin verified.

Colonel Andrei Lazarev stood behind the podium and said, "Colonel Yurievich wanted to do this, but he's still at the destroyed Officers Open Mess looking for the type of explosive used. Would Sergeant Antoliy came forward, please?"

Antoliy walked to beside the Colonel and stood at attention.

A Captain neared with an opened wooden box in his hand and the Colonel reached into the box and pulled out a Hero of Ukraine military Order of Gold Star. "This medal is being presented to Sergeant Antoliy for heroism on January 1st, of this year. Senior Sergeant, then Corporal Antoliy, killed three partisans attacking his Commander and the last one he killed with a bayonet. Wounded severely in his left thigh by one of the Americans, he made his way forward and led a group of men to victory over the enemy. Those men were not usually under the Corporal's command. During the attack, the Corporal continuously refused first aid until the last American was dead. Having personally killed at least five of the Americans, one by the blade, Corporal Antoliy displayed unusual bravery, dedication to victory, and brought great honor to his airborne unit and Russia. I am extremely proud to present Sergeant Foma Antiliy the Hero of Ukraine military Order of Gold Star. Congratulations, Sergeant."

The officers all stood and began clapping their hands, most envious of the young boy that had become a man in America, but they said nothing.

"I want all of us to line up and shake this brave man's hand. I understand our newly combat promoted Sergeant is offering free drinks for friends and comrades at the NCO club for one hour. I intend to be there. Come gentlemen, line up."

Everyone moved forward and Antoliy shook hands until his arm was sore and then he went to the club. He vaguely remembered walking home near midnight.

At exactly 0400 hours, Senior Sergeant Petr Vova picked up a trashcan and as he made his way down the middle of the all male dorm, he beat the metal hard with a piece of a rake handle he often carried when working with his men and women. Senior Sergeant Yoga Salvicha was copying his behavior in the women's barracks. Coming to his newly promoted Sergeant, he leaned forward and pushed the double bunk to its side on the floor.

The noise was loud and Antoliy climbed from his blankets looking worse for wear. He stumbled to the foot of where his bunk used to be and stood at attention, as he fought the urge to puke. His bunk mate was moving beside him, as the Sergeant chewed his ass for being slow and drunk. Senior Sergeant Vova knew half the barracks was drunk, because they'd all been at the club, guests of the newly promoted Sergeant. He figured they'd sober up during the ten kilometer run in full gear.

"Drop your clocks and grab your socks! Wake, my little boys, so we can form up outside for our morning airborne run. We will do ten kilometers today and work our way up to 30 by Wednesday."

"Sergeant, we no longer run in the mornings."

"What did you say? Are you calling me a liar, Private?"

"Uh, no, sir. But, we have never ran in the six months I have been here."

"Everyone! Listen up. Thursday, we are going to make the first mass combat assault landing in America for our unit. We will be in shape and we will kill our enemies. All of us will jump, and unless you are in the hospital under a doctors direct care you will jump too. Now, all of you men have 10 minutes to shave and then fall out in full combat gear, move!"

The men scattered and all headed to the bathroom to shave, and since there were only 20 sinks for 40 men, some shaved behind others as they followed the Sergeant's orders. Ten minutes later, 40 nicked and cut men were standing in formation, dressed as the airborne troops they were. Each wore a full combat pack, loaded with everything they'd need to fight a fierce battle after being dropped by parachute.

As they ran, some stopped and puked, others began sweating the alcohol from their bodies, and others fought severe headaches from drinking, but all ran and said nothing. They were running with a Russian Senior Sergeant, with a promotion coming soon to Master Sergeant, so he wasn't concerned at all about their hangovers or how they felt. They would run and then move on to practicing leaving the door or ramp of a moving aircraft. It was jump school all over again and come the 24th, they'd be ready to kill.

CHAPTER 2

Partisan High Command Headquarters, near Dallas/Fort Worth, was on a high stage of alert because of a warning that the Russians were suddenly making their airborne forces visible and what looked to be a build up of supplies and material for them. Having used the units as traditional infantry for years, the buildup caught the eye of the photo interrupters who analyzed the images taken by some very brave men and women on the ground. If caught, the images would have meant instant death, without a court date. The Russians were a hard army and they played war for keeps.

So far, America had turned into Russia's Vietnam, with no more of a win in sight now than 8 years earlier when they started. Some even compared the war to the Russian's war in Afghanistan years ago. They'd fought like two cats with their tails tied together, only they had never come close to winning a conventional war. Most of their civilian acts and plans were outdated and the military used fear to insure compliance, but emotions didn't work. Americans were willing to sacrifice everything, including their lives, to get the Russian Bear to leave.

In Russia, many folks were tiring of their sons and daughters coming home in aluminum caskets and many were marked 'Do Not View Remains'. So far, over 80,698 Russians had been killed in the war with America and over 12,000 were missing. Many of the missing had blown up when they activated a mine and left nothing but a smoking hole in the ground. The war was crude, and the partisans actively took the war to the Russians. It was no longer safe on any installation due to bombings, assassinations, and sniper attacks off base that killed folks on base. The folks back home were growing angry because the war should have been over years ago.

Over a million people had marched and protested the war effort at least four times and small assemblies were formed to protest as well. The smaller groups were more frequent and growing violent the longer the war continued. Russian politicians were now being elected by promising to withdraw from the war in America. So far little had been done, but it was suspected by everyone that the Russians were about to call it quits. The hatred of the war was one of the reasons the partisans were making every effort to increase their body count of dead Russians in every battle. After large battles, with the Russians losing large numbers of men and women, the protesters were always out in force.

"John, the latest intel states that the Russians will be using airborne troops soon because of the large number of material and replacement troops sent to them. Now, not once in all the years have the Russians actually used their airborne as a real airborne unit. They have been used as conventional troops over the years, but now they seem to be making them ready for an assault someplace." a Major said as he placed a stack of images and papers on the Colonel's desk.

John, wearing the silver eagles of a full Colonel, thought for a minute and then asked, "Any increase in materials that would be used only by airborne troops? You know, parachutes, packs with lanyards, lowering devices, or anything that will prove they will soon be dropped?" He then began going through the documents and images the Major had given him.

"You're looking at photos of containers marked 'Parachutes, harnesses, and Bison sub-machine guns'. The Bison is their airborne weapons for those above the rank of Corporal. Our eyes on the bases claim the Russians are suddenly running in the mornings, and practicing exiting aircraft mock-ups by the door and ramp. This training is being done out in the open, and sand has been laid to reduce the numbers of injuries the trainees might have during training. I'd say we have an excellent chance of one or more airborne attacks and they will hit, most likely, near Partisan Headquarters or our larger Partisan groups in the field. They have no idea where our small field units are and their base camps move frequently."

"I want both areas prepared for a warm welcome for our parachutists. Since we have no idea when they will land, place everyone on immediate alert. Have the Partisan groups in the field leave this evening and do so after dark. I want everyone to move at least twenty miles or more. Have them report to you after they have moved. As for us, I want any and all openings large enough to land a company size airborne unit mined and prepared to make life rough for them once they land. I know we may not have much time, so get the alert sent out and get this place to hopping. I'm due to return to the Missouri Ozarks and my old unit in three days, but until then, I want security on this base fixed up and made stronger against airborne troops. Now, get this started, and right now."

"Yes, sir. But, what about the General? He needs to be told, sir." Major Fan Woo said.

"You get the base ready and send the messages by radio to all others. I'll take care of the General. Go."

As soon as Woo left, John, picked up the phone and dialed a number.

"Office of the Fort Commander, Sergeant First Class Windwood. This line is not secure. How may I direct your call?"

"Windwood, give me General Thomas, please."

"Morning, Colonel, I'll pass you right into his office."

"General Thomas." The General answered almost immediately.

"Sir, this is John, and I have some security information that I will brief you on as soon as you have an open hour. But, I need to have your response today."

"That important?"

"Yes, sir. I certainly feel it is."

"I will have our lunch delivered, so be here at 1200 hours and we'll eat and talk. Keep up the good work, John, and I may have some good news for you when you arrive. See you at noon."

At 1150, John arrived at the General's office, got past three doors of guards, and walked into his outer office. A crusty looking man of about fifty sat at a desk cleaning his 1911 .45 pistol and an old M-16 was hanging from a nail behind him. John noticed the rifle had a magazine inserted and it was squeaky clean.

"Intelligence. I have a 1200 hours appointment with the old man." John said.

"Go right in, sir, he is expecting you." the man said without looking up from his disassembled pistol.

John knocked once and entered when the General said, "Enter."

He walked to the General's desk, saluted, and when told to take a chair he did, and then began telling the man all he knew of the buildup of the Russian troops. When he finished, the General thought for a long time and then said, "You've taken the proper procedures to keep us as safe and sound as we can get, but I want a battalion on ready status until this happens or two weeks, which ever comes first. I want the men and women in your intelligence section to monitor this closely and our eyes on the ground might even see the fully loaded aircraft take off. If so, we need advanced warning they are coming."

"I'll see to it. I'll also see that all personnel are issued rifles, sidearms and combat gear for the time being. I agree with you, I don't see any attack coming later than two weeks from now. If all that gear was issued for replacement of other gear, they'll not move, but my belly says we are in for a fight. I've never heard of the Russians issuing all new gear and then not putting it to use."

"I agree with you, John. I trust you to handle this and if you need anything, anything at all, just contact me. Now, I have a surprise for you that I think may confuse you. Over the course of this war, medals and awards have been stockpiled until it's all over. The mission you were on to place a suitcase bomb in Pearl, Mississippi years back has been evaluated by a team of combat senior officers and you have been approved for the Medal of Honor, effective six years ago. Now, if the Russians win, your medal will be on hold until they leave."

"Gener—"

"John, we will not discuss this. I know you don't want the medal, but you're not being asked. The impermanent Chief of Staff thinks you deserve the medal and by God, you'll accept it with open arms. Once the Russians leave, the medal will be presented by our first President, whoever that may be. John, you continued your mission even when severely wounded, refused morphine for your pain, and the whole mission was a mess by then. Your action alone killed over a quarter of a million Russians and to this day, they have not reported the loss of a single man."

"How many innocent citizens died, sir?" John asked, his voice hinting at anger.

"It simply does not matter. Look, the civilians were expendable, just as we are. Many were in gulags, or homeless and sleeping in the street. Hell, over half of them were eating human flesh and were the dregs of society. John, you didn't make the decision to kill a single civilian, we Generals did that, and you were only our delivery system. I had hoped the medal would have made up for the fact your mission was a tough one and one no other man could have completed."

Giving an ill felt grin, John replied, "Yes, sir, I will accept the medal, but you know my feelings on the subject well."

"There will be more than you getting our nation's highest medal that day. There will be six other brave men and women, if they survive this war. The Russians are about at the end of their efforts in

America and the people back home are tired of no progress, and the numbers of Russians soldiers killed and maimed is high. Combined, over 290,000 of Russia's men and women have been maimed or killed in action against us. But, it has cost us, too, with almost the same number, 275,000 recorded dead or wounded. We have no idea of how many civilians have died through all acts of this war. We are not presenting the Medal of Honor to heroes like you to feed your ego, but to show our civilian population that our men made great sacrifices for our freedoms."

Silence, because John had nothing to say.

Opening his right top drawer, the General pulled out a bottle of excellent Kentucky whiskey and poured a double shot in two glasses. He handed one to John and then said, "We have unofficial word that this airborne assault will be the last combat of the war, if the Russians lose. So, with that said, we must make it fail. We had no idea what exactly was being planned, but obviously it was this airborne unit. If they win a great victory over us, their army will then continue the war. That makes the coming fight the most important in the history of our current warfare. At all costs, *all costs*, we must win this battle."

"I have the information being distributed as we speak, sir. All our field units and units here will know what is planned to happen, to a point. I will not provide anyone but my staff and yours what I learn from now on, such as the date of the attack or the number of troops to be dropped by the Russians. The information I provide you, sir, you can do with it as you wish. I suspect you'll want to inform certain members of your staff."

"I will do that." Standing, the General moved to a dining table and said, "Let's eat now, John, and relax a little. Once the meal is behind us, we both have jobs that need done. Come and join me. It's not everyday I get to eat with a Medal of Honor recipient."

"Sir, our eyes on the ground in Saint Louis have stated the Russians are currently loading aircraft with supplies and pallets of gear, but no personnel are moving yet. They expect the troops to load tomorrow or the day after. They have heard nothing, but they have seen the activity and it's obvious to them the Russians are ready to fight." he was speaking to Colonel Joshua the Commander of the Communications section, and in John's tent.

"Tell them if the troops load wearing parachutes, we need to be notified as soon as possible and at all costs." Joshua said as he looked up from the 8 by 10 images he was looking at with a magnifying glass. The image showed a Russian forklift moving crates and pallets of supplies and gear to a Russian transport aircraft.

Major Woo knocked on John's removable door frame, entered and said, "The Russians will use the 38th Guards Air Assault Brigade. The unit is the Special Forces brigade of the Armed Forces of Belarus. It is currently based in Saint Louis, Missouri, but in Russia it's based in the city of Brest, which is a historic site of a variety of cultures. I'm pretty sure you're not interested in their culture, Colonel. The most important thing to remember, sir, is these men are Special Forces, and are able to operate in units as small as only three men. I think if you think of them as equals to our US Army Rangers, you'll be almost correct, sir."

"Thank you, Fan. How are the sharpened poles and land mines coming along?"

"We now have thousands of sharp poles in the ground around the area, but it would take years for us to put them in every clearing. The mines take less time and we have over 50,000 planted so far, and each have minefield warnings placed around the areas. It is estimated that by tomorrow at 1600 hours, we'll have over 150,000 mines planted and four times the number of sharpened poles. The poles will also keep helicopters from landing, so that may or may not help us."

"I want command detonated mines placed on all trails leading toward our base. Plant an explosive with a 55 gallon drum of old aviation gas and a gallon of liquid soap, which we have in storage, but we don't have nearly as many 55 gallon drums as I want. I suspect we will need over a thousand, but at last count, we had fifty. The older gas and soap is lethal and I'm sure the new stuff will be too, but the soap breaks down in the drum after a month of storage, then it makes the whole mess sticky when it blows."

"There are other traps in use that you suggested too, Colonel. The toe poppers, using shotgun shells with the primers resting on nails are all over the place, and the punji pits and snake pits are also being used."

"Smear human waste on the sharpened stakes so they cause an infection from the smallest cut. The more that become injured or killed the better chance we have of ending this war."

"Do you really think you or I will live to see the war end?" Woo asked.

"I do, and it is not a secret that the Russians need a big win to stay here. That alone is why I think we've been targeted. But, remember, they may have Spetsnaz or other units looking us over and probably today even. I'm sure our increased activities have been reported to the Russians in Saint Louis, I really do."

"Once they have a big operation moving, they can't stop it now, boss. They're committed, no matter what they discover we're doing. They may alter their drops to locations with no mines or poles, but eventually some of them will have to cross our mine fields. I expect more than one booby-trap to slow them down too."

Standing, John said, "Yes, they will slow them down, maybe kill a few, but the majority of their troops will arrive here, ready to fight."

"Have the Chinese been notified?"

"Oh, yes, and they are on standby with fighter jets, attack helicopters, and even bombers to help."

"Good, because when they attack us in force we'll need all the help we can get. One of our eyes was caught this morning, and the reason you don't know is I just got the notification from a Chief Master Sergeant, Partisan Air Force Ground Defense Section. They run twelve sets of eyes for us and this one killed was taking images of Russian Paratroopers practicing leaving the door of a transport aircraft. He'd taken about a dozen photos, when a Full Colonel arrived and while taking images of the Russian Colonel, two guards caught him red handed. The Colonel, who has been identified as Colonel Andrei Lazarev, personally shot the man in the head. He was made to kneel and you know the routine. The dead man's name was William R. Barnes and he lived in the local area. He was hired as a janitor at the start of the war and furnished us information for 8 years."

"Not much we can do about him now, but he knew he could one day be caught. See he is awarded a medal for his actions, Silver Star, and another medal for his long service to our unit. When the war is over, we may find a relative to give the medal to, but if not, we'll add his name to those patriots that have given their lives to the effort of recovering their homeland."

"A medal for a life. That doesn't sound hardly fair, does it?" Colonel Joshua asked.

Thinking of all the deaths he'd caused with the suitcase nuke, John said, "No it doesn't, but there is a war on and people die. In the morning, have the staff, all of them, here at 0400 hours and working, because at 0500, I have a staff meeting with the General. He will be briefed on all the information we have and he'll make the final call for defensive steps we need to take. I feel this attack will come sooner than later, perhaps in a day or two. My feelings tell me it could happen any minute, and I've rarely been wrong in this war. When I return, I'll have a staff meeting of my own and starting today, we're on 12 hour shifts. After the meeting, release our night shift to get some rest and we'll do as the General wants done. See to this, Major Woo."

The next morning was cool but not cold as the Colonel walked into his office at 0410. He looked around and spotted most of his staff in place. After getting a cup of coffee, he moved into his office and noticed his classified safe had been opened and reading the name of Major Woo on the access roster, he opened it to see what new information was added overnight.

He removed a manila envelope, which was 8 by 10 inches and a good 2 inches thick. He quickly untied the back and opened the envelope. He pulled out the papers and photographs and began reading. Five minutes later as he was trying to put all the information he'd read together, Woo entered, smiled and asked, "Does it all confuse you?"

"No, not overall, but the part about the additional transport aircraft and helicopters does seem confusing."

"There are images of an Ilyushin Il-76 "Candid" aircraft; 20 of them are currently in Saint Louis loading supplies and gear. Our eyes saw the bulk of them, oh, fifteen maybe, land the last few days. We know they are also used for airborne troops. As a drop platform, they are similar to the old American C-5, Galaxy, and are capable of not only dropping troops, but also LAPES, and on the same mission. The helicopters, mostly the Mi-17 general purpose transport helicopters, are also new to the base in the last 48 hours. Our eyes indicate two squadrons, and with them came a division of standard Russian Infantry, which we think will be transported by the choppers."

Scratching his beard, John said, "Interesting, and almost proves to me that the attack is imminent. I read something about attack helicopters, but it was confusing with some varieties in Saint Louis and others in Kansas City. What do you know about them?"

"Our people spotted Mi-28, Ka-52, and even some old Mi-24P Hind-F attack choppers on the ramps of both locations. Saint Louis has the newer Mi-28 and Ka-52, both estimated at two squadrons of birds, on both bases, even where the older Hind-F was in Saint Louis. The number of Hind-F's were guessed at three squadrons. We suspect the attack helicopters will provide support to the non-airborne troops using the transportation choppers as a way to move men to the fight."

"What can you tell me about the unknown movement of supplies, gear and artillery?"

"The cargo was in nets and covered well with canvas tarps, and our people were unable to tell exactly what was being carried by the Mil Mi-26 cargo choppers, but the big guns were easy to spot because of their shape. They suspect the big guns were transported to areas near their targets, meaning us and other Partisan Headquarters. We are currently waiting on word from our Partisan field units to confirm the guns are in position there."

"Great job, Major, and I mean that. I'll take all of this to brief the General and I'm sure he'll be very sat—"

"Sir, our tower reports a huge number of unidentified aircraft nearing us and none will respond to radio calls. The base commander has placed the entire facility on alert, with security at Apha Stage 1. He thinks this base is their target and all personnel, including us, are to prepare for an assault. I have Corporal Brown issuing weapons and grenades to the troops." Master Sergeant Mary Dias said as she stuck her head in the door.

"Bingo!" John said and met the eyes of Major Woo, who looked concerned. He then added, "Major, call the General and inform him I will not be at standup today, and I honestly think it will be cancelled with an attack coming. Let him know if he needs me my radio call sign is Cobra One. He should have it, but tell him just to make sure. Gentleman and ladies, prepare for war."

Major Woo asked, "Sergeant Dias, how far out are the aircraft?"

"The tower said about twenty minutes and the ETA could vary as much as five minutes either way. Most of the base is still asleep, but with the siren blaring, that'll soon end."

"Get our troops ready to move and then check their gear. Within fifteen minutes, I want us near the eastern perimeter. Now, move!" John said and then thought, *I wonder if any of the booby traps we have out will slow any of the Russian troops down. There is also a chance some troops will intentionally be dropped on the base proper. I need to get to the command post and see how things are moving. Protect us Lord, as we enter combat and fight to free our nation.*

CHAPTER 3

S enior Sergeant Petr Vova was standing next to Master Sergeant Adam Slava and Vova was standing in the opening where the door used to be on the big Ilyushin Il-76 "Candid" aircraft. He could feel the cold air as it struck him hard. They'd already done their equipment check and all was a go. Slava was the jump master, and would be the last man out the door. The light beside Senior Sergeant Volva was a constant red now. He kept his eyes glued to the light.

"Steady, Petr, the light will change soon. Steady." The light suddenly showed steady green and the jump master screamed, "Go, Petr, go!"

Vova jumped with his chin down, slightly bowed at the waist, and his feet together. His hands were on his reserve parachute and he was ready to pull the handle if his main chute failed to open. As he twisted and turned in the cool morning air, he saw he narrowly missed the hard horizontal stabilizer on the aircraft, so he stiffened out of uncontrolled fear and continued to fall. A few seconds later he felt a hard shock as he immediately stopped falling. He heard a loud 'uuummmpppphhh,' and realized the noise was from him, and it was his opening shock. He looked up and his chute was in excellent shape and fully inflated. Looking between his legs, he noticed his forward speed was normal. He then glanced at the horizon in front of him and saw his rate of descent was normal as well. Weather had stated the conditions in Texas were excellent, with visibility around 12 miles.

He'd jumped from 800 feet and immediately saw, when looking at the ground, that there were long sharp poles positioned to impale paratroopers, so he grabbed his risers and moved away from the poles. One of the larger men passed him and Vova realized the weight carried combined with the weight of the jumper added to a person's descent rate and the heavier the load the less control.

Watching the man below him, he was surprised when the man touched ground and then went up in a narrow wall of red-white flames and smoke.

"Damn me, land mines!" the Senior Sergeant said to no one in particular. He realized the whole field was probably mined. He made the decision to land standing up. He could not risk a standard hit and roll landing, due to the explosives. He then released a lanyard with his 27.2155 kilo pack attached and it now hung below him on a long lanyard.

Just before he touched down, he got a glimpse of the man on the ground, and his left leg was missing and he was removing his belt to use as a tourniquet. He was heard screaming. The Sergeant touched the ground hard, staggered a little, but did not move. All around him explosions were heard and they were almost always followed by loud screams of pain. He looked up and about one third of his unit was yet to land. The aircraft was banking and on the way home.

As he watched, a missile was seen leaving the ground and he watched in horror as it struck the left wing of the Russian aircraft, the lowest one in the turn, and exploded. The aircraft, now in flames, was starting a nose down sharp angle. He saw three parachutes open, but one was in flames. Less than a minute later, the man hanging beneath the burning parachute fell when the fire on his canopy grew too large. He must have fallen 500 feet to his death.

"No one move, and I mean not an inch! This field is —"

There sounded a loud explosion, a scream and then another voice yelled out, "Don't move! Listen to Senior Sergeant Vova! Mines!"

"This field is mined! I need my men with mine detectors to mark a way out of here."

An hour later about 75% of his men were alive and uninjured. Three men had landed on the sharpened poles and were impaled. One man had the end of the long pole sticking in his rear and the tip was out his chest. He looked ghastly because his mouth was open and filled with bright red blood, which ran down his lips and chin, to fall on his chest. He made no movements.

"Form on me!" Vova yelled. It was then he realized the man on the pole was his Captain, so the responsibilities of the unit were suddenly his. Not overly worried to be a leader, he knew he could run the company with his eyes closed. He'd ran it many times after getting drunk and that was during peace and war. While he'd not felt drunk, he'd been legally intoxicated at the time.

As men neared him, he called out, "Radioman, post!"

An attractive blonde with big full cherry colored lips, wide hips, narrow waist, and large bust neared and handed the radio handset to him as she said, "Here you are, Sergeant."

He nodded and then took the headset and said, "Monsoon Two to Hotel Actual. We have landed, but approximately 25% of my troops were killed or seriously injured when we landed in a mine field. Do you copy, over."

"Copy Monsoon Two. Where is your One?"

"KIA, Kilo, India, Alpha, and I am in charge, sir. Request immediate recovery of my dead and wounded, but do not land in the field. The field is mined, over."

"Copy, Monsoon Two. We will collect your dead and wounded but not land on the field, due to mines, correct? You have orders to break your company down into squad size units and harass the enemy until you get new orders."

"Roger, correct on the mines. Monsoon Two, I will break them down once away from the landing zone, and we will harass the enemy, Monsoon out." He handed the handset back to the radio carrier and then began forming his people. After organizing, he called out, "Jora and Ilyich, I want Jora on point and Ilyich you are my drag. Let us move, but expect booby traps along the way. Keep your ears and eyes open and you may be alive tonight."

The first hour went well, then Private Jora stopped and said, "I need the Senior Sergeant here. I see something that looks wrong."

When the Sergeant neared, Jora said, "The soil looks a different color in the center of the trail and I think it may be a booby trap."

"Take the end of your rifle, push it under the soil and then lift it up. It looks like a pungi stake trap to me. Once you feel the weight on the end of your rifle, flip the mat off and we'll take a look."

The mat flipped off and in the hole were about 20 sharpened stakes, with the barbs smeared with human waste.

"What now, Sergeant?"

"Mark it and carefully move around it. The sides may be booby-trapped as well. They often do that. As soon as you are around the trap, clear any dust or dirt from your rifle barrel and continue moving."

Once Jora was moving again, Vova moved back to the center of the group and smiled when he realized the young paratrooper was learning and in the most deadly way, on the job training.

Less than ten minutes later the sound of an explosion was loud, followed by continuous screams from up front. Vova ran forward and found Jora on the ground and his left leg was missing at the knee. The severely damaged limb was not bleeding much and the Sergeant knew the heat from the mine had cauterized the wound as it removed his leg. He moved to the man's position and yelled, "Ikovle, you take point, but stop out maybe fifty feet and wait for us to treat our comrade. Medic!"

"Yes, Sergeant." Ikovle replied when beside the older man.

A short, stocky man ran forward and, according to the red cross on his helmet and sleeve, he was their medic. He instantly began working on Jora without a word spoken. Vova remembered the man and his name was Nititovich, Private Yakov Nititovich.

"Makarovich, post on me!" He then remembered his radio operator was the attractive blonde with the full lips he'd seen earlier.

When Olga was near, she handed the handset to the Sergeant, and waited.

"Uh, Hotel Actual, Monsoon Two here, and I am requesting an immediate pickup of a male with one leg missing, numerous wounds to his crotch and chest. We have excessive bleeding and my corpsman is currently doing all he can for the man."

"Roger that, Monsoon, and I have a Mi-24 with two Ka-50 Attack Helicopters I can send you."

"I request the Mi-24 and the two Black Sharks at my current location as soon as possible. The man is bleeding profusely."

"Copy and fully understand. The medical evacuation helicopter has a well trained medic on board and will give your wounded additional blood if that is required."

"When can I expect the aircraft?"

"Three minutes or less. They are picking up wounded in your mine field. Get someone ready to pop smoke. His call sign is Medic Two Zero, over."

"Copy, over and out."

A minute later the radio grew loud, "Uh, Monsoon Two, this is Medic Two Zero and I am about a minute out from you. Have someone pop smoke, so I can see wind direction and your location, over."

"Copy, Medic Two Zero. Rostislavovich! I want you to move to me and pop smoke in the small clearing to my left, move and do the job now!" He spoke to the pilot of the medical aircraft and also to his Private, to pop smoke.

Orange smoke began to rise in the cool morning air.

"Uh, Monsoon, I see your smoke and have you visual. We are coming in now for the patient."

"You four, pack Jora to the clearing and place him on the helicopter. Move, he will land in less than a minute."

The helicopter neared the ground and as the chopper hovered, a medic jumped from the aircraft and made his way to Vova's men. He had the wounded man placed on the helicopter and then the handset in Vova's hand came alive, "Taking ground fire, taking ground fire from the west side of the landing zone."

"Cover the aircraft and now! Place your fire on the left side of the helicopter, in the bushes on the far side." The Sergeant ordered.

The sound was loud and when the Sergeant glanced at the helicopter, the engine was smoking slightly and it was climbing for altitude as they left the area.

"Do you think they will make it back to the base smoking like that?" Private Makarovich asked.

"Probably, but if not, someone else will pick them and their patients up, I am sure of that." he said and then added, "Private Ikovle, start moving and lead us west by south. Keep your eyes open for booby traps and snipers."

"Snipers? Sergeant I will never see a sniper."

"Move. We will talk about this later tonight."

"Yes, of course, Sergeant."

The afternoon was coming to an end with about an hour of sunlight left, when the radio suddenly blared, "Monsoon Two, this is Hotel, over. Monsoon Two, this is Hotel, how do you read me, over?"

Makarovich neared and handed the radio to the Sergeant.

"Uh, read you five by five, over."

"Uh, your man Jora is in recovery and will be returned to Moscow in the morning. His left leg was lost, his left eye and part of his left arm. He is expected to make a full recovery, over."

"Copy and glad to hear that. Our evening coordinates are . . ." Vova starting giving their night position to headquarters so no one would fire on them by mistake that evening. When he finished, he looked around at the tired troops he had and then said, "Call it a day. I want you to team up with a buddy and two to a fox hole. Let us get to digging, folks. Makarovich, you will share a hole with me. I need the radio close to me at all times."

"I like that idea, Senior Sergeant."

Petr glared at her and then said, "We are professionals, Private, and it will remain that way until we are discharged, understand?"

"I understand, Sergeant, just making conversation."

"Make it about something other than sex. I am not married, do not intend to be, and have no urge to be with a woman young enough to be my daughter. Now, get digging our fox hole. Open your mouth again about you and I, well, I will report you to the Colonel." he said, but didn't mean it. Actually, he was flattered she made the comment, but a man couldn't lead a woman into war if he's sexually active with her or even worst, fell in love. He liked women, but this was not the time and for sure not the place to be climbing in the blankets with someone, no matter how attractive she might be.

He looked the men and women over, saw all of them digging in, so he moved out a ways and set up three MON-50 mines, the Russian version of a Claymore mine. He knew if the enemy approached during the night, they might reverse the mines and that took big balls in his opinion. The person moving the mine never knew when the man or woman on the other end would squeeze the clacker and set the mine off, sending 540 steel balls or 485 short steel rods (depending on variety chosen) out in an arc, killing most of those within 40 to 60 meters.

He moved back to his fox hole, picked up a small shovel and began to help his radio operator dig their fox hole. Once the hole was done, they both pulled out their rations, affectionately called green frogs because of the color used in packaging, and ate his supper. His meal was filling but the taste left a lot to be desired, but they would keep them alive forever. They were high calories, bland, and most of the food was covered in grease. They were good hot, but only a fool would start a fire while invading an enemy's country. It was a guaranteed death sentence. The chemical tablets used to heat the rations had been stolen and were not available anyway.

As he leaned back against the cool soil, he heard a helicopter nearing and didn't give it much thought since most were Russian aircraft, and he'd called their night position in earlier. He was sure it was Russian, because the Chinese Helicopters had a different, higher pitch, sound. He suspected he and his troops were on Infrared radar and relaxed. He was exactly where he was supposed to be.

Suddenly a loud zipper coming down was heard and bullets began to strike all around his position. Men and women screamed as the big slugs hit them hard, with most losing arms and legs if the bullets struck a limb. One woman was there one minute and blown in half the next.

Grabbing the radio handset, he screamed, "Unknown attack helicopter attacking at this instant, break, break, you are firing on Russians! I repeat, stop your damned attack right now!"

The firing stopped and a confused voice said in Russian, "Uh, unknown contact, what is your uh, call sign? I am Warrior uh, Four, over."

"I am Monsoon Two, Warrior Four, and I have dead and wounded down here now. Get the hell out of here, now!"

"Uh, Monsoon Two, I am sorry! I was informed by headquarters anyone in front of latitude 32.768799 and -97.309341 longitude was fair game."

"You were told wrong. Now mark my position as I —"

"Monsoon Two, this is Hotel Actual and go easy on the Warrant Officer, because your position was not marked on our map. Warrior Four, return to base. How many medical helicopters do you request, Monsoon?" It was the base.

"Uh, unknown, wait one." Vova said and then yelled, "Corporal Lukovich, quickly get me a body count and a good number for our wounded. Do it now and quickly, I have headquarters on the phone!"

"Yo, Sergeant! Will do."

Five minutes later, Lukovich said, "Sergeant, I have three dead, fifteen wounded with three critical. The medic, Nititovich said one of the critical will only live with an immediate dust off."

Vova contacted Headquarters gave them the numbers and a request for immediate removal of his wounded, was confirmed with, "Roger that. I have some Mi-54's that have just unloaded troops less than a Kilometer from you and they will be on your position quick time. I suggest you get a flare lit up."

Knowing a flare would silhouette the person holding it, he stood and ignited a flare from his vest. As the flare sputtered and spit, he held the handset in his free hand.

"Monsoon Two, this is Bus One, over. I am a Mi-54 out of Saint Louis turned medical helicopter for your dead and wounded. I see your flare and have you on my infrared radar, so get rid of the flare."

As Vova was in the process of throwing the flare away, a bullet struck his left hand, taking off his little finger. His pain was fast in coming and blood spurted in all directions. He wrapped it in a bandage from his first aid kit and replied, "Be advised, Bus One, the area is hot, I repeat, the landing zone is hot. Over."

"Just load them quickly and get them ready to move now! I am coming down."

The walking wounded were loaded first, then the more seriously wounded were placed on the second helicopter and the seriously wounded, along with the dead, were loaded on the last aircraft. As it left the area, Vova heard the pilot say over the radio, "Taking ground fire from the right, over. Heavy ground fire." The sounds of bullets striking the helicopter was heard during the transmission.

Screaming to be heard, the pilot came back on and said, "Hotel, Bus Three, and I have all of my console lights blinking or turning solid red. I will try to limp home, but not sure I will make it."

Suddenly, off the left of Vova a bright light moved through the air and then there was a loud explosion.

"Hotel, I am going down. I repeat, mayday, mayday, mayday. Bus three and I am going down. I was struck by a man launched missile. A FGM-77 is my guess. I am going down!" a crash was heard over the radio and then silence.

"Black Shark One, this is Hotel. I request you move to the crash site and provide security until I can get a rescue team on the spot, over."

"Uh, copy Hotel, will do. The darkness is well lighted by a fire and I do have three survivors moving around on the ground, according to my advanced infrared screen. Over."

"Uh, Black . . . Shark One, uh, this . . . is . . . Bus . . . three. I am . . . trapped in . . . the wreckage . . . and . . . cannot . . . uh . . . get out. Please . . . make a live . . . fire pass . . . with Gatling . . . guns. Please . . . I do not . . . want to . . . burn . . . to death."

"Uh, Black Shark One, do as requested." Hotel added quickly. "No need for the man to burn to death. This is an order, destroy the Mi-54 on the ground, copy?"

"I copy and will obey, but I dislike doing this, over."

"Understand, Black Shark, now do the job. This is Hotel Actual."

By telling the Black Shark pilot he was Hotel Actual, he was telling him he was the Commander and his order was to be obeyed. The Black Shark attack helicopter made three passes, and on each pass he fired his Gatling guns until the aircraft exploded into countless pieces of metal and glass.

"Black Shark, return to base to rearm and refuel, copy?"

"Roger that, copy and will do. Black Shark One, over and out."

The helicopter was heard turning and moving away from Vova and his troops. The shock of the murder stunned the younger troops in their fox holes, but the old man had seen it done more often than he cared to think about. Handing the headset to Makarovich, he stretched out in the hole and tried to sleep. Death had reared it's ugly head killing a whole helicopter crew and five of his wounded. Three had been critical, but now they were all dead. Minutes later, he drifted off to sleep.

CHAPTER 4

John was in the communications bunk deep underground and he'd been in there since the Russian paratroopers had landed on the base proper. He wanted to be out in the fight, but the General himself had ordered him into the bunker. He was frustrated and wanted to be with his people. Communications were coming in from all over and the battle was going rough. A couple of companies of airborne troops had landed on the base proper and the battle was intense. Most had landed away from the buildings and as such, actually in a wooded area on the base. A few unlucky ones had landed near the buildings and were killed within minutes of landing. Now a battle raged far overhead on the facility.

"The Chinese have a squadron of attack helicopters due here in less than five minutes. So far we've held the base, but if the Russian ground troops happen to hit the base from the outside, we'll be spread pretty thin. It looks like the booby-traps and mines have greatly slowed down those who landed outside our fences." an unknown Captain said.

"John, I need you to take a radio and go top side to direct the choppers. Do not, unless you have no choice, get involved with the fighting. I need a good man on top that I can trust and will follow orders. Any questions?"

Smiling, John replied, "No questions, sir. I'll leave now, sir."

"And John?"

"Yes, sir?"

"Watch your ass, son. The Russians are giving this much more attention than any prior attack. This, or so I feel, is the big make it or break it for them. Now, go."

Minutes later, topside, John stood beside a Corporal named Johnson, his radio operator.

"Johnson, see if you can reach the Chinese, but their English will probably be bad."

"Any Chinese aircraft, this is Cobra, over."

Silence.

"Any Chinese aircraft, this is Cobra, over."

"Uh, go Cobra. This is Panda One, over." Come a reply in excellent English.

Two Russian airborne troops ran right for the two Americans using the radio beside the entrance to the underground bunker. John raised his Russian Bison and squeezed off a quick burst and both men fell to the ground. Blood and gore had splattered out their backs, so he knew they were down for the count. Using his pistol, Johnson fired twice, and both shots hit the men in the center of their chest. Both were now unmoving.

"Uh, Panda One, Cobra Two and I need your flight to hit the south side of the base, near the trees. Hit them hard and with everything you have."

"Roger that, and that is what we'll do."

The aircraft began moving toward the trees and the Chinese CAIC Z-10 attack helicopters looked deadly with their black paint with sleek bodies and loaded down with armament and munitions. Almost immediately the aircraft Gatling guns began to fire, and to John, the guns sounded like a long zipper being pulled down. Tufts of dirt were thrown fifteen to twenty feet in the air.

Russians in the open began to fall, and all knew the big Gatling guns were tearing the soldiers of the Russian Bear apart. As soon as they neared the woods the choppers fired missiles, and then turned slowly to the left or right as they broke from the attack. As one bird turned left, a missile was seen coming from the ground and it exploded right beside the tail rotor. A second later, parts of the rotor flew into the air and the aircraft began to slowly circle horizontally. It looked as if the rotor blades were still and the aircraft was in a flat spin.

Listening to the radio, he heard a calm voice speaking in Chinese and suspected it was the crew of the hit chopper. Since he didn't understand Chinese, he had no idea what was being said.

The damaged aircraft hit the open field halfway between the trees and the base proper, and hard too, but no explosion. The two man crew quickly exited the aircraft. Minutes later they were seen as prisoners of the Russians and were moving toward the trees under armed guard.

A CAIC Z-10 attack helicopter lined up and approached the men in the opening and John thought he was confirming who was taken prisoner, until his machine gun began barking and men began to fall. Body parts and gore flew in all directions as the big slugs burned holes through Russians and Chinese. They all fell and no one moved.

Taking the radio, John said, "Panda One, this is Cobra Two, your attack helicopter crew just killed all of the Chinese and Russians."

"Affirmative, Cobra Two. He was only following orders. It seems China wants none of us taken prisoner, so that will happen to all who crash and cannot be rescued. I know you find it harsh, but without a live prisoner, the Russians cannot prove we are here. Copy?"

"Roger, copy. Cobra Two out."

The Chinese attacked the woods three times and then Panda said, "All of the attack helicopters are returning to refuel and rearm. They will be gone about three zero minutes, over."

"Copy, what about you, Panda One?"

"I will remain on station to keep the Russians busy and when my men have new targets after they return, I will return to base for my turn rearming and refueling. Copy?"

"Copy, Panda One, Cobra Two out."

For the next thirty minutes the Russians stayed in the trees, probably licking their wounds and treating their injured. Soon the tell tale sound of the attack helicopters were heard and looking up, John saw them attacking from the left.

Panda One was heard speaking in Chinese and then he said in English, "They will attack targets of opportunity while I'm gone. Panda Two speaks some English if you get into trouble. Over."

"Copy, understand Panda Two is an English speaker."

"Roger that, but his accent is thick. Panda One, returning to base to refuel and rearm." As soon as he'd spoken, the aircraft turned and began moving south.

Over the next twenty minutes all was well, but then about 200 Russians ran from the trees toward the base. The attack helicopters were all over them, only the men were now firing shoulder launched missiles and in less than two minutes two birds were down. One landed on the base and was rescued. The other struck the ground at a fast speed and blew to hell and back, leaving a smoking crater behind, just slightly in front of the Russian advancement. The explosion killed at least five Russians.

The Russians just reached the perimeter wire when a Chinese Jet, it looked like a Su-27 Flanker, which was made in Russia but many were sold to the Chinese, zoomed down and dropped two canisters of napalm, burning the hell out of the attacking force. They slowly withdrew, taking their burned and smoking comrades with them. Others were seen dancing in the flames as they died. The flames were high and the smell of burnt flesh soon filled the air.

Chinese Jet, Su-27 Flanker, identify yourself, this is Cobra Two." John said.

"He is Balls Niner One and he is here to help. He is ready to do the most damage, but his English is poor. I will tell him your desires, Cobra Two. Copy?"

"Uh, yes, copy. Have him hit the trees with more napalm if he has it."

"Roger, understand. Wait one."

A minute passed and then Panda Two said, "Roger the napalm and he is making his approach now."

Without warning, there was a tremendous explosion that shook the ground and when John looked around, they were under an artillery attack.

As the jet made for the trees, two canisters of napalm left the aircraft and were seen flipping tail over head as they dropped into the trees. An artillery shell hit close to John and his radioman, so they both hugged the ground. Looking at the jet, now pulling away, the world under the aircraft was an inferno of red and yellow flames. Dark black smoke rose to the sky.

"Panda Two, can you find where those big guns are firing on us? They are causing casualties here on the ground."

"Copy, Cobra Two." Then orders were given in Chinese and two gunships moved to the west. There was a volley of artillery fire as five shells struck at the same time. Men and women screamed as the hot shrapnel stuck them in various parts of their bodies. Some fell to never get up, while others wrapped a wound and kept moving. Then it grew quiet.

"Cobra One, the big guns have been silenced and for good."

"Roger and copy that. Thanks, Panda Two."

"Cobra One, Panda One, and I am back on the target. It looks like you made excellent use of the fast mover I sent."

"Panda One, we did at that. If Balls Niner One is still around, have him place some rockets around our shrinking circle, please."

"Will do," Panda said and then passed John's words on to the jet fighter.

Explosions were heard just outside the fence and shrapnel was heard flying through the air with a loud buzzing sound. The Russian fire grew less and less, and then stopped. They were seen running from the battle, moving south. The attack helicopters and the jet made their way after the retreating army, hurting them with each pass.

"Tune in the base radios." John said and when the handset was given to him he said, "Cobra One to all Base radios, we will wait for the Russians to leave and then we'll clean this place up. I want all Russian dead piled in one pile and all of their wounded treated with compassion. They fought a good fight. If you meet any resistance, take it out quickly. I want all Commanders and section leaders at Stand Up in the morning at 0600 hours. Do not send a representative, unless you are dead or wounded. Any questions? Call me on a landline in an hour." He handed the phone back to his radio operator.

"What now, sir?" the radio operator asked.

"I need to report the battle to the General and we need to increase security here until all Russian troops have left the immediate area."

L eaving the bunker after filling out an after action report for the General John was tired but noticed his men and women were making headway in clearing the destruction and bodies from the base proper. The Russian bodies were being placed in huge nets and then picked up by helicopters and taken to areas near Russian facilities, to make finding the bodies easy for the Russian Bear. Times had changed and just four short years ago, the Partisans didn't even take prisoners.

As he moved, he thought, *I'm so tired. I think I'll shower, eat, and then hit the bed. I can't believe I get this tired after a single day of combat. I also need to send out some patrols to look for the Russians. I need to lead one, too, because I don't want to get rusty. I've found my people are easier to lead if I share the risks of a patrol and the chance of death. I'll lead them out in the morning, about an hour before dawn.*

He arrived at his quarters, found it as he'd left it and then cooked a quick meal of beef steak and a fried potatoes. He had a glass of water to wash his meal down. He finished eating, closed his eyes, and in seconds fell asleep. He woke when his head nodded and fell to his chest.

Walking to his phone, he called his office and said, "Sergeant Dias, alert my section, including you and all others, that we are moving into the field in the morning, two hours before dawn. Draw a full load of ammo, grenades and rations for seven days. I want a backup radio and a backup medic along for the trip."

"What is our assembly time?"

"O400 hundred hours. Now, see it is done and enjoy your evening."

"You as well, sir. Goodnight."

"Night, Sergeant."

He then showered, and went to bed. He was thinking about his life before the fall of America when he drifted off to sleep.

Morning looked cloudy, from what little he could see in the darkness, and turning on a television in his room, he listened to the weather as he dressed in his battle dress uniform. Pulling a small tube, he pulled the covers off both ends and began applying his camouflage face paint. He then placed his brown cowboy hat on his head and walked out the door. Over the next few days, someone would die.

When John neared the formation of this troops, he heard Lieutenant Joyce Jones grunt, "Teeennn-hhhuuuttt." All the troops snapped to attention.

"All ready and accounted for, sir. We lost two members yesterday during the attack. Private Barnes was killed by a grenade and Sergeant Armitage lost his left arm and eye to rifle fire. Armitage will recover and then be reassigned to other duties besides combat." she said as she saluted the Colonel.

"At my command! Teeen-huuut!" John then bellowed, "At ease."

Twelve people relaxed as the Colonel then said, "We are going into the bush today to look for Russians. We will be out for at least a week, or until our losses grow too heavy. All of you have bush time, so this is nothing new to you. As an experienced squad, I want nothing but professionalism once we leave this base. We all know just a split second of goofing off in the woods can get you killed. Keep alert and you'll come home alive. Any questions?"

Silence.

John then said, "Dismissed, but remain in the area to form into fighting groups. We'll be leaving in just a few minutes."

"Sir, did you want Major Woo along too?" Lieutenant Jones asked.

She was an attractive woman, mid twenties, short, maybe five feet and two inches tall, 100 pounds, with blonde hair and big deep blue eyes. Her teeth were white and even, and she had a beautiful smile. All of her curves and bumps were in the right places, but John actually thought she was a very intelligent woman. He was attracted to her mind and not so much her body. Even a blind man could see she was stunningly beautiful, but once past her looks, her logic was sound and she was an excellent and fast mind in combat. John deeply respected her, professionally.

"No, Woo is to mind the store while we play infantry for a few days."

Jones nodded.

"Gene Green, post! You're the radio operator, so I want you closer to me than my shadow. Jason Smith, stay in the middle of the group, so you can respond as a medic in either direction quickly. I want Leroy Carrier on Point and Vernon Lee on drag. Let's move, people."

The two men he'd called out for point and drag were both near six feet tall, thin due to poor food, and wore their brown hair clipped short. Lee sported a short brown beard, while Carrier wore a long shaggy mustache. Both men were good in the field and with Lee being an ex-country boy, he could track and kill silently. How did John know this? He'd seen the man kill just that way and more than once. Lee carried a set of deadly throwing knives and loved to use a garrote. While only 18 or so, both men were experienced and professional in their duties.

John then said, "Forward at a slow walk and once off the base, keep your eyes open for booby traps, both ours and theirs." He moved in between Msgt. Mary Dias and Ssgt. Tom Prings and they moved toward the main gate.

The closer they got to the main gate, the more dead bodies and destruction they saw. Many of the dead had been disfigured by the bullets and bombs that had struck their bodies. Piles of dead Russians lay in a small river of blood. Their eyes open, but unseeing. John shivered as he watched a fly go into a dead Russian's nose and come out his open mouth. He spotted movement and then saw a fly walking over the still open eyes of a dead man. Once again he quivered.

The morning passed uneventfully, except a few booby traps had been marked. Carrier was good on point and probably John's best. They stopped in a grove of walnut and hickory trees for a 30 minute lunch and break from walking. Sixty pound packs grew heavier the more tired the carrier got. John was paying for being out of shape and his back was already hurting him early in the mission.

Whispering, John said, "We break for 30, so we can eat a bit. No talking."

They started opening the stolen Russian Green Frogs or the issued Chinese rations and everyone got a mixture of both. John didn't care for the Chinese food because it was spicy, almost too hot to eat in some cases, especially the pickled turnip or the spicy rice. At times he open both rations and mixed them together. The Russians had a nice thick stew that John usually poured over the rice from the Chinese rations. By mixing the two, both foods were improved.

"Cobra One, this is Copperhead four, over."

"This is Cobra One, go ahead. Over."

"Radio check."

"Uh, read you five by five, over."

"Copy. We have unconfirmed reports of large bodies of Russian troops in your area. I suggest stealth. One partisan unit, 'Possum One, confirms there are T-90 tanks and BMP-3 fighting vehicles about five miles north of your current position. The General wants you to confirm them and then move back as he sends in a squadron of H-6k Chinese bombers."

"Copy, we'll eat and then find the tank farm, if possible."

"Colonel, someone is nearing our position. I got a quick look and they appeared to be Russians." Carrier whispered as he neared John.

"Cobra One, over and out." He said and then turned to his troops and said, "Everyone hide, and we'll ambush them if possible." He wasn't super worried about his troops being seen, because from head to toe they wore camouflage, including face paint and flat olive green Nomex® flight gloves.

They had just hunted cover when the Russian point man neared. He glanced at where the squad had been eating and then walked closer. Someone had left some green paper from their Green Frog ration and it had caught the man's eyes. He bent over, picked up the paper and then walked back to his group, who were stopped maybe a 100 feet from him.

John saw the man showing the green paper to a Captain and then some words in Russian were exchanged, but the Captain laughed and sent the man back up front. Obviously the Leader thought another Russian unit had stopped there to eat. He did send the man in a different direction though, just to be safe. As the men moved north, John released a loud sigh.

Five minutes later, the Russians were out of sight.

Crawling from the brush, John said, "I thought we were going to have to fight our way out of here. I'm glad that officer thought the paper from the ration was left by a Russian soldier. I think we need to move more slowly toward the tank farm.

CHAPTER 5

S enior Sergeant Vova was a little confused until he realized he and his men had been dropped miles off course and nowhere near where they should have been. Supposedly he'd be within a mile of the stockyards and he smelled nothing. He knew stockyards smelled, because he grew up on a farm. His nose picked up nothing and from triangulating his position on a map he knew they were at least 20 miles off, and that meant many of the men dropped in waves would not reach the base in time to place pressure on all sides as the attack took place.

"Okay, we are a little off course and not where we are supposed to be, so we will correct our course and rush to the base. I doubt we will reach it before the attack, but we will do our best. Makarovich, give me the handset."

Private Olga Makarovich handed it to him and then smiled, enjoying the burning touch of his hand on hers. She wanted Sergeant Vova and would have him, but not out here. She'd get him drunk back at the base and then see if he was the lover she thought he was. *Right now, I need to be totally professional, so when I go to see him in his quarters, he will not know I have plans to take him to bed.*

"Hotel, Hotel, this is Monsoon. Do you read me, Hotel? Over."

"I hear you fine, Monsoon, what is your location? Over."

"Hotel, the aircraft dropped us at least 20 miles off the planned drop zone. Over."

"Uh, understand you were dropped away from your drop zone (DZ). Hotel One will not be pleased because at least half of the drops were off target. What is your status? Over."

"No wounded, killed or hurt. We are at 100% and continuing our mission. Over."

"Your mission is over, and it did not go victorious for the Mother Land. The attack on the base gave us 40% casualties, with

23% of them dead. Wait one, while I get guidance from Hotel One on where to send you or if you are to return to base. Over."

Vova waited patiently; the battle was over now, and he was not rushed for time. A couple of minutes later the radio operator at the base said, "Monsoon One, this is Hotel. Hotel One states he wants you to remain in the field and pester the hell out of the Americans. A classified message will be sent within an hour. Additionally, I expect you to be returned to base by the time the General arrives from Moscow and the court martials start over the missed drop zones and drinking on duty. There was no way the aircraft should have been that far off target and the Colonel will have some heads before this drop is ever close to being forgotten. Anything else? Over."

"No, I will remain in place until we get the classified message. Then we will do as ordered. Monsoon One, over and out."

Looking at Makarovich, Vova said, "Prepare for a classified message from the base."

"Yes, Sergeant."

Less than ten minutes later, she handed him a decoded handwritten message.

"This message is classified Top Secret. Your unit, Monsoon One, will proceed to the enemy base and harass them each time someone leaves the base on patrol. Your sniper will kill any and all senior officers above the rank of Major. You will then defend your sniper at all times. If pressure gets to be too much, pull back and wait a day or so. Your whole mission is to harass the enemy and keep them off guard until another attack is drawn up. Your needed supplies will be dropped to you by parachute. You will be returned on the first day of next month, and two days after your return, you will appear in a series of Court Martials where you will be a state witness. This message is classified Top Secret."

"Well, every one, we will not be returning to base for at least a week. We have our marching orders and they will be followed. Rostislavovich, as my sniper, you will soon be put to work, but only killing senior American officers. The rest of us will be ambushing American patrols and killing as many as we can. On the 1st of the new month, we will be picked up and returned to base. Now, I want Ilyich on point and Pavovich on drag. Keep the pace slow but steady. We are not in a race with anyone. Mark any booby-traps."

"Yes, Sergeant. When should I start?" Ilyich asked.

"Uh, right now, unless you are busy." Vova said, his tone indicating he was getting frustrated.

"No, Sergeant, I am not—"

"Move to the front and get us moving! We need to cover some miles before dark, and I want you on a compass bearing of 310 degrees and remember the magnetic north here is 8 degrees. Now, move." the Sergeant said and then thought, *He's a good trooper, but a little slow at times. I need to try and instill some sense of mission here, or they may keep us out here forever. If I can motivate them to complete a successful mission or two, then headquarters might remove us and we can return to base. The problem is most are just out of secondary school and know little.*

The next hour was passed without any booby-traps found and they moved at a fair but not really fast rate of speed. Then, Ilyich froze and called out, "I need the Sergeant here!"

If that boy has seen a snake or is messing around, I will kick his ass, Sergeant Vova thought as he moved forward. When beside the young man, he whispered, "What do you see?"

"See the mine about six feet from me? Straight ahead. It is a big one, and I am not sure what to do since it is at least four times bigger than most."

"All mines are treated the same, unless they are command detonated. This one is one of the larger personnel mines. Now, Mili, move close to the mine, pull your knife and prepare to follow my orders."

Private Mili Ilyich took three steps, screamed, was jerked off his feet, and his body was pulled into the air, where he struck a camouflaged 4 foot by 8 foot sheet of plywood. The plywood had a handmade nail placed every six inches in the surface and he struck it with his back first. Each nail was approximately 14 inches long with barbs on the end. His body was penetrated by eight of the nails and they were protruding from his chest, stomach and neck. Blood dripped from the board, to land in the lush green grass of the forest floor. He tried to speak, but the words would not form in his mind, as he ran his fingers over one of the nails in his chest.

"Get me a medic up here and fast!" Vova ordered.

"Nititovich, get to the point and now!" someone said, their voice filled with urgency.

When the medic neared, he took one look at Ilyich and said, "I can do nothing for this man. The barbs have torn and punctured most of his major organs, Sergeant."

"I know that. Give him a double dose of morphine, because the shock will soon wear off and no man or woman should die in pain. Do it now."

Pulling a syringe, the medic loaded morphine from a vial, and gave the victim a shot in his left arm. He then refilled his needle of death and gave him another, a fatal amount. Ilyich gave a great quiver as the medication entered his body and his eyes turned glassy, as the strong pain killer made it's way though his blood system. A couple of minutes later, his body jerked a couple of times, his breathing stopped, and with his eyes fixated, Milli Ilyich died.

"He was only 18, Sergeant."

"Now he will never be 19. I warned all of you that the traps usually have traps around them, but I can see now that no one listened. The Americans are not a bunch of dumb asses running around looking like cowboys. Most of the men are prior service and they will kill you in any number of different ways. Never blindly approach a booby-trap without checking all along your intended path for other smaller or, like in this case, larger traps. *They will kill you!*"

"Should I have his body removed?" the medic asked.

"No, because the tree he is in could have any number of traps. Leave him, but report him as confirmed dead, unable to recover his body. He will not be the only one that never sees Mother Russia again. Now, Corporal Igorevich, you take point *and watch where in the hell you step.*"

The next four hours were uneventful and the Corporal found a few mines, which he marked, and continued on his way. It was about an hour from dark when the squad found a suitable place in some trees to spend the night. The area whey were traveling was lacking trees overall and was on the edge of the great plains. While teams could move over open ground it was difficult, and a man's stress level went up a great deal. There was little cover, except for gullies, old buffalo wallows, ditches, and dry stream beds. Once standing, you could turn around after a full day of walking and see where you spent the previous night.

"We will rest overnight (RON) here and continue in the morning." He was tired and the death of Ilyich still bothered him.

As they stopped for the night, Vova thought, *I like to have enough cover to move unseen but not so much cover it is a jungle. I can remember attending jungle survival training in Vietnam 60 years after the Americans had been there, and I hated the place. At night, everything imaginable, and some things one could not imagine, would come out to feed and mate. The floor of the jungle became almost a living thing, with all the insects, snakes, crocodiles, and other critters moving around. If nothing else, I learned to sleep in trees, and I hated the place. I had almost been snake bit a number of times and once had a huge crocodile attempting to pull me and my sleeping bag into the water. No, jungles I will avoid if at all possible.*

The Radio Operator neared and said, "Headquarters just called and they want us to join a tank farm tomorrow and start hitting the partisans in this area. One squad per tank, and we are to work together as a team. All houses are to be attacked and destroyed by the tanks, while we shoot those running from the house for safety. We are to take no prisoners."

"I will not murder those unable to fight back. So, if we are not to take prisoners, we will doctor those hurt and leave them unharmed. By God, I have to be able to sleep at night and murder would make that hard to do. I have been in this man's army longer than you have been alive, Olga, and I will be damned if I will start murdering now. That part of the order is illegal."

Olga smiled, because she had him using her first name. She knew it was common for superiors to use first names of those they knew well. She had him half way in her bed already, only he didn't know it. If she could get him hot in some way, nature would take over from that point on, or so she thought.

"Tell them we will comply with the orders, and in reality, what we do or do not do is none of their business, not as long as we kill Americans. I have found murdering members of the partisans is not healthy for a Russian. Simply say Monsoon Two understands and will comply with the orders."

Olga made the contact and passed on the Senior Sergeant's words. Base then signed off and as she placed the handset in the cradle, she wondered if she could get him hot enough tonight in their fox hole to play a little. While she thought about sex a great deal, her real experience was limited to one time in a hayloft of an old barn, a couple of times in the back seat of a car, and once in a dark barracks with another woman when everyone was asleep or gone. That experience had been fun with the woman, but she didn't count it as much. She'd discovered she enjoyed sex with either gender, but preferred to be with a man. The love of a woman satisfied her immediate needs, while the love of a man filled her with a contentment that lasted for a few days.

They quickly dug a foxhole, placed all their grenades and other gear within easy reach and then began eating their supper. She intentionally bent over her pack low, as she looked for a ration, and knew the Sergeant could see much more than just cleavage, but her complete breasts, if he looked long enough. When she stood, ration in hand, he caught him looking. She simply smiled and gave him a wink. Petr blushed a little, turned his head and began opening his meal.

As she ate, Olga made it a point to run her tongue over her meal, and knew she was being watched because she'd caught him, but neither of them said anything.

Shortly after dark, they were to stand 50% awake all night, which meant one of the two troops in each foxhole had to remain awake. It was not unusual for Petr to get up and check the foxholes, looking for both sleeping. Then he would place the edge of his sharp knife blade on the guilty person's throat and wake them. The fear they felt for a few minutes was intense and more than one had peed their pants in fear. It kept those on guard duty awake because a sleeping guard was useless, and rumor had it if the Senior Sergeant caught you sleeping he'd cut your throat, which was of course a lie. He never brought the lie up because it was better if they believed he'd kill them for sleeping. So far, his new organization was better than most and he'd caught no one sleeping in the last six months. The sad part was, under Russian Army law, he had the power to cut their throats and no charges would be filed against him for killing. The Army was a brutal life where sergeants and officers could kill those who did not obey orders. However, only a fool would try to kill those who worked for him or one day he would probably find a grenade in the bathroom with him. The troops knew how to fight back and without witnesses too.

"Do you wish to sleep now, Sergeant?" Olga asked.

"Yes, I will sleep now and wake me when half the night is over. I think midnight would be a good time."

"Good, you sleep and I will bathe in my helmet. I cannot sleep covered with dirt and sweat from walking all day. Sleep, and I will wake you later."

An hour after they'd spoken, Olga poured water into her helmet, took a wash cloth from her pack, along with a bar of scentless soap, and began washing herself clean. She didn't get so wrapped up in her washing that she wasn't looking around, because she was, and some of the men were watching her. She unbuttoned her camouflage shirt and ran the cloth around her full breasts and moaned just loud enough Petr heard her.

Opening his eyes, he watched her for a few minutes, found himself interested in her, so he closed his eyes and rolled over on his side, facing away from her.

Seeing her bathe wasn't working on the old Sergeant, so she quickly finished cleaning and then sat in the darkness fuming mad. *He actually turned his back on me and I know he saw my breasts. He saw the shape of my hips too. How can a man do that? He is not normal,* she thought as she scanned the darkness looking for movements. Over time her anger disappeared and she grew sleepy, but she knew if the Sergeant caught her sleeping, he'd at least ridicule her in front of the other troopers and probably after slapping her hard. No, she had no desire to get on the powerful man's bad side or the rest of her army career would be rough.

Over the next five hours she listened to the crickets, tree frogs, whippoorwills, and quail calling in the night. At one point the night sounds stopped, but for less than five minutes. A little later they started up again. All experienced soldiers knew the night sounds assured them no one was in the area, but when the noise stopped, something big was moving around. Each person on guard flipped their rifles off safety until the noise returned.

It was midnight by her watch when she woke him, and then curled up with a wool blanket on the damp floor of the hole in the ground. She was asleep in seconds.

An hour before dawn, Sergeant Vova said in a voice loud enough to be heard by those awake, "I want everyone awake. We have a tank farm to visit and work to do for Mother Russia. Eat, gather in all mines, and pack your gear away. We leave right at dawn."

Corporal Adam Igorevich mumbled awake from his sleep and said, "My father told me, join the army, it will make you a man. I joined the army thinking I could catch up on my sleep. I never imagined that for two years, I'd be getting up earlier than any damned farmer, but here I am and in a place I have never heard of. I know only that they have a lot of cowboys here in Texas. Maybe I will kill one and take his hat."

"You would be handsome with a cowboy hat." Private Tima Yermolayevich said and then she gave a low sexy laugh.

"That's enough clowning around. Stop the noise and prepare to leave." the Senior Sergeant ordered as he placed his overnight gear in his back pack.

Igorevich walked to the edge of their camp, peed and then returned to his foxhole to finish packing. He'd only been in country a little over two months, but the Sergeant was correct to say something to them. Snipers often waited for the enemy to relax and then started their killing spree. He cut the small talk instantly because the old Sergeant was experienced and his word was law. Adam wanted to survive his tour in the American War, return home a hero, and go to college and then to a good paying job. At some point he'd marry, have a family, grow old and then sit around with other veterans and sip vodka as they spoke of times long gone. Yes, he would survive, because he'd listen and follow orders.

"Get your gear on, and it is time we move. Nititovich, I want you and Ikovle to guard the women as they pee and do their morning toilet. All of you men who have not peed and emptied yourselves yet, do so before we leave. Hurry, I want to be moving by the time the sun is clearly seen."

Ten minutes later, all the Russian troops were moving down a little travel trail toward a tank farm. Junior Sergeant Ekel Pavovich was cursing the army in general for the ungodly hour they started to work, when a look from Senior Sergeant Petr Vova shut him up instantly. The look clearly said, 'Shut your mouth.'

It was near noon on a beautiful day and the man on point was Rostislavovich; they rotated the point man every two hours and that was because so many booby traps were being found. A tired person might pass up an obviously dangerous place where a fresh mind would not. The position was hard for some of the troops, because your adrenaline was high; one mistake could get you killed, and the traps were expertly hidden so a good eye and attention to detail was needed. Some men, like Ikovle or Rostislavovich enjoyed point and lived for the high the position brought. Every sense a person has was on edge and finely tuned while walking point, but a minute of slack would get yourself and probably others maimed or killed. It was, to some of them, an interesting job.

"Monsoon, this is Hotel, over." The radio came alive.

"Go Hotel." Olga said in a flash.

"Be advised a flight of Chinese attack helicopters are currently hunting in your area on the map. They found Captain Grigorievna's squad and there are only three survivors out of twelve."

"Copy, understand we have unfriendly helicopters in the area. Over."

"Correct and they are reported to be very aggressive. Over."

"I will inform Monsoon Two. Monsoon out."

"No need to tell me, I heard it all. Okay, spread out. I want ten meters between you and the next person in line. If we see a helicopter, fall to the ground and hope they do not see us. If they do and line up for an attack, scatter and spread out. Make them work if they want to kill us. We have two missiles, both are shoulder fired and four Grenade launchers, keep all of them out and ready to use. Pull them now and make ready."

"Can we not just hide now, before they see us?" Junior Sergeant Ekel Pavovich asked.

"We could do that, but then we would not get to the tank farm, now would we? No, Russian soldiers do not hide, comrade, we stand and fight. Come, we have more kilometers to cover and I expect to reach them in the morning, unless the Chinese kill all of us. Let us move it, people, we have things to do."

Whispering to Igorevich beside him, Pavovich said, "Nothing scares that sonofabitch."

Vova heard him and didn't say anything, but he did smile.

CHAPTER 6

John and his people were moving again, and things were slow and the stress rate was out of sight. They'd seen three more groups of Russians within the two hours they'd been moving and things were not normal. Never in 8 years had the Colonel seen so many Russians in such a small portion of land. The big groups of them had broken down into smaller cells, which the partisans did all the time, and they were all moving in different directions in a hurry.

The Colonel was squatting over a map, removed his cowboy hat, ran his fingers through his sweat saturated hair and then put his hat back on. He was attempting to find their location on an old map he had from a gas station, and was having little luck. He saw little in the way of a landmark and without landmarks, it was difficult to triangulate his position. He was finally able to find his location, near Mesquite, Texas or so he believed, and discovered he was about 18 miles from the tank farm at Rockwall, Texas, if his guess at their location was even close.

"As near as I can figure, we're near Mesquite, Texas and if we follow the highway, about a hundred meters from here north by east, we'll come to the tank farm before the end of the day."

"What highway is it?" someone asked.

"Interstate Highway 30, but stay off the road and about a hundred meters from the edge of the road. Be watchful of Russian traffic on the road as well as mines too. Before we reach the tank farm, we'll find a huge lake, named Lake Ray Hubbard. We'll find Rockwall near the northern end of the lake, and the tanks are just a mile or so north of the small town."

"How small is the place?" Private Larry Brown asked.

"I'm not sure but this old map says around 45,000 people so give or take a bunch now. It's hard to say how the fall of America hurt this place. As we all know, the war has killed millions of civilians. I don't think many still live there, or the Russians would not be using it as a tank gathering spot or farm. Surely most populated places have members of the partisans there and I've never heard of a group from Rockwall, Texas. Now, let's get saddled up and walking. If we work this properly and make good time, we'll be there way before dark. Let's move, people." John said and stood, placing his sixty pound pack on his sore back.

As they moved toward the small town by a lake, John thought, *I'm getting too old to be out here with these youngsters. I'm 40 years older than most of them, have a bad back and carrying more than my fair share of scars from previous battles. On top of that, my back hurts, my fingers are sore and my damned hair tingles under my hat. I don't think I'll go on more missions in the future, but I have to go on this one, because it may be the last big battle of the war. I'm tired of living alone, with no one to love me or to make me feel special. War is bad enough, but being alone in combat is hard, very hard. Then again, worrying about a person you love is hard to do as well. I need to remember I'm in a war and keep the relationships down to meeting a physical need. I am damned if I love a woman, and damned if I don't.*

It was near 1600 hundred hours when Ssgt. Tom Prings, the point man, stopped, held his fist in the air balled up and everyone knew he spotted the enemy. John quickly moved forward.

Whispering from beside the point man, John asked, "What do you see?"

"I see nothing, but listen and tell me what you hear?"

John cocked his head to the side and then grinned as he said, "Tanks or bulldozers."

"I suspect, sir, that's your tank farm. The lake is off our left side."

"Move forward and do the job slowly. When you can see the tanks stop, and I'll move forward to your location. Move, but remember, this is not a race, and we're in no rush."

"I fully understand, sir. I will use caution, and when do you want to leave?"

Smiling, knowing Prings knew his intent, John replied, "We need to leave now, Sergeant, and watch your ass, because booby traps will grow more frequent the closer to the big beasts we get."

Prings smiled and then walk in the direction of the loud noises, his every sense on high alert.

Less than a mile later an explosion was heard at the front of the squad and when John arrived at the point man, he discovered

Pringle sitting on his rear in the middle of the trail, a smoking two foot deep hole in front of him.

"What happened?" John asked as he looked for blood on the man but saw nothing but a small puncture wound on his right earlobe.

Shaking his head, the Ssgt. said, "I'm sorry, sir, but I can't hear you. My ears hurt and the noise may have busted my eardrums. I think I activated a small bomb, maybe 100 or 200 pounds. I tripped over the activating line and I suspect that saved my life. As it was, I was on the ground when the bomb exploded, sending all the shrapnel over my head and into empty air."

John pulled a small notebook from his shirt pocket and an ink pen from another shirt pocket. He then wrote, "If you cannot hear, you are no good as a point man. Join the main group and send Corporal Brown to me as your replacement. Understand?"

"I'm a bit confused, but I fully understand, sir. I can return on my own and I will send Brown to you."

"Good, now go. I want to get to the tank farm today." John wrote and then slapped the Sergeant on his back.

In a matter of a couple of minutes, Corporal Larry Brown was beside John as the Colonel discussed how to approach the tank farm. The new point man was all ears.

When he finished, John asked, "Any questions?"

"No, sir. I'll move out right now. I will be about 50 yards in front of the main group. If you hear gunfire, don't rush forward, because I will drop and attempt escape and evade back to the main group. You rushing forward might get you killed for nothing."

"I understand, now move toward the tanks."

Less than an hour later, Brown made his way to the main group, moved to John and said, "Sir, if you'll come with me, you can see your tank farm and it's not only full, but busy."

Smiling, the Colonel said, "Lead the way and I'll take a look. Private Green, I need you as my shadow, and I want the phone at arms length at all times."

"Uh, yes sir." Green said and then began to walk with the other two men.

Minutes later, with all three on the ground behind some brush, John moved a few leaves and clearly spotted about fifteen tanks. A good twenty men were working on the big beasts or talking to others near their tank. Slowly John counted and when he reached the sixteenth and last tank, he said in a whisper, "I need the handset."

Private Green handed the handset to his Colonel and waited. Speaking, John said, "Copperhead, Cobra Two, over."

"Go Cobra, this is Copperhead, over."

"I am at the farm and I count sixteen tanks, with four BMP-3 troop carriers. Ten of the tanks are the T-90 and the other six are T-14's. I see close to 25 men out in the open, working on their tanks."

"Roger that, Cobra Two, and I copy. Wait one, as I determine what Copperhead Actual wants done. Over."

"Will do, over."

Two minutes later, Copperhead said, "Cobra Two, Copperhead Actual wants you to pull back to the nearest hill or highest tree and for you to watch and provide a damage report. The Chinese have been notified and they are on their way to strike the tanks. Estimated time of arrival is ten minutes, over."

"Copy and we're pulling back now. Cobra Two, out."

"Everyone make for the slight hill to our east and we'll sit there and watch the show. When the attack helicopters arrive, bury your asses as deep in the ground as you can, to avoid any mistakes. In the meantime, once there, I suggest you all try to dig at least a partial foxhole. We need to double time to the hill, now."

Once on the hill looking down a slight valley, he saw the tanks moving into a defensive position, so it was very likely they had advance warning Chinese aircraft were coming to visit. Most of the tank commanders stood in the turret, ready to override the electronics and fire manually. It was then the *whop-whop-whop* of the attack helicopters were heard.

There were three counted by John, and he grinned as the fast choppers fired their first missiles of the attack. One struck a T-90 right where the turret meets the body and a huge explosion resulted as the tank stopped moving. Dark black smoke began to pour from the engine of the tank and men were seen climbing from the destroyed vehicle. The Gatling guns on one chopper began to fire and tufts of soil were tossed twelve feet into the air as men were cut to pieces. Bodies flew in all directions and when completed, a mist of cerise floated in the air, right above the dead. There were no more movements.

One chopper took a missile from a tank and began to smoke. Listening to the radio, he made no sense of the Chinese being spoken. The chopper gently moved for the ground, still level, but auto rotating as it dropped. The last six feet or so, it dropped hard and the other gunships lined up to attack the bird now in the ground and in flames.

"Cobra Two, to any Chinese attack helicopter attacking the Russian tanks. If you speak English, reply please."

"I speakie little English." a Chinese pilot said in a heavily accented voice. "This is Snow Reopard One, ovah."

"Do not kill the crew, because my men will try to rescue them."

"Uh, okay, but you no lescue, we kill."

"I understand, One. Give us five minutes and you can continue to kill tanks, over."

"Loger and out."

As the battle was being fought, John and his troops move toward the two Chinese, now in a shallow but wide ditch. He stopped about 100 feet from the men and sent Sgt Wolfgang Hanish to the two men. When the two Chinese saw Hanish, they were scared enough that they almost shot him, but he yelled, "American! American! I come to help you."

Once with the men, Hanish said, "Come with me and I'll take you to where you will be safe."

"I am Tam and I speak English. My co-pilot is understandably as frightened, as am I. Go, we will follow."

As the three began running, the unnamed Chinese man fell only to be scooped up by the somewhat larger man by the name of Tam. From what Hanish could see, the man had taken a bullet to the right calf. A few long minutes later, they were in among the Americans.

The injured man, introduced as Jong Wang, was bleeding and one of the medics, Private Marriann Toms, was all over him working. Ten minutes later, his wound dressed and him given morphine for pain, he drifted off to sleep.

"Snow Leopard One, this is Cobra Two and we have your two pilots with us."

"Copy. We must attack again and again. Busy now."

The last remaining tank, a T-14 fired a round and the lead chopper suddenly exploded with absolutely no chance for the crew to get out. Small pieces, along with a half dozen larger pieces began to rain down on the battlefield. The tank took a rocket to the turret and then exploded, sending the turret a good twenty feet into the air, where it fell back to earth to land beside the burning chassis. The one surviving attack helicopter said, "I have notified my base you hab Tam and Wang. I go now."

"Copy, you have notified Chinese Headquarters that we have your pilots. Good luck and have a good flight home." John said into the handset and then to his troops he said, "Prepare to fight, the Russians will come for these Chinese men."

His people began to lay magazines, grenades, bayonets and even shovels with the edges sharpened within reach. The Russians were still fighting fires and rescuing people, so John thought maybe they still thought the two Chinese were in their destroyed chopper, but once the fire was out, they'd find no bodies.

"Disregard the fight. They seem confused by the battle and to lose that many tanks, even if two of the three attacking helicopters were downed, it was a small prize. Millions if not billions of dollars in heavy armor and the small personnel carriers, the BMP-3, were totally destroyed, not to mention the loss of life as well. Someone in this group is in serious trouble when Moscow calls next time."

"Gather up your gear," MSgt Mary Dias said as she began placing magazines filled with bullets, back into her pack. She even retrieved a Claymore mine she'd set out earlier.

Minutes later, John said, "Green, give the radio to Carrier. I want you and Smith to carry the injured pilot. Come, we need to get the hell out of here. Every minute the fire is burning is time better used getting away from here. Someone give Tam a gun, pistol or rifle, it matters little. Let's move, people and now."

"I will stay near the injured man." Marriann Toms said.

"No, Smith is carrying the man and I need you to be prepared to give medical care to our troops. Since the two of you are both medics, Smith can care for the patient and you're needed for us. Stay near the middle of the group, so you can respond to either end quickly."

"Yes, sir." Toms replied and moved down the line a little.

"Lee, you're on point, with Hanish bringing up the rear on drag. Let's move, and now."

An hour later, during a break, Tam pointed out, "Do any of you hear the dogs barking? I count two dogs by the sound."

John listened and then said, "I hear them too. We will soon be coming to one of our minefields; we'll go through it and if they attempt to follow, we'll ambush them."

A few short minutes later, a small field between two groves of trees was seen.

"There's the minefield." Toms said and then added, "and they're closer now. Hurry."

Pulling a map from his shirt pocket, John moved to the front and they were soon across the field but they'd lost valuable time. He had his people hide and prepare to fire on the Russians when they were half way across the minefield.

Minutes later about fifty Russians appeared and they were totally unaware they were about to enter a minefield. About half the group moved quickly into the field with dogs leading, and the animals seemed to be unable to smell the explosives because not a one went off, then off on the right side there came an explosion, followed by a horrible scream of deep pain.

John lined up on the closest dog team and yelled, "Fire!"

Hanish was on the M-60 machine gun and Brown was his loader. The big gun swept the path clean of any standing Russians and mine after mine began to explode as people and bullets struck the detonators. The air filled with screams, prayers in Russian, and yells for help. The M-60 then moved to the very rear of the Russians and began its killing and maiming.

Now grenades were exploding with the mines and the Russians, many of them, were in hell before they knew they were dead. Ables stood and gave three long squirts with his flamethrower and men and women engulfed with flames walked aimlessly as they fought to extinguish the flames eating at their flesh. Some stepped on mines and were killed in the explosions that followed but what the mines didn't kill, the big M-60 did.

"Cease fire! Ables, no more flames, the Russians are all down for the count. I want everyone to gather their gear and let's get the hell out of here before Russian aircraft arrive. Lee, you're on point and Irving, you're on drag. Let's move, people, and I mean now!" John began moving at a fast walk. Soon the rest were behind him and each was filled with a deep sense of satisfaction knowing they killed the half of a company size group that was after them. They'd killed as a part of a huge killing machine and each knew in the war it was them or the Russians and when given a choice, like today, the Russians would die.

"Colonel, the wounded Chinese man has died. During the battle he must have taken a round to his chest. I just moved back to check him and he was gone. That is when I saw the injury to his back."

"Take the body to the small river ahead and find a ridge of soil and collapse the dirt on him. We cannot not carry dead weight, just so he can be buried Chinese style or any style. We need speed and we'll have it now."

"Colonel, I appreciate what you did for my co-pilot and weapons system operator. He was a good man with a family." Tam said as he neared John after the impromptu burial.

"And, your rank?" he asked the young officer.

"I am a Captain, sir. Captain Tam."

"Tam, I did for your man exactly what I'd do for an American. I'd like to recover his body and take it with us, but our stretcher carriers don't need that. There are only twelve of us, so we have to make every effort to survive. Two men away from a stretcher are two more guns and four eyes helping to make us safe."

"Thank you anyway. I have marked where his body is and one day my country may return and recover his body or bones." Tam nodded seriously and then moved up the line.

"What was that all about, sir?" Msgt Dias asked, her voice revealing her interest in the conversation.

"Not much. He just thanked me for sort of burying his flying buddy. I wouldn't call collapsing an overhang of dirt on a body a burial, but he did."

Dias nodded but said nothing. She found the little Chinese men interesting, but knowing they were communists she avoided them. She had no political beliefs but they would not include that form of government anyway. She believed in democracy and a republic, not socialism.

"Uh, Cobra Two, Copperhead."

John took the handset from Green who had gotten it back when Wang died, "Cobra Two Actual, go."

"The Chinese government wants the live man brought out if possible, but if things turn rough, he is to be killed, understand?"

"No, Copperhead, I do not understand. Are you asking me to murder him?"

"No, not murder, but he must be silenced if he is about to be captured. At all costs they do not want the Russians to get their hands on him or any Chinese. He must be terminated immediately if it appears you are about to be captured, understand?"

John then acted as if he had radio trouble, "I cannot hear you, Copperhead. Cobra One to Copperhead do you read me?"

"Roger that, Cobra. How do you read, over?"

"Come in, Copperhead. Copperhead do you read me, over."

"Cobra Two, this is Copperhead. Do you hear me?"

"Copperhead, this is Cobra, you are coming in broken up, so I'll try to contact you in an hour. Maybe by then I will be in an area with better reception, over."

"Copy, over, Copperhead out."

Tossing the handset to Green, John chuckled and said, "I hate radio trouble."

Tam laughed and said, "We were warned we'd be killed if at all possible before we would be allowed to be taken prisoner. My government has been fighting this war for years and they still deny they are here."

"Let's move, and quickly. Toms, you're my point and try to find us a place to RON."

"Will do, sir." She replied, stood and began walking toward base.

"I thank you for saving my life." Tam said as they moved over the rough ground about twenty feet from a well traveled trail.

"It was God that saved you, not me. I was just his tool."

"Perhaps, but I was raised with no religion. Most of us in Communist China have no religion because it is forbidden. Some of the very poor attend church or a temple of some sort, but those of us in society have been trained not to call on a man who is a fairy tale."

"Well, my new friend, that fairy tale just saved your ass."

Silence as they continued to walk.

Finally, John said, "We can talk later, because it is not smart to travel over lands our enemy may be in as we chatter like magpies."

Tam nodded and continued walking. He looked as if he was going to say something, but changed his mind and kept quiet. They could talk later.

CHAPTER 7

Senior Sergeant Vova woke up earlier that day pissed because Headquarters had him out looking for members of the resistance, and all they cared about was partisan body counts. His people were well trained and they were airborne troops, but they cost more per man than regular infantry. It was his opinion that the "mud walkers" should be out searching, and not his people. Rumor had it that even Spetsnaz was out looking for their enemies.

"We will stop in those trees and bivouac. I want mines out, guards posted, and meals eaten before dark because we will have no fires after sundown. Sgt. Katenka, see my orders are followed."

"Yes, Sergeant." She replied and then moved to where the troops were and repeated his orders.

"Private Makarovich, bring me the radio so I can call in our night position and see if our orders have changed. I figure the tank farm is just a few more miles. Tomorrow night we will be surrounded by the armor and we will not have to pull guard. Their food is flown out, too, so our meals will be better."

Once on the radio, Vova said, "Copy, Hotel. Any change in our mission?"

Olga Makarovich watched the Sergeant, and when his eyes closed and he shook his head, she knew he had bad news for all of them.

"Roger, Hotel. Monsoon out." he handed the handset to Olga.

"Everyone listen up. Headquarters, in their great wisdom, has changed our mission. We are now looking for an escaped Chinese pilot. Apparently this Chinese man escaped after his attack helicopter crashed and burned. He was seen being rescued by an unknown partisan unit. We are to try and find him."

"I do not see, with all the land out here, how they can expect us to find the unit much less the man. It is a very difficult mission." Sergeant Vera Katenka said, and then shook her head.

"Nonetheless, we will do our best to find the man."

"We cannot look for campfires at night because our attack helicopters will kill us. While the night belongs to the resistance, our helicopters even things up for a few hours."

"There will be no aircraft out tonight, mainly because the crews need rest, but partially to allow us to search and not worry about getting our arses shot off."

"So, what now, Sergeant?" Olga asked.

"We rest until about 20 hundred, then we go looking for campfires." Vova said and then he added, "From now on, we sleep in the day and work at night."

As they rested, Vova gave thought to where the Chinese man was and knew the Americans would try to get the man to the closest military base, which was at Dallas/Fort Worth. *While we damaged the place, we killed very few Americans, especially when compared to the number of dead sons of Mother Russia. We lost thousands of men and women. They will make a beeline to base, that much I am sure. We need to get in a straight line from the crash site to the base,* he thought.

He pulled out his compass and drew a straight line from approximately where the helicopter had gone down and the main gate on the north side of the base. He chose a spot about 100 meters from the gate, near a stream and a grove of trees. He marked it on his map and then pulled out a Green Frog for supper. As he ate, he unknowingly smiled.

Olga was watching him and she wondered what made him smile. She hoped it was the memory of her "sponge bath," from her helmet, but suspected it was something else. *He never thinks of women, I do not believe, but give me 30 minutes alone with him and I will have him hotter than a firecracker,* she thought as she ate her bland rations.

Right at 2000 hours, he had his troops moving through the forest, with all looking for lights of a campfire or the scent of burning wood. They made great time using the night vision goggles (NVG) and the whole world had a nice eerie green glow. For over two hours, they didn't see, smell or notice anything out of the ordinary.

Near 2200 hours, the point person, in this case it was Junior Sergeant Pavovich, neared Vova and whispered, "I see a light ahead."

"You are about the best of us in the woods, so you come with me and we will check out what we see. If they are Americans, we will attack them. If nothing else, we will be able to send Headquar-

ters a body count. Let us go now. The rest of you remain here."
Vova said and then walked off into the darkness.

They approached the Americans downwind because both knew at times people could be smelled way before they really turned gamy. They were still fairly clean, but sweat and dirt marked them after only 24 hours in the bush. They crawled the last fifteen meters so they would not be seen. They then saw a group of partisans sitting around a small fire, talking in low tones. One man had a map and was pointing to this and that, but neither could hear the man. Seeing motion to the left, they quickly saw a guard and then looking right, they spotted another.

This group is well trained and security conscious. They will be hard to kill or overrun, but we can do the job, Vova thought as he watched the Americans.

After about thirty minutes, he tapped Pavovich on the shoulder and began to slide away from the brush. Once about fifty meters from the camp, Senior Sergeant Vova said in a whisper, "Let us go get the others. We will return and kill this group."

An hour later, everyone hidden around the group of Americans, Vova checked camp security and discovered the guards were half asleep. Only two men were still up and they were talking in low tones as they ate a Russian ration.

The Sergeant pointed to the man on the left, beside the fire, and when Olga looked at him, he mouthed "When I shoot, you kill that man."

She nodded in understanding. Two others had been designated to kill any other guards, and after that they'd rush the camp.

The Senior Sergeant lined his sights up on the man he was to kill and took a deep breath and then started to slowly release it. As the air was released from his lungs, he gently began to squeeze the trigger. His shot surprised him, but he knew he'd hit his target hard. The man screamed loudly and then fell from his log. Glancing to his left and right, he saw both guards were down and losing blood. A loud shot was heard from beside him and the man on the left dropped without a sound, due to a red hot lead slug that punched a hole completely though his heart. Others in the American camp were coming alive now and a firefight started.

Every single one of the Russians tossed hand-grenades at the camp and the explosions brought screams of fear or injury, and it mattered little to the Sergeant which brought the noise. Seconds later the firing on the American side stopped.

"No one move, not until they have time to bleed out and stiffen up a lot. Anyone of you hurt?"

"I lost my little finger on my left hand, right at the second joint. I have a rag on it now, stopping the bleeding." Zinon Ikovle said.

"Stay in place until you see me moving for the camp." Vova ordered. He then dropped a magazine, pushed a fresh one into his weapon and gave Olga a smile. The empty magazine went into his pack, so he could fill it later once he returned to base.

Forty five minutes later, the Sergeant stood and made his way into the camp. One of the guards tried to sit up with a gun in her hand, so the Sergeant fired one shot and struck her in the center of the chest, right between her breasts. She fell back as she kicked and moaned. Seconds later, she was dead.

"Use some caution, people, because some of them are not dead. If they threaten you, kill them, but otherwise take them prisoner."

"I have a prisoner over here. He is alive, took a bullet to his shoulder, and he is knocked out."

"Secure him with the plastic ties you have and leave him in place. Nititovich, as the medic, I need you to treat the injured man. His hands are behind him, so you will be safe enough."

"I will do it, Sergeant."

There was one more gun shot and Ikovle said, "He had a rifle he was raising. If he had kept the gun out of his hands, he would be alive right now."

"How many dead, wounded and captive Americans do we have, Pavovich?"

"I see one wounded American captive and 10 killed, Sergeant."

"Olga, give me the handset." the Sergeant took the handset and said, "Hotel, Hotel, Monsoon here."

"Uh, go Monsoon."

"We ambushed eleven and have one wounded American as a POW. Poppa Oscar Whiskey, over."

"How many dead?"

"No injuries on my side, ten dead Americans, and three wear the rank of officers."

"No Chinese among the dead?"

"No, no Asians. Do you want me to booby-trap the bodies?"

"Roger that. Booby-trap all of them."

"Roger, copy. I will proceed with my search for the Asian."

"Hotel Actual said good hunting on your kills. You are the first unit to call in any dead so far. Yes, Actual wants you to continue searching for the Chinese man and if you find him, you will all get a fifth of vodka, a week off, and some women or men, depending on what your desires are. By all costs this Asian must be found. Hotel out. Over."

Handing the handset back to Olga, he said, "I cannot believe they offered us men or women if we discover the Asian."

"Most of the men and women I know would make good use of someone who wanted some hot, wet and sticky love making."

"Good God, even you?" Vova asked as he met her eyes.

She licked her lips, gazed deeply into his eyes and replied, "No, not me. I want no male or female whore, but a real man I know. You will discover when we return how well I can please a man in many different ways, Senior Sergeant."

"Enough, Olga! Private Yanovich, you are my point man, come to a heading of 120 degrees and remember the magnetic declination of Dallas/Fort Worth is -6.76°E. Keep the pace brisk. With the NVGs on there is no reason we cannot hunt all night. About an hour before sunrise, lead us to a good place, in trees or brush, so we can sleep during the daylight hours."

"No problem, Sergeant." the young man replied and took off at a good speed.

At 0200, there came a slight yell from Yanovich. Vova moved to the man and asked, "What is wrong? Why did you yell?"

"I am standing on a booby-trap."

"What makes you think so? It has not exploded on you yet."

"I felt something give under my right foot and then heard a click. It is a mine, but I have no idea what kind."

The Sergeant squatted beside the young man, pulled his bayonet out and began digging. If he could uncover enough to see what kind of mine it was, then he'd have a better idea of what to do next.

Ten minutes later, his face sweating although it was not hot out, Ikovle asked, "Can you tell what it is yet? I am terrified, Senior Sergeant. I do not want to die this way."

"No one does, but they do everyday here. Looks like a mine for tanks or personnel carriers. I do not think you armed it at all."

"So, what does that mean . . . to . . . me?"

"Step off the mine."

"Are you crazy? It will explode!"

"I am not crazy, but I can understand you thinking I am. No, honestly, step off the mine and remember I am right here beside you. So, if you blow up, I will too."

"If you are one hundred percent sure, I will step off. When should I move?"

"Right now, step off."

Yanovich stepped from the mine, but the instant his foot touch the dirt, he pushed a shotgun shell resting on a nail down and it exploded, sending pellets into his crotch and lower stomach. They were called toe poppers, and they did a good job of maiming a person. Usually the shot would hit a soldier in the lower belly or crotch, removing or damaging the person's sex life. More than once in his career, he'd seen balls and penises removed by the cowardly mine. No soldier, male or female, wanted their sex organs rearranged by a shotgun shell.

Yanovich fell to the ground and began to scream.

"Medic!" the Sergeant yelled

"On the way!" Nititovich yelled in return.

As the medic leaned over the injured man, Vova heard a far off rifle shot and then turned to look at Nititovich when a large caliber round, probably a 30.06 struck him in the middle of his chest, pushed its way through his body and exited his back, taking blood, bone and gore with it. The medic collapsed without a sound, dead.

Grabbing the arm of Private Yanovich, the Sergeant pulled him as fast as he could into some brush. He then returned and grabbed the medics first aid kit. Once back in the brush, he put bandages on his balls and penis, lower belly and one eye.

Senior Sergeant Vova yelled for Olga and soon she was right beside him.

"Give me the handset, now." She handed it to him and waited.

"Hotel, Hotel, I have one man KIA, Kilo, India, Alpha, and one WIA, Whiskey India Alpha. The wounded has serious lower belly injury and needs a medical evacuation by helicopter, over."

"Monsoon, wait one."

"Roger, waiting."

A minute later Hotel said, "I have a helicopter heading in your direction. His call sign is Nurse One, over."

"Roger that. How many minutes is he away from me?"

"About six, and get ready to pop the flare end of a smoke flare. Hotel Actual said he will send a squad out to you in the morning. It will be led by a Captain Vera Grigorievna."

"Copy. We will be ready when the aircraft gets here, over and out."

"Get him ready to move." he said as he looked at Povavich.

The Sergeant pulled a flare from his pack and waited.

The sound of a helicopter was heard and then the radio came alive, "Monsoon, Nurse One. How is the landing zone? Over."

"Green, but we did have a sniper kill my medic, so watch your butt as you come lower."

"Will do. I need a flare, and I will be lowering with my nose west, pointing into the wind."

"Get him ready, and now. Katenka and Pavovich, pick him up and have him ready to place on the helicopter. Come closer to me and move toward the pilot's door when you approach the aircraft. Stay where he can see you. A crew member will come out to help you."

Both men nodded and picked the injured man up and made ready to do the job quickly.

"Monsoon, I am turning off my lights, so have your people rush the victim to me. My medic will help them get him on the aircraft. With my lights off, I am less of a target. I also have four replacement troops on board, and they now have orders to join you. They will unload first."

"Roger that, copy." Then looking at the two men holding the bleeding Yanovich, he said, "Now, rush in and out." He watched them race for the helicopter and then in the darkness they disappeared. His flare spurted and spit and then the flame died.

"Nurse One, Monsoon, do you need another flare?"

"Negative, Monsoon. I have your patient and I am leaving now. I just took two shots to the side of the aircraft but all lights are still in the green. The ground fire came from the east, over."

His engine grew louder and the Sergeant knew the helicopter was coming straight up, then he would nose down and begin to gain altitude.

"Copy that and good luck."

"Same to you, Monsoon. I am hard to see and flying fast now, so we made it. You call and we haul your wounded to the hospital." the pilot was heard to laugh, and Petr knew the man had been scared, but who wouldn't be?

While the man wore NVGs to land in darkness and then take off, it gave any man a real tight butt, and only the bravest would do something like that. The Sergeant made it a point of seeing the pilot was given a medal for his bravery.

"Where is Nititovich's body?" the Sergeant asked as he turned to look at his small group.

"Igorevich loaded him on the helicopter too. We cannot bury him and he was a brave man. His remains should be returned to his family."

"You are correct in loading him." The Sergeant replied and then added, "Saddle up, we need to be moving."

Near 1400 the same day, a helicopter landed and 10 men and women joined the squad. The total now was 20 troops. After all the meeting and greeting, Vova met with Master Sergeant Adam Slavam and they discussed the control of the blended squads. As the senior man, Slavam had the responsibility of the squad, but he agreed to allow Petr the control and command. He would, however, keep a close look on the overall operation.

"Kartenka, get everyone ready to move. We have about four more hours of walking time before we will be in the area I want to RON. Saddle up, all of you." Vova stated.

Most of the new members were on their second tour in America, except for the Privates. They would soon come around to thinking like veterans or they would die. They found countless booby-traps and avoided all but one.

They had to cross a small, thigh deep stream and as they did so, there came a loud explosion as water was thrown high into the air. Men in the water screamed as the underwater booby-trap broke their ankles from the compression of the explosive. Two men died instantly when their bodies were torn to shreds by the grenade.

As the medic worked on three men with open wounds and injured ankles, the two top Sergeants began looking for evidence of what kind of booby-trap had been used. Finding an old soup can tied to a small tree beside the stream they both knew what had happened.

"What do you see, Senior Sergeant?" Yefim, a replacement asked.

"An old school booby-trap. See that can? A grenade with the pin pulled was placed in the can, a line was stretched across the stream and anchored on the far bank. Once a foot pulled the cord or line far enough the grenade was pulled from the can and exploded five seconds later. The partisans also knew anyone in the water would have their feet and or ankles injured. So one grenade killed two men and injured three others. Not bad for a booby-trap, and they may have knocked out five or six people."

"The cost to the partisans was one grenade and some fishing line, huh?"

"They always strive to apply the most damage to their enemies while having no risk or cost to themselves." Then, walking to his new medic, he asked, "How are they or is it to early to tell?"

"The wounded are all serious, but not life threatening. While two of the wounded broke both ankles, one woman has only one ankle broken with the other severely injured. We need a helicopter pick up for all the wounded and the dead. There is no way these people will be able to walk, no way."

The Senior Sergeant said, "Olga, call headquarters and request a medical helicopter to pick up our wounded and dead. If they give you any shit, give the phone to me."

"I will do it right now, Sergeant."

Five minutes later, she walked to Petr and said, "Inbound medical helicopter to pick up our wounded and dead. Replacements will be onboard too."

"Okay, listen up. I want everyone to move to the clearing on our left, but do not move out onto the grasses. I want you to take up positions to cover the landing zone (LZ) as the helicopter lands, loads, and then takes off."

"Sergeant, I spotted movement on the other side of the clearing. They were too far away for me to determine who they are."

"One man?"

"I really cannot say, but I believe it is a small group of soldiers."

CHAPTER 8

John and his group, along with the Chinese pilot, were making a beeline straight to the front gate of the base. They all knew there were Russians in the area and they had spent the night sitting in a crude circle of bodies, back against back. Guards were assigned and the night had been uneventful, but everyone was tired now. The colonel estimated they'd be at the base in less than eight hours unless the clouds off to the west brought rain. It was late afternoon, so rain was very possible overnight.

"Cobra Two this is Copperhead, over."

John took the handset and replied, "Go Copperhead."

"Be advised of possible Russian unit in your area. Catfish One reported hearing an explosion and then seeing Russian troops moving near a clearing just a few minutes ago. He suspects a booby-trap wounded or killed some of the Russians."

"Has there been a change in my orders?"

"No, your package is too valuable. We wanted you aware of what was going on is all, over."

"I will keep my eyes open and we should be there tomorrow, so warn the guards at the main gate. Over."

"The guards are already warned to expect you. Oh, one other thing. Chinese attack helicopters were out flying over you in a circle last night, out to ten miles from you, and they used their infrared radar. They counted twenty-three groups in the circle. Now a few were partisans, but how many? How many were Russian? We have no way to tell who was who, over."

"Understand, and we'll do our best to not be seen. Over."

"Roger that. Copperhead over and out."

"Smith, you're my point man today and Prings, you're my drag. Keep the pace normal and keep an eye out for booby-traps, from either side."

A s the Russians walked, Slavam walked beside Vova and asked, "Our mission is almost insane. How can they honestly expect us to find this Asian when half the time we do not even know where we are, except in Texas?"

"It would be hard enough knowing where the man would be taken, but we do not even know that much. I assume it was to the base but I do not know for sure, and I am assuming which is a dumb thing to do in combat."

"We have good troops, so that much is in our favor."

"We need to hush. I have a rule that no one talks as we move, and I think it has saved our lives more than once out here."

Slavam nodded but didn't speak.

It was four hours later when Leonid was on point when he knew suddenly he'd walked too far into the woods near the trail. Looking over his shoulder, he heard the sound of lots of gunfire and knew he'd led the squad into an ambush. While he'd seen nothing, heard nothing and smelled nothing, his senses had been at their highest when he'd walked through the trees behind him. He was alert then, but why? Since he'd seen nothing unusual, he'd kept going.

There were explosions and each brought screams from those injured and dying. He cautiously made his way back, noticing the gun shots were fewer now, and then, abruptly they stopped. He squatted behind some brush and saw most of the Russians on the ground. Then the Americans came out of the woods, pistols drawn, to quickly dispatch the injured.

One pistol shot was heard, followed by many more. Then silence.

An American called out to his friend and then they both laughed.

Leonid backed into the brush and listened. While he didn't speak English, except for the words, Cowboy and Horse, he knew the tone would tell him what he needed to hear. Within ten minutes the Russians were stripped of things the Americans wanted, like guns, rations, ammo, and watches. They then left. Twenty minutes later, the Private stood and made his way back to the killing trail and saw a number of white bodies laying on the trail, in many cases unnaturally. Clothing and boots had been taken as well, in some cases.

What do I do now? I am at a loss on what to do. I must get back to our base, but I do not even have a compass. I need to check and see if anyone here is alive, he thought as he neared the Senior Sergeant.

Petr was still alive and had taken a piece of shrapnel in his left arm. A bullet had creased his head and while the wound looked fatal, it was not.

Leonid quickly bandaged the Senior Sergeant and said, "I will be back. There may be more of us alive."

The next person he found was Olga and while she was bloody as all hell, none of the blood was hers. Two of the Russian dead were laying on her, so she looked dead enough.

"Are you hit?" he asked.

"No, not at all, and I was terrified they would shoot me if they found me breathing."

The next twelve were all dead and some in horrible condition. Ekel and Katenka must have been standing right in front of a claymore mine when it detonated, because they were torn apart. Leonid only recognize them by the heads of each. He did find six others alive, but two were near death. Firsov Sergei was missing his left arm, while a new woman, Mara Sabitove was missing her left leg. He placed a tourniquet on both victims and then looked the others over. The rifleman, Klokov Gavrila, was alive and had a minor wound to his back so out of seventeen, a total of seven remained alive.

Anfisa Petrovna, the drag man, walked up the trail and when he saw the dead, he said, "Oh, my God! What do we do now? I have no idea which way our home base is."

"I do, and I will get us home too." Senior Sergeant Vova said. "But, first we need to get away from this spot and hide. The Americans may return. Give me about five minutes to clear the fog from my brain and we will leave. It looks like all but Sabitove will be able to walk. Make up a litter for her and you two will have to carry her. Gavrila says he can walk. I will lead us to safety."

"The radio is useless, Senior Sergeant. It has been shot to hell and back."

"We need to see what we have to survive with."

After ten minutes of looking, Private Leonid found a pistol and two clips of ammo near the body of Master Sergeant Slavam. He'd died with a bullet through his head. Then, Firsov Sergei began to shudder and as he attempted to sit up, he fell back to the ground, dead. Now there were six.

Private Petrovna found an AK-74 in the grasses, but only one magazine available for it and it was in the weapon.

Forty minutes later they stopped, and the Sergeant thought they'd covered about a kilometer. They were too tired to continue walking, especially the wounded.

"Move up under the trees and we will give everyone medical treatment. See to Gavrila first, he is bleeding an awful lot right now. I wish we had a radio, because the two hit hardest need to be in a hospital."

"I will do what you ask, Sergeant." Private Makarovich said, "I was a medic until I transferred to the infantry, who had plenty of medics but not enough riflemen. I will have Olga assist me in treating them."

"Good, and let me know the condition of each person, please."

"Will do and it will not take long. The two most serious have been given morphine to kill their pain, but it makes them sleep a lot. It is all we had, so it was use the drug and keep them quiet or do not and listen to them moan and cry all the time."

"Okay. Just try to keep them comfortable as we wait for rescue." the Sergeant said.

"There is a helicopter nearing, but we have no idea which side." one of the Privates said.

Vova said, "Stay hidden until you see which side the aircraft belongs to. We do not want the Americans to know we are here and if we signal a Chinese attack helicopter they will soon know. I will go see and do what is required."

He picked up his Bison sub-machine gun and moved to the edge of a nearby field.

Five minutes later, a Mil Mi-14 still camouflaged in the Navy white and blue, flew overhead. Senior Sergeant Vova moved into the clearing and waited for the aircraft to pass over once more. As the aircraft approached, obviously looking for someone or something, the Sergeant waved. The aircraft stopped about fifty meters from him and then lowered to the ground. Never had the Sergeant been so happy to see an Ellie before. That was the nickname of the helicopter.

A single man ran from a side door and once near the Sergeant, he asked, "Are you the only survivor?"

"No, I have them hidden in the trees. I had no idea you were a Russian aircraft and if you had been Chinese, I would not have waved. I have wounded, so can you take them out?"

"Yes, of course, but hurry. If we are caught on the ground, the Chinese will make short work of us."

"I will be right back. Oh, I also need a radio, personal gear for five people, rifles, sidearms, and rations with ammo. You can call that in while I bring the wounded to your aircraft." the Sergeant said and then ran to where he had everyone hidden.

Ten minutes later, with two of the injured in the aircraft, a radio was handed to him, half a dozen Green Frogs, two AK-47 rifles, six magazines, and one grenade.

"We have called in your needs and once we get your people to a hospital, we will return with your supplies, people, and gear."

Good, now go!" Vova said.

Two minutes later the helicopter was gone but the *whop-whop-whop* could still be faintly heard.

Colonel Andrei Lazarev stood in front of his commanders and it was early, 0600, and everyone was meeting for Stand Up. That was where if the Base Commander asked questions, the one providing answers stood up at attention out of respect for the senior man's grade, and providing him answers. This morning, the Colonel was not in a happy mood.

"So, Colonel Isaak, the reason our attack failed was our navigational systems were off and we dropped troops all over the place but none landed close to the partisan base?"

"That is correct, sir. We even had a company dropped right on the base and they were slaughtered as they fought to stay alive. That was 100 men and they died for what? No, our navigators messed up too, and should have overrode the electronic gear when they knew it was malfunctioning."

"And they did nothing?"

"No, they did nothing. One Navigator was overheard saying that he had almost forgotten how to navigate without electronic assistance."

"That is horrible, and well, uh, my next question is to Operations Commander, 'What have you done to correct this problem?' It is serious enough I should court martial someone."

"Remedial training on navigation is being given as we speak. Each navigator is to attend a week long course, refresher course, and will not fly until the course is completed satisfactorily."

"That may work. I have been getting calls from Moscow about our mission and I keep them at bay by telling them it is still continuing. That is why it is so important we find that Chinese pilot who was rescued by an American squad. Thank God Moscow does not know about the pilot, or we would all be out looking for him, and I tease you not. I think if we can produce a Chinese pilot, Moscow will suddenly have a great deal of satisfaction with us. They have not brought him to the partisan base yet, or the news would be all over it. Gentlemen, I learn as much by watching the news as I do here, at Stand Up."

Silence.

Then the Colonel said, "Colonel Zubov, as my operations officer, how many aircraft did we lose on the partisan base attack?"

Standing, the Colonel replied, "Fewer than we originally thought. Right now it appears we have twelve helicopters either crashed and burned, with sixteen sustaining some damage, with a total of 28 helicopters out of service as of right now. Some of those will be returned to us within a couple of days. The cost, however, is staggering and I do not have it tallied as of right now. We are, nonetheless, looking at billions of rubles."

"Ummm, not good, because the General will wonder why we had such heavy losses." Colonel Lazarev said and then, placing his hands behind his back, he walked to the closest window and looked out.

Lieutenant Colonel Zubov said, "Sir, I have news that will, perhaps, be a bit brighter on the attack. Seems the attack on all the other bases have failed too, but at even a greater cost than what we paid. The Fort Leonard Wood attack cost them 4,000 troops dead or wounded, 43 aircraft destroyed or out of commission. The New Orleans attack was a complete disaster with 5,000 killed and over 3,000 injured, with a loss of 64 aircraft from helicopters to transport planes. They are by far the worst in cost, and I suggest you inform the next caller from Moscow that you still have troops in the area and as far as you are concerned the mission is still being carried out."

"Well, now, Colonel Zubov, your information is good to hear. I think I can rest better now that I know we lost much less than any other unit. Colonel Isaak, I want all available troops put into the field with the others to look for a Chinese pilot. I mean every man or woman not used in the protection of this base and our resources is to be inserted into the field. Do you understand?"

"Yes, sir, I fully understand and I will have troops air dropped this day and others brought in by helicopters and transport aircraft."

"Good, now if that is all and you do not have any additional questions, this meeting is over." Lazarev said and as he headed for the door, Master Sergeant Luchok Katin yelled, "Teeen-Huuut!"

Everyone stood until the Commander was gone and then they began to talk between themselves.

"How many airborne troops can you provide me to drop around the American base?" Zubov asked Lieutenant Colonel Vera Ginovich, the vice commander for the largest unit on the base.

"I can safely provide you with 2,000 of my paratroopers, but they will want to jump into combat."

"I do not know about direct combat, but they will be able to jump into a potentially hostile environment. I would actually like them to be dropped and never seen by the Americans. Stealth is the only way to end this battle."

"When do you want to drop them?"

"I want to drop them tonight at 2200 hundred hours. You will need to mobilize your soldiers as soon as you can. I will plan as if we can get them on the ground by 2300 today. That means in the morning, right at daylight, they will all get their marching orders from me and I will send them after the Americans."

"I understand, sir, and we will not let you down. Give me to-day, and by tonight you will have your paratroopers ready to drop."

"Good, very good." Zubov said as he turned and walked to the door.

It was getting late and all of John's troops were sleeping except for him and his radio operator. The colonel was sitting on a log as he held the radio in his left hand. He'd just been sent a classified message that Private Porter was translating into something that could be read.

"Sir, about all it says is the Russians may risk another parachute drop in our vicinity within the next 48 hours. Our eyes have photos of them rigging the transport planes with jump cables and topping off their fuel. Seems to be a lot of hustle and bustle there right now. Headquarters suspects the Russians want the Chinese pilot and right now."

John chuckled because he was just four hours away from the base with the Chinese pilot, and if all went well, he'd be on the base before the Russians were even airborne.

"What are our orders?"

"To reach the safety of the base as soon as possible."

"I was afraid of that. I'm worried that if we rush returning, we'll end up being ambushed and all of us, including the Chinese Captain, will be killed."

"We have our orders."

"Yes we do." John said and then looking at Master Sergeant Dias, he said, "Mary, get the troops up, including Captain Tam, and we need to be moving. This will be a long hard tramp, because we'll be walking about four more hours. There will be no rest stops. By then I suspect we'll be at the main gate of the base."

"Some just went to bed."

"Get 'em all up, because our orders have changed."

Soon everyone was up and moving around, which brought some cursing from those that had just gone to sleep.

Growing tired of the complaints, John said, "I don't like not getting a night of sleep too, but our orders are for us to return Tam immediately, with no breaks taken to rest."

The noise grew less and finally, Msgt. Dias said, "Saddle up and let's move. Jones, I want you for my point man and keep an extra eye out for booby-traps. The traps you find will probably be ours and that won't matter much if you trip one. All mines are equal opportunity killers."

"Captain Tam, you need to move to the middle of this group, sir. That spot is the safest and in the long run safety is what it's all about."

"I can do that." Tam replied and, as for himself, *he was enjoying the way the Americans thought and lived in a combat zone. A quick thought ran through his mind. Americans were more relaxed than a Chinese unit. The NCOs and Officers in Chinese units kept the conversation more formal and with full rank spoken when addressing someone else.*

Minutes later they were all on a little used path leading toward the base. The area was full of various trees and brush, so there were a thousand places that were open for ambush sites. Then suddenly, fifteen minutes later they were out walking on the plains. While the plains offered few places for an ambush, a squad of people could not hide as well and could be seen for miles.

"Base just called." Private Gene Green said as he moved closer to the Colonel. It was just a few minutes after sunup.

"Oh, and what did they say?"

"We are to stop here as they send a helicopter out to pick up the Chinese man. They had to fight tooth and nail just to get one helicopter to do this with. Sounds like we have some serious supply problems. The word I got is anything with a rotor blade is moving supplies. At any rate, the call sign for the rescue aircraft is Angels Three, and supposedly he is ten clicks out."

"Everyone, stop and relax a bit. I have a chopper coming out to us to pick up our Chinese pilot and, Lee, I need you to pop smoke when I tell you to, and visually lower the chopper using your rifle. Any questions?"

"Not from me. I've done this many times." Lee said with a slight grin.

"Get into position now and wait for word or a sign to pop the smoke."

"Cobra Two, this is Angels Three, over."

"Go Angels Three."

"I have you visual, so pop smoke now."

Lee pulled the pin, tossed the smoke grenade about 5 feet from him. He now stood straight with his rifle overhead. "I see them," Lee said and when John looked up, the aircraft was right in front of Lee, maybe 50 feet in the air. As Lee lowered his rifle, the chopper lowered, until it was resting on the grasses.

"Captain Tam, get your ass on that chopper and go home. I've enjoyed having you for our guest."

Tam extended his hand and as they shook, light gunfire from across the field was striking the chopper. The Asian suddenly turned and ran to the helicopter, where he was placed in the cargo hold and the aircraft began to rise up into the sky. Bullets were heard smacking the aircraft and each hit brought a pinging sound.

"Copperhead this is Angels Three. I have the Chinese pilot in my aircraft and have taken a little ground fire from the west side of the opening. I request —"

The Chinese pilot suddenly made a reactive move and then dispensed chaff. A heat seeking man held missile just missed him, to explode behind him, which damaged his tail.

"Uh, Copperhead, I have a damaged rotor blade and am declaring an in-flight emergency."

"Roger that and I am sending two fast movers to Cobra Two's position, over. Eagle One is their call sign, Cobra."

"Eagle One, this is Cobra Two and what is your estimated time of arrival over my position, over?"

"Five Mikes. Over."

"Roger that, five minutes. Line up on a group of trees, on the opposite side of the clearing we are on. Hit them with napalm if you have any. Over."

"What is five Mikes?" Private Light asked.

Private Joe Kelly said, "Five minutes is what five Mikes means. Mikes is used because the word may confuse the Russians. There is always a chance the enemy is listening and they have English speakers too."

"Each aircraft has two canisters of what we call shake and bake, over." Eagle One said.

"Drop all you have on those trees. Over."

"Will do, get down, it may get hot down there, over."

CHAPTER 9

Most everyone with Vova was exhausted when he called for a stop to RON. They'd been moving all night, but saw no one or even any lights the whole night long. As far as the Senior Sergeant was concerned it was a wasted night to him. Now his people needed rest because they had another night of searching ahead.

"Radio for you, sir." Olga said and passed him the radio.

"Monsoon, this is Hotel Actual and you are to be returned to base. I have a helicopter in the air coming for you as we speak. ETA is three five minutes, over."

"Roger, Hotel, understand we are to be pulled and mission terminated."

"Correct, Monsoon. Find the nearest clearing and your taxi home is called, 'Rescue One, over."

"Got it and thank you for the ride home."

"No problem, Monsoon. Hotel over and out."

Handing the headset back to Olga, Petr said, "We will be picked up in less than 35 minutes. I want everyone ready to board a chopper as quickly as possible. Now, just because we have not seen anyone, does not mean no one is near us right now. We will return fire as we move if needed, and then board the helicopter. Then once in the helicopter the aircraft machine gunners will take over."

"Private Leonid, you will lead all of us to the aircraft and you will be the first to board. Any questions?"

"Why are they removing us from the field?"

"I have no idea, but maybe they will pick us up after or before they complete their mission."

"Let us hope it is after and not before. I do not mind a fight, but I would like a little rest first." Private Petrovna said with a weak smile.

"Uh, Monsoon, Rescue One, I have you visual. Pop smoke, over."

"Will do. Wait One." Olga said and then turning to Vova she said, "He wants smoke."

A minute later the helicopter pilot said, "I have three smokes, so which is your color? I see red, maroon, and white."

Olga said, "We are the white, over."

"Uh, Rescue One, this is Bulldog Six and I have rockets or napalm. I am a fast mover out of Omaha, over."

"Roger understand. I am making a straight in approach and request you drop napalm on the maroon and red smoke, over."

"Roger. What I miss my wing-man will hit, over."

"Go as I land. Maybe we can keep the Americans busy and I can load soldiers faster."

"Copy and do as you have said. I will go around after dropping my napalm and using my Gatling gun. I suggest all of you keep your heads down, starting now."

The helicopter was just sitting down on the grass when a great wall of flames were seen after hearing the napalm canisters hitting the trees. Then glancing up, the helicopter pilot on the ground screamed into this microphone, "Wing-man break, break, over!" He screamed to be heard and the aircraft was lining up on the helicopter, not the woods.

As the helicopter pilot watched in horror, the canisters came off the wings of the aircraft and began to tumble while in the air. The canister went over his head and crashed into the woods where the Senior Sergeant and his troops were. Already the men and women in the squad were running full speed across the field for the helicopter. The canister struck the trees, burst open with flames and the sticky fire moved like a wave, up and over the trees to land a second later. The Russians were lucky, because if the squad had started running a second or two later than they did they would have all burned to death. The momentum of the napalm canisters had the wave of fire moving away from the Russians, but breathing was hard, with the flames sucking up most of the air.

"Damn you, Wing-Man, you have dropped your napalm on the known position of other Russians. Break, break, over."

The squad with Vova reached the aircraft on the ground and began to quickly load. It was then Captain Griovich realized the soldiers were safe.

"Bulldog Six, Rescue One and I am coming up and out of here. Hold off on any attacks until we clear your air space, over?"

"Did you copy Bulldog Seven?"
"Roger that and sorry about my last run. I was confused by your radio transmission, over."

"Coming up now." The helicopter pilot said and then grinned as he rose without taking any ground fire. He intentionally did not answer Bulldog Seven because he planned to file a complaint once back at home base. The fool had almost killed him, his crew and the soldiers he was trying to rescue.

"How far to the base?" Vova asked as he yelled at a door gunner.

"Twenty minutes, maybe. Relax, we will be flying as high as we can without oxygen masks. The skipper hates missiles, rockets and ground fire." A door gunner replied.

The Senior Sergeant nodded and said, "Good, I need a hot shower and some good food."

The gunner didn't answer, because they were just a thousand feet or so high and he was busy scanning the ground under them for threats.

"Rocket locked onto us!" the copilot yelled.

Checking the ground under them, the gunner saw something long and thin moving toward them and at the last second he said, "Break left and then reduce power."

"Copy, guns." The pilot said and then did as directed.

The gunner smiled when he saw the missile pass over them to explode about a hundred feet away from the helicopter.

Two minutes later, "Crew, this is the pilot. We just took some damage to our fuel tank and engine with the explosion of that missile. I have called in an in-flight emergency and we have been approved for a straight in approach and we are cleared to land. I need everything, especially the heavy machine guns tossed over the side. If you pray, right now would be a great time to speak with God."

Gray and black smoke began to stream from the helicopter and due to the slipstream around the aircraft, some entered the cargo hold. Vova felt his stomach tighten from fear, when a large piece of aluminum fell from the engine. He correctly identified it as the engine cover.

Now smoke from boiling hydraulic lines was filling the cabin and the occupants were having a hard time breathing. The two machine gunners wore the only smoke masks so the passengers had to make do with covering their faces with parts of their clothing.

"Pilot to crew, we are almost to the runway. Prepare for a crash landing. I will try to set us down off to the side of the runway and just over the fence. Here goes."

A minute later the aircraft began to shake as they lowered toward the ground. Then, without warning, the aircraft dropped from about six feet. It landed on the wheels, bounced into the air and then fell to the side. The big rotor blades denigrated as they impacted the ground, sending dirt and parts of the blades in all directions. After a minute or so, the rotor blades now gone, the noise and movement of the helicopter stopped. Smoke now filled the cargo compartment and the passengers were all terrified of a fire.

Crew and passengers all began to exit, scared of leaking fuel starting a fire, but the pilot reached down and turned all power to off. They were safe. There was still a danger of the hot engine catching any flammable liquids or fuel on fire, but turning off the power reduced the odds of flames a good 80%.

As they evacuated the destroyed helicopter, Vova heard an emergency response vehicle start their siren as they approached. He ran about 100 meters to where others were gathering in front of the destroyed aircraft and listened to them talk. All knew they were safe and nervous laughter could be heard at times.

I need a glass of vodka and a steak for supper, Vova thought as the firetruck and ambulance arrived on the scene.

A fireman neared and said, "Everyone in the two vans that are coming. All of you are to see a doctor before you are allowed to roam around on the base. Get checked out and then the day is yours. I consider you all very lucky. From what I can see, five more minutes of flying would have resulted in an explosion of your fuel tanks. All of you are lucky to be alive. Now, here are the vans. Load up and see a doctor."

At the hospital all were free to go except for the pilot who suffered a severe back injury. The rest had swallowed a little smoke but not enough to cause them to be hospitalized.

Vans then took the enlisted to their temporary quarters, the Lieutenant co-pilot to his officers quarters and finally Vova to the senior enlisted quarters. The Senior Sergeant quarters were visiting quarters for NCOs. It was a suite, and beautiful. He immediately walked down the street to the closest package store and picked up a quart of top shelve vodka. While out he picked up a potato, an inch thick steak, a bag of salad, and a gallon of milk.

He was leaving when Olga entered and their eyes met.

"Stay out of trouble." Petr said and then laughed.

"I will visit you tonight, Senior Sergeant." she said and then winked.

"You are all talk." he said and left before she could answer.

You will find out about 2100 I am not just talk at all. When I visit then, you will have been in your cups and probably a little drunk. Once you see me naked, you will desire me. I am young enough to turn you on and, while not beautiful, I am hardly ugly either. I know my body is fine, because I have been told that many times in the past. This date will be different than other meetings with men, because I have a deep hunger for you, Senior Sergeant, she thought. *I will turn into a cougar and come for you.*

Later, after cooking and eating his steak, he enjoyed a long hot shower and changed into lounge pants and a tee. He relaxed with a tall glass of vodka. He was sitting in the overstuffed chair, close to falling asleep, when he heard a knock at his door. He glanced at his watch and noticed it was 2100 hours, or 9 pm to most civilians. He took a big drink from his glass and then stood as he called out, "Stop knocking, I am coming!"

Pulling his pistol and sliding a round into the chamber, he opened the door a crack a looked out. There stood Olga, with half her big breasts seen, her nipples poking on the material of a thin short cut tee, and wearing a cut off pair of camouflage pants that covered little. He opened the door wide and said, "Come on in, and I am sorry about the gun. It is an old habit of mine, and I have been doing it for years."

"I did not think you would still be up." Olga said and wiggled her rear as she moved past him to his sofa and sat.

"No, and I did not think you would visit. What can I do for you this evening?"

"It is more like what can I do for you. I told you in the field I desired you and I have come here to have you, if you like what I have to offer a man."

She stood, pulled her tee off and thew it on the floor. Petr was surprised at the firmness of her breasts, which stood up on their own. Next she removed her shorts and moved slowly to get his attention. Then standing with just a red thong on, she said, "If you like what you see, remove my thong and we will play for a few hours.' She then pushed the Sergeant into the overstuffed chair and climbed in his lap. As she kissed him, she wiggled her rear on him and heard him surrender with a loud moan.

Morning dawned wet and with cold rain. The weather man on the television in Petr's room reported the freezing rain would soon be covered by a half meter of fresh snow. Olga was still sleeping and he wasn't happy to wake up in bed with her at all. He had a rule about never sleeping with his troops and now he'd violated his own rules.

"Do not worry, Petr," Olga said the evening before, "I will tell no one that we were lovers."

"Were is right. If I had been completely sober tonight I would have never done this."

"Is my loving that bad?" She asked, now confused, because he was supposed to love her after what they'd done with each other.

"It has nothing to do with good or bad, but sleeping with one of my people is not smart. I may have to send them in harms way and sleeping with one would make me hesitate to send them." "It does not matter to me, do what you must do, because I wanted you last night and still do."

"What are you thinking about?" Olga now asked from the bed and it surprised him, because he thought she was still asleep.

"Not much, except sleeping with you was a mistake, I think. But only because I am your Senior Sergeant."

"If you come to bed right now, I can make you smile the rest of the day"

"No, I think it would be better if you got dressed and left."

She got out of the bed naked, smiled at him and then moved toward him. Stopping within reaching distance she asked, "Are you sure you want me to leave? I see no reason we cannot be together until we leave for our return trip to our home base. Our secret is safe with me."

His eyes took in her beauty and he sighed as he pulled her into his arms and almost smothered her with deep kisses. She felt her smoking fire burst into flames, so she pulled him to the sofa, where she fell on her back. Petr landed on top of her and his mouth soon discovered her neck. She wrapped her legs around his middle and began to moan softly.

An hour later, while having coffee, he said, "If you stay here, we will need more food. My rations are bigger than yours, so I will take my ration card to the store and stock up with what we need."

"That is fine, and while you do that, I can return to my room and gather some clothing."

Just like in Russia, certain foods, like meat, veggies, beer, strong alcohol, and fruit was limited by the use of a ration card. No one could exceed their monthly ration, but many bribed the cashiers so they could get more. It didn't bother Vova, because that was just the way the system worked. He had money to buy what he wanted with a bribe but he'd never do that because he wanted to obey the system. If too many bribed, then some families with children would not get the needed foods they wanted to feed their young. He knew an unhealthy diet would cause children to be raised undernourished, with possible learning problems or other abnormalities.

An hour later he walked into his suite and placed two brown bags of food on the aluminum table in his kitchen. He then poured a water glass about half full with vodka and began putting the foods away. For tonight he had two thick beef steaks, a baked potato, and lettuce for a salad. He had to admit, compared to most Russians, he was a big meat eater. He'd also picked up a nice big bottle of French wine and another bottle of vodka. He hated to admit it, but he found Olga to be the sexiest woman he'd ever been with, and he'd bedded a few. He never bragged about his success at loving women. To him, a real man had no need to keep numbers or to pat himself on the back because a woman may have wanted to share sex with him. He felt that was between him and the woman, and no one else should ever be told. He liked to think he was a hard nosed gentleman and he would not have been surprised that most of his lovers thought the same of him.

Near 5 pm, Olga entered the apartment and found Petr asleep on the sofa. She used care not to wake him and showered and changed clothes. She placed her work uniform in the dirty clothes hamper and then dried her hair. Then, seeing it was close to 6, she woke him and began cooking supper. Both liked their steaks medium rare and neither liked a tough steak. The steaks had soaked in soy sauce all afternoon, which Petr thought tenderized the meat.

They both enjoyed supper, and after helping Olga with the dishes, they moved to the sofa and cuddled up close as they watched the government news channel. They only got one channel, so they were limited in what they could watch. The partisans had a channel now from some place in Arizona, and the Russians hadn't gotten to that state in their invasion. Since the Sergeant spoke very little English, he only watched it after a big battle or before one, to see the images and to listen to some things spoken in Russian. They were constantly showing propaganda in an effort to get Russian troops to desert and come to the American side where they'd treat them well.

Finally a documentary about World War II came on and both were interested in the women snipers, especially the one with over 450 kills. The woman they showed looked more like a child than a young woman. It showed her on camera killing Germans at almost a two kilometers. Most of her shots were supposedly head shots, but Petr found that difficult to believe. She was the highest decorated soldier in the Russian army's history.

When it came time for bed, Petr pulled her close, licked her ear and whispered, "You are mine until morning."

"Ummm, nice. What will you do to me?"

"Anything you or I want, my dear. Once in bed, give me some suggestions."

"Yes, oh yes, I can do that."

They'd been sleeping for three hours when there was a loud pounding on his front door. They were both surprised and Petr said, "It must be an emergency or they would never bother me. Let me answer and see what is the matter."

Picking up his pistol, he yelled, "Just a minute, please. Stop the pounding because you will wake up the whole building."

He cracked the door, saw a Junior Sergeant and asked, "What do in the hell do you want at this hour?"

"A military cargo plane has gone down, destroyed by Partisans, and the commander wants all Senior NCOs and commanding officers to report to his stand-up room at 0400 for an intelligence briefing. I was ordered to tell you that you are expected. Uniform is battle fatigues with full combat vest and helmets. That is all I was told to tell you."

Opening the door wide, Vova said, "Tell your boss that I will be there and I will be a little early."

He closed the door, told Olga what was going on, changed into his uniform, and kissing her on the forehead he said, "I have no idea how long I will be. Be patient and sleep while you can. Right now it is just a briefing, so I may be back before breakfast. I hope they keep it all short but do not count on it. They will have to find answers for Moscow and that means the safety team and the various commanders will be working long hours today. I hope they allow us airborne troops to go home after the presentation, but you never can tell."

Putting his helmet on, he said, "I will return when I can. Stay in here and keep the bed warm, I hope to return soon."

The briefing room was filled by 0330 and Vova got one of the few empty seats left. He heard all kinds of rumors floating around and one said a traitor had his body wrapped in explosives and killed himself. While another stated the man and woman, they were a team, killed the pilots and flew the aircraft into the ground. The black boxes had been found and right now the things were being copied on paper. He had no idea what had happened, so he paid no attention to those talking and spreading rumors.

"Teeen-hooouuut!" a crusty old Senior Sergeant yelled as the Commander entered. Everyone stood and then once in the room, Colonel Pudin Luchok said, "Take your seats."

The Colonel took a sip of coffee from his mug and said, "Ladies and Gentlemen, at 0120 hours this night, a missile fired by a partisan unit struck our resupply aircraft in the left wing, bringing it to the ground nose first. The aircraft was approximately 500 feet above the runway. At this time all inbound and outbound traffic has ceased except for aircraft with emergencies, until we finish our preliminary investigation. We suspect it will be complete within 24 hours. All aircraft are being diverted to other airports and our goods transported here by truck. We have witnesses who saw a missile fired from the woods and then five men running across an open field. I have three dog teams on them right now."

The Colonel took another sip of his coffee and said, "I have called you all here to order you to increase security and to have roaming squads out and about the airport. We cannot allow this loss of life and equipment to continue. I want the guilty men caught, punished with death, and increased security all around the airport."

"Any dead or wounded, sir?" someone up front asked.

"We currently have identified 23 dead and two survivors with horrible burns over most of their bodies. The doctors expect them to die as well. 18 of the known dead were infantry replacements and each will be shipped home once an autopsy is done. As of right now, we expect all of the 43 men and women on board to be dead. The aircraft body burned almost completely, leaving two wings, about 4 feet of the nose, and very little of the tail still intact. Right now, I want all of you to send your squads of men to protect our airport and to find the guilty party."

"Sir, I am Senior Sergeant Petr Vova and I am here temporarily with my troops; are we called to provide security as well? We were on the crashed helicopter that landed yesterday, sir."

"No, Sergeant, this is not your base of assignment and not your responsibility. I appreciate your asking, because it identifies you as a real professional. It reminds me that all airborne troops are some of our nations best. Now, all of you not involved in security may leave the briefing. The next part is classified secret and if you do not have a security clearance, you need to leave too. Dismissed."

Vova hurried back to Olga and when she asked what was going on, he simply said, "It's classified." She never asked another question.

CHAPTER 10

John and his troops watched the napalm hit the wooded area and instantly burst into flames. A huge ball of reddish yellow flames with black edges and smoke then rolled in the air as it fell on a number of Russians. Once the containers hit and detonated, the flames could not be put out easily. Those covered from head to foot died quickly, but those splattered with the sticky jell would burn for what seemed like hours to the victims. While they were a good quarter mile away, the Colonel would have said in a court of law that he could hear people screaming, but that was not possible due to distance.

"Eagle One, you are right on target. Have your wing man drop about a hundred meters deeper into the trees."

"Copy, Cobra, and will do. Eagle two, did you hear my conversation with Cobra Two, over?"

"Roger that, One, and I'm lining up now for my approach."

The Americans and Russians watched as the aircraft lined up, headed for the trees at a great speed, and just before he flew over the heavily wooded area, he released two canisters that flipped end over end as they fell. There was a huge flash of flame when the napalm struck and a wall of flames went up and over a good acre or more of land. When the wave fell, John knew Russians were dying by the dozens.

"Copperhead, Cobra Two."

"Go Cobra, over."

"We are now moving and on a heading of —" John spoke into the handset a few minutes and then handed it back to his radio operator. "Okay people, listen up. We're leaving, and no need to search for any tank farm. According to Chinese intelligence, they are no more. We are to find and harass the enemy anyplace we can find them. Saddle up, our threats in these woods are now gone. Brown, get to the point, and Smith, you are my drag man. Let's move so we can finish this day and then see what our orders will be tomorrow."

They moved until noon and seeing his people were tired, he stopped. He stopped for the night early, because they needed some rest, food and sleep.

"Msgt. Dias, we'll spend the night here and catch up on some rest and sleep."

"Roger that, and all of them need some sleep time. It's hard to sleep at night sitting and sleeping back to back, but it keeps us alive."

"Yes, not much sleeping takes place sitting like that, but we're better ready for battle in that position."

It was near 1400 when Green handed the handset to the Colonel.

"Cobra Two, go Copperhead."

"Uh, you have a classified message coming to you, so read it closely. You are to follow the orders given in the message even if you cannot complete your mission on time. If you cannot comply immediately, move to your location and do it then, after the fact. Read the message and then contact me if you have questions."

Private Green decoded the message and handed it to John.

"Colonel, it looks like we're attacking the Russian air bases, all of them, tonight. I suspect that will be hard on a number of partisans. Many will die, sir." "Our leaders want to force the Russians out of America by increasing their losses each month. Eventually public opinion will force the Russian Bear to leave, or so our intelligence guys and gals tell us, if we just make each day costly for them. Right now we are averaging a hundred dead and maimed Russians a day."

"So, win or lose tonight, we have won a political battle?" Green asked.

"More or less, yes. I don't know if you are old enough to remember our war in Vietnam. While the United States won the war we lost the American people and media, so we lost the war. Once the media and people turn against something, that something goes down hill from there. While we had won the war right at the end of Tet 1968, the media assumed we'd lost and they kept throwing out the number of dead we had following the battle, and the fact a US embassy was overrun for a few hours. The American public grew angry and bitter. The North Vietnamese Army said later if we'd only have pushed them a bit more, they would have collapsed and surrendered. But due to protesters, politicians against the war, and the news media, we chalked the battle up as a loss."

"But the Russians don't have the freedoms we do."

"No, they don't, but no one will allow their kids to be butchered year after year with no end in sight. While it's illegal to protest there, the police and military allow it because they both need the public's support. Now, if a protest turns into a riot, the military and police will strike back and often with deadly force, too. They will not put up with destroying private property or attacking others with different beliefs. Peaceful protests are actually supported."

"I see, and our orders are to not enter the battle, but assist hurt and sick partisans that will withdraw from the battlefield. If we see no Americans, then we are to harass the enemy to the best of our abilities until relieved." Green said after reading the decoded message.

"That is correct. Wake Msgt. Dias and have her get everyone up and ready to move. I want to be moving within the hour."

"Okay, sir. I had better eat something this morning too, because I think once the attack hits, we'll be busy."

"Probably." John replied.

After Dias was awake and finished her morning toilet, John told her their orders and she took it all well.

"I want the troops up, awake, and moving within the hour. I realize it's early evening and many just went to bed, but we have marching orders."

"Okay, I'll get 'em up, but they'll not be happy about it at all."

"They'll get over it. Now, wake them and get ready to leave. We will leave in —" he said, then looked at his watch and continued, "45 minutes. Get them up and moving."

Soon the camp was up and busy with the normal amount of throat clearing, sneezes, coughs and cursing of any military unit. Forty five minutes later, they were moving down a narrow path and all wore NVGs. Brown, the point man, was scared and he had a right to be. If he missed one booby-trap he would never see home again or find a woman. His remains would likely be left where he fell.

As he moved he thought, *What is that on the trail? Oh, a piece of grapevine and not a tripping line. Why is the ground a different color here instead of like the other ground? I need to stop and test it with my knife blade. Oh, God, it is a pit with stakes in it! I need to mark this, to keep others safe.* He then marked it, stepped over the trap and felt the edge of his boot contact something and then it pushed it to the side. There came the sound of a shotgun shell going off and the blast just missed Brown. He knew he'd stepped on a toe popper, but his movement must have pushed the shell to the side slightly. He was unhurt.

John ran forward, saw the marked trap and Brown was standing there looking sheepish.

"Are you injured, Larry?"

"No, but look at this thing."

Using caution, John made his way to the man and there in the soil was a 12 gauge shotgun shell laying on its side.

"Looks to me like you didn't step on it 100%, not flat anyway, but just enough to push it down and off to the side. Of course your body weight was enough to cause the shell to detonate. You are one very lucky man. I'll go back and send Carrier to take your position. I want you to then move to the center of the group and walk there. One saving by God a day is all any person needs."

"I'm okay, but thank you, sir."

"Not a problem. Wait right here for Carrier."

"I'll be here."

John returned, sent Carrier forward and waited for Larry to return. Once the private was back in the group they started moving again. Some were complaining about their backpacks and the weight they carried. Many carried mines, ammo, and even a M-60 machine gun with 500 rounds. Finally, after carrying about 70 pounds day after day, their packs seemed to double in weight. John fully understood the complaints, because he was years older than most of his troops. However, once in a firefight, you could only fight with what you had on hand. It was then that everything back-packed in was worth its weight in gold.

Hours later, near 2100 hours, John heard a noise beside the trail and he slipped the safety off his Bison. He pulled his weapon to the ready and said, "Come out and now! Come." He then slipped his weapon off safety.

A minute later, two men parted the bushes and stood in front of John. Both were in torn and dirty Russian uniforms and they looked terrified.

"Da." The taller of the two replied. The man was about six feet tall, blond hair, blue eyes and a thin frame. He looked intelligent, where the man beside him looked as if John was going to kill and eat him. The man was thin also, brown hair, green eyes, about five feet and five inches. He was shaking, and obviously he was facing their enemy and he'd heard horrible rumors about how partisans killed their prisoners.

"Brown, Green and Lee, come to me." John said in a loud voice.

When the three men arrived, the Colonel said, "Secure these two and get Sergeant Hanish to talk with them. They are not to be harmed, understood?"

"Yes, sir."

"Sure."

"They're safe with me." Brown said.

"Go and do it now, we have some distance to cover. Tell Hanish he'll have to wait until we stop for the day before he can interrogate them. Corporal Brown, I'll hold you responsible if these prisoners are hurt or killed. They are to be protected and treated with respect."

"Why me, sir?"

"You, as a Corporal, have rank over the others."

Lowering his head, Brown said in a weak voice, "Yes sir."

Less than a mile later, knowing he needed to stop for the night, John said, "Never mind my previous orders, move the two prisoners over by that big cedar tree and we'll spend the night here. I see a small stream about a hundred feet from here, Smyth, go check it out."

After Smyth returned to the group, he said, "All clear, Colonel."

John said, "Okay, we'll spend the night here. Those of you not on guard right now can catch up on your sleep. I suggest you eat before sleeping, but it's your choice. We will leave here two hours before dawn in the morning."

Moving to Hanish, John asked, "How good is your Russian?"

"I attended college there and was working in a government job selecting quality imports for the United States. I can carry on a conversation, but I'm not fluent. Why?"

"I need for you to talk to the two Russian prisoners we have."

"Oh, I can do that for sure, sir. When?"

"What about right now?"

"I can do that," Hanish said laughing, "because I follow orders. No, seriously, I can do it now, which is as good as any other time."

"Then come with me." John said and they walked toward the two captives.

"First ask them their names and why they are out here alone."

Hanish spoke and then got an instant reply, which he said, "The taller one is Private Gavrila and the other is Ivakin Vodavochov. They are both Privates. My guess is they expect to be executed, because we have a hard reputation. I have told them they will be treated kindly, as long as they answer my questions."

"Good, let's use their fear of us to our advantage. Ask them why were they in the field and how come they are the only ones we found."

A minute later, Hanish said, "There were with a squad and they were out looking for Americans getting ready to attack their base. When they went to pee, the unit moved on without them. Both are lost in the woods and they feared starving to death."

"Tell them they will be taken excellent care of and they will soon be taken back to the base and placed in a jail cell. Tell them their war is over. Give both of them a ration to eat and a canteen of water."

Once again John waited and then Hanish said, "The tall one asked if we will kill them. I told him no, not as long as he obeyed orders. The other one is scared of jail and asks if he can be let free. He promises he will never shoot at Americans again in his life."

"Tell them both they will go to jail and neither of them will be freed. I need to make a call on the radio, but get friendly with them and try to learn some military information if you can."

"Yes, sir. They already trust me because I speak Russian."

"Good, you stay friends with them." John said and then walked away.

Near Green he said, "Gene, hand me the handset."

"Yes, sir." Private Green said and handed the handset to the colonel.

"Copperhead, this is Cobra Two, over."

"Go Cobra."

"I have captured two Russian privates, so do you want to send a chopper for them or do I keep them with me? Over."

"Wait one, let me talk to Copperhead Actual, over."

"Roger, I'll wait, over."

Five minutes later headquarters said, "Get them ready for a chopper ride back to the base. We will be in a ball game this evening, so they need to be locked up. The boss is concerned they may make a break for freedom if left with you. ETA on the bird is one hour from now, over."

"Smart man to pick them up." Green said.

"Yep, if this place gets to hopping this evening, they could easily escape in all the action going on around them." John said.

"Understand. Cobra Two, out."

Less than five minutes later the radio turned live again with, "Cobra, this is Copperhead Actual, over."

John still held the handset so he replied, "Go Copperhead, this is Cobra Two."

"I just had a change in plans and we can take your prisoners in fifteen minutes."

"The sooner the better, and fifteen minutes is ideal. I just don't want to lose them because it's rare for me to capture one, much less two. Have the chopper contact me five mikes out, over."

"Copy, five mikes out. Copperhead, over and out."

"Hanish, get the two prisoners ready to take a chopper ride. Let them know they are leaving in about 12 minutes or so, and on a chopper."

"Will do, sir."

John stood with the handset in his hands waiting to hear from the chopper.

Ten minutes later, "Cobra Two, this is Coon Dog One, over."

"This is Cobra, go Coon Dog."

"I am five mikes from your position. In three I want to see a night flare that marks your position and keep me in an opening, not too close to the trees. I am approaching with my lights off. Over."

"Don't you know night landings must be rough." Hanish said.

"I've not given it any thought. Lee, pop a night flare and help me land this chopper."

"Yes, sir." Lee said and they pulled out a Mark 13 Mod O flare and ignited the flare end. The flare lit up the whole surrounding area.

"Cobra Two, I have your flare and man visual. ETA is less than two minutes. Get the POWs on, and fast. There are reports of many Russians in your RON area."

"Roger, we'll load them quickly." Then turning to SSgt Prings, he said, "I want you, Prings, to take Tom and Carrier to provide security for the chopper. If you see the aircraft take any ground fire, I want you to fire back. Scan the area constantly and hopefully with any shots you'll see the muzzle flash. Now, go."

The chopper landed with all lights off, except a huge spotlight, and the prisoners were thrown on the aircraft. They were on the ground for less than two minutes. The chopper was rising when the tell tale sound of bullets hitting the bird were heard. The big light on the helicopter went off when the first bullet struck. Every gun in John's squad returned fire by simply shooting where the tracer rounds were coming from, as well as the flash from the weapons. The hostile firing on the aircraft stopped and so did John's return fire.

"Cobra Two, thank you for watching my six. We are going through 2,000 feet and they can't see me now."

"Copy, and have a good flight home, Coon Dog."

"Roger that and remember, you call and we haul. Coon Dog, over and out."

"Master Sergeant Dias, get everyone up and lets move about a mile south before we relax too much. I expect the Russians to come and see who they were exchanging bullets with as the chopper went up. Line 'em up and let's hurry."

Their night at the new location was uneventful and as the sun came up, they were all walking down a narrow trail and each was wearing his NVGs. They had been walking for over two hours already. But, they'd not seen or heard anything.

"What is going on? The two prisoners stated a bunch of Russians were out looking around, but we've seen none." Hanish asked the Colonel as they walked.

"Give some thought to camps off the trail that are campfire free. If they remain in cold camps, we may have passed a dozen squads just this morning."

"Maybe, but I don't think so. I get a feeling when I'm close to Russians and I don't have that feeling right now."

"Everyone stop, I hear an engine of some sort. Listen and be quiet, please." John said and then cocked his head to the left.

"It's a prop driven airplane, look it's overhead now."

Everyone was watching the aircraft as John said, "It's an Antonov An-22 "Antei" and they are the Russian's C-130, so to speak."

"Look, men are jumping out the rear doors!" Msgt. Dias said as she flipped her Bison off safety.

"Spread out and shoot them, because everyone we miss will land on top of us. Fire at will." the Colonel yelled as he fired and watched a Russian Paratrooper suddenly go limp.

Out of a hundred men dropped on them, less than fifteen made it to the ground safely for one reason or another. Most seemed to land in a huge field maybe a hundred yard from John and his people, so they quickly moved there and continued the fight.

Of the fifteen, less than five men made it to the trees on the other side of the clearing. There they took up defensive positions as the radio operator attempted to make contact with the base. Five minutes later, he finally noticed two bullet holes in the side of the radio, so he tossed it to the ground.

The leader of the group, a Captain Vasilyeva Nadka was in shock. She'd been in combat many times but it was her first combat jump and so far she didn't like it. Over 95 men were now dead or seriously injured and she was left with a small group of five counting her. The fear she had of being shot while still helpless in her parachute made her shiver.

Master Sergeant Robert Sergeyvich said, "We need to escape and evade until we meet another group of Russians, or we can hide and hope any battle that takes place is not fought here. Right now, I have the urge to join others and fight Americans."

"What do you think, Captain?" a corporal asked.

"We . . . we do, uh . . . as the Master Sergeant said, we try to find other Russians troops to join. That is the only honorable thing to do. Now, let us ignore the Americans here and slip into the woods. Once there, I will pull out my map and determine where we need to go. Alright, everyone, let's move."

CHAPTER 11

Senior Sergeant Vova was in his room cuddled up with Olga when he heard an explosion and it sounded very close.

"What was that?" Olga asked.

"Sounded like a grenade in this building, and we are to have visitors tonight. It may be Americans."

He quickly dressed and grabbing his nylon combat vest and weapons, he said to Olga, "Stay in this room and if you hear footsteps, do not pick up a gun. Let them take you prisoner, because it beats death." Then, he made his way from the room.

His NCO quarters were three levels, and the two highest grades slept on the top floor so they'd not have noise from people walking overhead and their walls were more or less soundproof because of the crazy hours they worked. He and Olga had just been outside, sharing a drink as they watched the sun go down. When they came in, they'd left the balcony door open or they wouldn't have heard the explosion. He now picked up the *pop-pop-pop* of small arms fire in the building. He cleared the third floor, then the second and knew someone was on the first floor. He'd avoided the elevator and stood outside the first floor in the stairs, and he was right beside the door.

Suddenly the door swung open and three American partisans moved toward the hall. Vova fired three rounds and saw them go down. Blood, now running toward the floor, was splattered over the walls. He moved to the dead men and took two grenades from each of them, as well as their sidearms and ammo. They were carrying Bison sub-machine guns, like he was, so he collected six more magazines and another weapon.

Opening the door, he peeked out and saw no one so he entered the stairs and went to the ground floor. The first three rooms were open and the occupants dead on the floor. As NCOs they were allowed to carry their weapons all the time, but few did. He looked them over, but knew none of them.

In the third room he discovered Senior Sergeant Vera Katenka laying on her back, her fatigue shirt off and her tee soaked in blood. Some of her blood had ran down her belly and legs to stain her white thong. She'd taken three rounds between her breasts. He noticed her eyes were still open and he moved to her and pushed her eyes closed. Her shoes were off, so she must have been relaxing when the soldiers burst into her room. She was a good soldier but she'd been caught unarmed, and all he saw as a weapon near her was a butcher's knife. The knife's whole long blade was covered with fresh blood, so she'd killed or injured one of them.

He left the room, made his way down to room four, and he heard American voices and he saw the door was open. Knowing any Russians in the room were now dead, he pulled the pin on a grenade, let the spoon fly and then counted to three. On three he tossed the grenade in the room.

"Grenade!" someone screamed and two men ran out into the hall, where Vova was shooting them down when the grenade exploded. There were piercing screams heard in the room where the explosion had killed two and left two severely injured. One of the injured had a leg missing and his whole body was leaking blood so he must have been close when the grenade exploded. The next soldier had a missing leg and arm, so Vova fired two rounds into his head. He then turned and fired two rounds into the other injured man, his plan to take him prisoner gone when he remembered Katenka and her fatal wounds. Near the front door was an American soldier, his body untouched pretty much by the grenade, but his stomach was ripped open and he knew immediately that Katenka had killed this one. He fired a round into the moaning man's head and left the room.

When he opened the door to look out, this side of the base was being overrun by Americans. He then went down the hall and knocked on all the doors. Some occupants were armed with pistols but in five minutes he led a squad of ten up to his room. Olga was scared and concerned, especially when Petr hadn't returned quickly. Waiting for Petr to return was very hard for her. She'd been in firefights before but she'd always been armed. Passing the men on the stairs, the Russian Sergeant cleaned them of every weapon and all the ammo they could find. Keeping the Bisons he had, both of them, he made his way to his room. Olga relaxed a great deal when he gave a Bison and half the ammo he had to Olga.

"What do we do now, Senior Sergeant?" a young Sergeant asked.

"We will leave here in a few minutes and fight. We are the best troops from Mother Russia and we will make her proud of us this night." Walking to his cabinet he pulled out a quart of unopened top shelf vodka and tossed it to a man. "You are now our medic. I want you to plug all holes we may get and give each patient a long chug of alcohol when you first treat them. Maybe as the night progresses, we can find a real medics bag."

"From what I saw from my window, there are sure to be many dead medics. The Americans are fighting well tonight and I have been here three tours, counting this trip, and all I have seen them do was hit and run."

"This is no hit and run. They are trying their best to overrun us and I think they will do so."

There sounded a loud explosion and the JP4 and JP8 fuel tanks both went up in flames. Shortly after, two large parked transport planes went up, followed by a number of attack helicopters. Without a word spoken, they all knew they would lose this battle this day. As far as they could see and in all directions, dead Russian soldiers lay. Partisans were dying too, but not nearly as many as the Russians.

"Damn me, Isaak, we have partisans all over the base like ants. Do something or we will lose this base and Moscow will have our heads." Colonel Lazarev said and his desperation was clearly heard in his tone.

"Not much we can do since you sent the last of the men, the bulk, away after the American base, but they all got their asses kicked and while most still live, they are straggling back in squads. No, my friend you kept just enough soldiers here to handle day to day operations, but not enough for defense. Now you are paying for your foolishness."

"We must leave then. I will have a helicopter made ready and it can land on our roof here."

"I strongly suggest you do not do that. Moscow would rather we fight to the death than to survive in defeat. If you survive this attack, my friend, you will be dead by the hands of Moscow within a month. It is better to die a hero of the Motherland than to live as a coward. I for one, will not be running away from anything."

"But, we will surely die if we stay."

"Some things are worth dying for and personal honor is one of them. No, I will stay and either survive or die, depending on the wishes of God."

"God? There is no God. You are a fool. You mean to stand there and tell me God can save us?"

"No, not you, because you do not think he is real, but he is. So, run and go now, before I pull my pistol and shoot you myself. I can tell you one thing, Moscow will never let you live if you lose this base. You will be a dead man, no matter where you are, only you have not been killed, yet."

Picking up the phone, Lazarev said, "Laura, contact my personal pilot and have him land on the roof. The base is being overrun and I must escape. Yes, of course you will go with me, my dear. Now make the call."

"I will leave then, and try to get the men organized and attack the Americans. I think it can be done, and we will not need you."

Reaching into an open desk drawer, he pulled out a bottle of vodka and took a long pull, and when he placed it back, he pulled out a pistol.

Grinning, he pointed it at Isaak and said, "I am tired of your talk and do not appreciate being called a coward."

"Oh, this is rich. Now you are going to start shooting your staff? May God have mercy on your useless soul."

Lazarev pulled the trigger twice and both bullets struck Isaak in the middle of his chest. After he fell to the floor without a sound, the Base Commander said, "Where was your God, Isaak? Why did he not protect you? Because there is no God."

Gasping, Isaak said, "You . . . you are . . . wrong. So . . . very . . . wrong." He then fell back limply and Full Colonel Dimitri Isaak was dead.

"Damn fool."

The door swung open and Laura said, "He is on the roof, we need to go now. The Americans have broken into the lower floor and will soon be in here!"

Turning to Laura, his secretary and lover, Lazarev said, "There has been a change in plans, my dear. It seems you were killed in the attack and I cannot take you with me." He then fired twice, with both bullets striking her center mass, and down she went. She screamed for him not to leave her, but he stepped over her and ran for the roof. Minutes later he was strapped in and the aircraft began to rise into the sky.

"Where to, Colonel?" the Captain asked.

"Any place as long as it is away from here."

As they raised, a beeper was heard and the pilot said, "Someone has a radar lock on us. I need to —"

Neither the pilot or the Colonel felt the shoulder fired missile when it struck them right behind the pilot's door. The aircraft burst into a huge ball of flames, as helicopter parts and body parts fell with the wreckage. Both men were dead before they seriously realized how much danger they were in.

Looking up at the falling ball of flames, a partisan Corporal said, "Nice shooting Private, we can claim one helicopter destroyed. Get another ready, because aircraft are starting to leave here. Maybe if we get near the end of the runway, we can down more of them." Three bullets struck the pavement in front of the men as they ran and both heard the bullets zing off into space.

Near the end of the runway, the man carrying a rocket propelled grenade (RPG) and one more missile said, "I can't run anymore, because this crap gets heavy. Place the two missiles you're carrying on the ground beside me. Hopefully we'll knock some aircraft out of the sky."

A huge transport plane flew over them and any conversation, thanks to noise, was quickly ended. Another transport aircraft was rolling down the runway as the Private opened a shoulder fired missile, and made it ready to fire. Just when it looked like the aircraft would never get into the air, it raised its nose and slowly climbed into the sky.

Just when the aircraft was almost overhead, the Private fired and the missile launched. Both men stood, waiting to see if it would hit the aircraft or miss. Since the missile was a heat seeker, it struck the outboard engine on the left wing. The explosion was loud and big, and the blast knocked both men to the ground. Parts of the jet began falling. Then there was a secondary explosion that blew the plane into thousands of pieces. It continued moving forward, but in the air it was no longer recognizable as an aircraft. Flaming pieces of the aircraft began to hit the ground. When the largest portions struck the ground, there was more noise and explosions as the oxygen systems and other flammables in compressed tanks blew due to extreme heat from the fire. There were no survivors.

Dropping the one time use empty missile container and launcher, the man picked up another missile and waited. A smaller aircraft that reminded the man with the missile of an American C-130 was next and he was a good 500 feet into the air before he crossed the end of the runway. The man sighted in the bird, squeezed the trigger and the missile system gave a short series of beeps, confirming the target was locked on. A split second later the missile fired.

The aircraft immediately dropped chaff and hot flares in an attempt to trick the missile from striking them. The system was used to confuse the heat seeking system on the missile by having too many hot flares. Hopefully it would cause the missile to go after a burning flare. It worked this time, because the missile followed one flare and then exploded right behind the aircraft. The horizontal stabilizer was blown half away, but the plane remained flying. Picking up an RPG, mainly because he didn't have time to open a missile container, he lined the cross-hairs on the nose of the aircraft and squeezed the trigger.

The grenade launched with more of a kick than a missile and the man stood watching, knowing the grenade could not be sidetracked by chaff or burning flares. Once again the pilot dropped burning flares in hopes of staying alive. The RPG struck slightly behind the crew cabin of the aircraft and the explosion was a big one. The aircraft wobbled a bit and then grew stable. On the aircraft, the pilot sent a chilling warning that Americans were using missiles and RPGs at the end of the runway. The tower quickly sent a team of soldiers to wipe the threat out completely.

The pilot said, "Tower this is Beach Boy One and I would like to declare an in-flight emergency. I have taken a missile or RPG in the passenger compartment just behind the cockpit. I can see my dead engineer and I have a navigator I cannot get a response from on the radio. While I partially can see him, I am a bit busy keeping us in the air. My console is lit up like a Christmas tree. Over."

"Copy, Beach Boy One. Please use runway two five west to land and visually clear your own approach and landing. I have over a dozen aircraft currently waiting for takeoff. Over."

"Uh, roger that. I will land on runway two five west."

"If you have problems due to aircraft traffic, land on the grass or any empty taxi way, over."

"Roger that. This is Beach Boy One and I am coming in on final now."

"Good luck, Beach Boy."

Back on the ground, the man assisting the shooter, Private Mark Gomez, said "Steve, there's a Jeep looking thing headed right for us. I suspect our surprise is over."

"Not as long as I have an RPG left. Let me line my sights up, Mark, and we'll see if I can take the vehicle out of the picture." The truck was easily sighted in and then Steve squeezed the trigger. The rocket flew straight into the grill on the vehicle and it went up with a loud boom. Bodies and truck flew high into the air and were then consumed by an oily ball of red and black flames.

"Forget about the truck, let's get this next plane, because it's huge." Mark said, his voice full of excitement.

Opening a missile, Steve said, "It looks to be an Antonov An-124 *Ruslan* and it carries about 150 tons of material; it's like our old C-5. It rarely carries passengers or airborne troops because the cargo area has poor pressurization." Both men would have been surprised to learn over 375 men and women were onboard the aircraft as the base began to fall. The pilots knew if they kept their altitude below 10,000 feet they would be able to transport people.

He was ready as soon as the big aircraft began its taxi for takeoff. The airplane looked huge to both men on the ground as Steve prayed he'd be able to down the aircraft. Minutes later the *Ruslan* flew overhead and Steve fired the missile. Again chaff and flares were seen, but the missile ignored the decoys and stuck the aircraft in the right inboard engine. The explosion was great and the complete engine dropped in pieces. Flames began to flow over the leading edge of the aircraft as the pilot tried his or her best to keep them in the air.

Two gunshots were heard and Mark dropped, dead as hell.

The aircraft became inverted just before impact with the ground. The aircraft struck the ground hard and with touch down the fuel tanks ruptured, spilling aviation gas that caused a huge explosion and fireball.

It was then Beach Boy One touched down on an empty runway and just as he landed his left tire blew, causing the left wing to drop and hit the runway. The aircraft began to cartwheel down the taxi way, nose, wing tip, tail, and finally wing tip as it scattered metal and parts down the concrete. Then there was an explosion that placed the aircraft in flames as it moved. Steve knew the passengers and crew were dead. It finally slowed down enough that it ended on it's side, the wing knocked off the frame and laying about half the distance from the point they'd sat it down to the end of the runway.

On board, everything was covered in red flames and the passengers and crew were all beyond feeling pain; they were dead.

Steve checked Mark, found him dead due to a bullet burning a hole through the center of his chest. Without help, there was no way Steve would remain here shooting at planes. He dropped the used missile launcher and picked up his rifle and his one remaining missile. He ran toward the smoke of the burning *Ruslan* aircraft, knowing he would get away clean if he could move through the smoke and get into the woods on the other side of the crashed *Ruslan*. Anyone following him would be forced to stop and look for survivors on the huge airplane.

As he ran near the crashed bird, he spotted people, obviously the passengers of the big aircraft, some still strapped in their seats in various stages of death. One woman had a pipe stuck in her chest and then poking out of her chair back. He spotted a man's body sitting in a chair, yet holding a magazine with both hands, but his head was missing. Wounded were seen crawling around, as if looking for something, and most had horrible burn wounds. It also sounded like 100 of them were trapped and screaming for help as the fire inside the cabin grew closer to them. Rescue trucks were approaching and Steve ran harder for the woods. He wanted to be in the foliage before the firetrucks arrived.

Minutes later, just as the trucks arrived, Steve slipped under the fence and into the woods. He then moved north, the direction all lost partisans were told to go so they could regroup and attack again.

About twenty minutes later, Steve arrived and discovered a large number, well over a hundred people, waiting to be organized so they could attack the Russians. There was one Major and while he was trying, no one was listening to him. They all milled around talking to each other in low tones.

Someone yelled, "Hey look at the way that jet to the north is lining up. Do you think he's lining up on us?"

The jet was now streaking for the group and Steve yelled, "Scatter, he's got napalm."

People began to run in all directions. Pulling his last missile, he stood on the grass and faced the Russian jet pilot. Just before the pilot released the napalm, Steve squeezed the trigger on the missile launcher.

Steve stood spellbound as the two canisters of napalm flipped over and over as they fell to earth. The containers struck the ground maybe 500 feet behind him and when he turned there was a huge wave of flames thrown up and over the running partisans. Then, a second later the wave fell and people were heard screaming as the sticky jell stuck to their bodies. Seconds later the screaming stopped.

The Mig was hit in the left engine and half of the wing was missing when the smoke cleared. The pilot was clearly seen ejecting from the aircraft and his parachute opened. The jet crashed about 200 yards from Steve; it caused a huge explosion and smoke, dense and black, began reaching for the sky.

Sighting in the pilot, Steve shot at the man, still in his parachute, and at one point the Russian went rigid and then fell limply. To insure he was really dead, the Private shot him four more times without any movement from the pilot. Once he landed, Steve shot him another half a dozen times.

The Major neared and called out, "If you are able to still fight, form on me! Hurry, the base is almost ours. Everyone, form on me!"

Steve walked to the man and said, "Can I help, sir?"

"You can and as of right now, consider yourself a Staff Sergeant."

"Yes, sir."

Few partisans formed on him because many had been killed in the fire, but some were alive and able to fight, while others were in pain from the sticky napalm jell. Out of almost 200 men and woman, exactly 21 stepped forward to do battle against the Russians. They ran forward and were soon grouped and roughly formed behind the Major. They then started over the base. Few Russians were resisting now and even the plane flights were stopped. Americans lined the runway, with machine-guns, RPGs, and missiles pointed in the general direction of the aircraft. One small commercial plane, a single propeller model, took off and was quickly brought down by ground fire, a mixture of machine-gun fire and three RPGs.

John, in the middle of the bunch, was happy they were now the holders of an entire Russian base and for the first time in the history of the partisans, they were winners of territory and not just a hit and run. Right after they'd killed most of the airborne troops that landed in a field next to them, they were picked up by Chinese Helicopters and brought back to the Dallas/Fort Worth base, so they could be part of the attacking force on this Russian Base.

"Copperhead, this is Cobra Two, over."

"Go Cobra."

"Send the deuce and half trucks in so we can start loading Russian supplies. I figure we have less than 12 hours before they counterattack. We need to strip this base bare and then get out of Dodge.

Over."

"This is Copperhead Actual, good job Colonel. I'm damned proud of you and your people. I want you back on the first truck, and as of today your time in the field is limited, understand? I will tell you more when you arrive. Copy?"

"Copy, sir. Okay, I'll return with the first run back to Dallas/Fort Worth, but it will be a couple of days drive. I may jump a helicopter and get back sooner. I know our intelligence people will be out in less than an hour to go through the files and images the Russians didn't have time to take with them. We discovered the Wing Commander dead in the office of the Base Commander, and his secretary was shot too, but not by us. From the looks of his office he flew the coup after shooting both of them with his pistol. We found four ejected pieces of brass and all four are from the same sidearm."

"That is tremendous news in my eyes. We not only took the base, we saw the two senior people kill each other. Any idea where the base commander is?"

"If he tried to fly out of here, there is a good chance he is dead. Our shoulder fired missiles and our RPGs downed about 7 out of 10 aircraft attempting to get airborne. I wasn't watching all the time, but I think he's dead because all the choppers I saw in the sky were blown up. But, he may have left on one of the bigger aircraft."

"Look for his body or anything that a Commander might have on him when he left. He may have had a briefcase, stack of papers, or whatever. I'd really like to think we killed them both, but indirectly. Copperhead Actual, over and out."

It was then a woman that John didn't know approached him and asked, "Are you the Colonel assigned to take this base?"

"I am. What can I do for you, and I'm called John."

"John, if you'll come with me, I have a few over 200 people who want to meet you. You indirectly rescued them from the base gulag. I am Major Joy Barnes and I'm your new executive officer."

"What happened to Major Woo? And, yes, let me speak to the released prisoners. I have some important words for them." They both began walking.

She chuckled and asked, "Would it matter if I took Woo's job over?"

"Yes, it surely would. He and I have worked together for a while and while he's no field troop, he damned sure knows intelligence." John said and then realized he sounded cold so he quickly added, "I have nothing personal against you, I don't even know you. All I see is an attractive young woman, but that doesn't mean you know beans about intelligence."

"I was always told military intelligence is an oxymoron." she said, and then broke out laughing.

John laughed too and then said, "You do have a good sense of humor."

"Relax Colonel, Woo is still your chief of intelligence, but I am your executive officer or in layman terms, your gopher." Once again she laughed.

They were quiet the last 100 yards to the gulag, where a crowd of people were waiting to be told something by a partisan in charge.

When John and Joy neared, she said, "This is the man responsible for your rescue and release. He has a few words for all of you, so keep the noise down."

"All of you, regardless of your gender, can join us in our fight against the Russians or you are free. If you join us, I can promise you nothing, except two hot meals most days, a life of living in the wild, and fighting your ass off to free your country. Out of three volunteers to join the partisans, two will be dead within the first year. Only the smartest will survive living our life. If you hate the Russians and would like to murder all of them, we don't need you. I'm wanting men and women who are willing, need be, to fight and give their lives in the name of liberty. I can only promise you more hunger, poor sleep, and a chance to be proud that you freed America from the Russian Bear. If you want to serve under me, then move behind me."

All moved behind him except for three women who were holding babies on their hips.

"We also need people to cook, wash clothing, work as nurses or in other noncombat jobs. If you ladies want the added security of a large group of fighters around you and on a military installation, join us."

Joy smiled as the three women joined the rest behind John.

"Now, Major Barnes, see these people are assigned to various units and try to keep family and friends together if at all possible."

"Yes, sir. I'll fill you in when I return to the base."

"Good. I have to leave, one of my men is yelling for me. Good luck to each of you." John said and then walked back toward Green and the radio.

Ten minutes later, John was informed by headquarters he and his squad would be relocating to near Fort Leonard Wood, Missouri. It was John's old stomping grounds. But as he spoke with Joy, because she requested to be assigned to his unit, he kept their destination out of the conversation. He wanted to make sure she didn't know much, not that he didn't trust her, but as the newest member of the unit she had no need to know everything.

CHAPTER 12

That afternoon, deep in the woods behind the base, a Master Sergeant that was good friends with Petr and had been for years, whispered to him, "Stay aware and keep your eyes and ears open tonight after dark. We are preparing an attack to take the base back from the Americans."

They were with a bunch of other Russians, and both men were there to get their rations. Vova found the whole situation upsetting that they'd been driven from their base like a pack of rats. He was used to airborne troops who would have died before they ran.

"I will do that. How do you like being out of an airborne unit, Rogov?" Vova asked.

"It is okay, but I am not as proud being in a non-jumping unit. Being airborne made me proud and I felt worthwhile. Now I feel we are simply cannon fodder. The spirit is not the same and the troops are not tough enough. Most are just kid draftees and almost useless."

"How much longer before you retire?"

"If I survive tonight I have less than a year. I have 121 days and a wake-up and I am a civilian again. I guess I will move back to the farm and take over from my father."

"At least as a farmer you will always have something to eat. Have you seen the price of meat here? Beef is insane. I have been saving half of my pay for 20 years and all I have to spend my money on is vodka because I can eat in the mess tent for free, but I like to cook and usually have foods in my room."

Glancing at his watch, Rogov Christov quickly said, "I need to rush. I have an appointment in twenty minutes with the new Colonel they flew in just to plan and lead the attack. You take care and remember, we may be returning to the base this evening." The Master Sergeant had less then six hours before he would be dead.

"You take care, and watch your ass when the lead starts flying."

When Petr and Olga finished getting their rations, they went by the foxholes of everyone in his squad and warned them to be loaded for bear this night. He also instructed them to request more munitions and ammo from supply if they had it to spare.

"What is so special tonight? I can see you expect an attack or something else, but why all the ammo and munitions?" Olga asked as they moved for the foxhole they shared.

"Did you see the Master Sergeant I was speaking to when we were getting this food? He warned me to expect us to attack this night, and I am taking his word very seriously. He used to be airborne, but hurt his back and failed his jump physical. They made him a top sergeant in a regular unit. He hates being a leg and I do not blame him."

"Leg?" Olga asked.

"We call people who do not jump, 'legs,' because they walk into wars. We, on the other hand, are transported over a target and jump into our fights. Our missions are always more glitter and sparkle than a leg's war."

Olga laughed and replied, "My first half a dozen jumps, I was kicked in the ass as soon as I stood in the door. The jump-masters knew they had to kick me from the aircraft. I froze every single time. Now, I have complete confidence in my gear and I love walking off a lowered ramp in the rear of a plane. I also get a big thrill out of jumping from a helicopter."

"To me, jumping is just another another way to enter combat. I never thought about dying from a jump, but I have had friends die that way. I have to admit it is very, very rare though. It is safer than driving in any large city."

"Should you and I go by munitions and load up for the attack? If we are going on the offensive tonight, I would like to provide a good time for my enemies."

"I have Dimitri collecting ammo for us. He will be by our foxhole within the hour. We need to eat and then relax; taking the base back may take all night and it is sure to be tough. I honestly do not know if we can do it without close air support."

"Can we not call another base for help?"

"At least one other base has fallen and a couple of others are in fights for their lives, so no, we have to make due with what we have. Other bases are too far away, like Saint Louis, to even consider and by the time they arrived, we would not need them one way or the other."

"I am scared, Petr."

"You have that right, and you would have to be dumb to not have fear. I am frightened too, but not for the same reason as you. I do not want you injured or killed, but that is why I try to avoid getting personal with anyone in my squad. Sooner or later, I know I would have to send them in harms way. If they are hurt or killed, then I would feel responsible, but I have to lead you into danger this night, maybe."

"I do not blame you because that is your job and in my opinion, you are the best senior NCO around. I trust your decisions and value your knowledge. We will both survive, but we may be beaten up a little when we return."

"It creates a problem for me. We will both be exposed to danger, maybe."

"I hope we survive."

"I do not know if we will or not, but tonight before we attack, we need to clean all bullets, check our gear, and make sure our weapons are all in good shape. Then we need to rest or sleep."

"I understand." she said, and began looking her Bison over closely.

Petr pulled an old oily rag out, tossed it to her and said, "Here, wipe it down as you look it over. I keep that rag for times like this. I use it all the time, except in winter when the oil cans freeze."

It was a little after midnight when the Russian army moved toward their old base, determined to regain ownership. Most of the troops were understandably nervous and Olga was fighting the urge to puke.

"Senior Sergeant, I need you for the radio." she said as she held the handset out for him. "It is Hotel."

"Monsoon to Hotel, go. Over."

"Spetsnaz indicates the Americans have gone as if they had never been there. Most of the supply buildings and bunkers have been ransacked, and stealing occurred, but all their troops have disappeared."

"Roger, understand. What are your orders, Hotel?"

"Continue with the attack and if no Americans are there, clean the place up and make it a home again. Moscow has called all troops from the field and they will start landing at your place at about sunrise. Copy?"

"Understand the troops in the field will start to arrive here near dawn. Will make them welcome and put them to work. Anything else going on?"

"Not at this time. Moscow will be happy we regained control of our base and without the loss of a single man."

"I am sure they left some booby-traps, because they always do. It is the young and dumb that find them. Let us hope this day no one touches anything until the Explosive Ordnance Disposal (EOD) team clears the base, but I expect us to lose a few. The partisans love to booby-trap Russian bodies or souvenirs."

"Copy. All I can suggest is you keep a tight leash on the young troops, so they can live long enough to be old troops. Hotel, over and out."

Tossing the handset to Olga, Petr smiled at her and said, "The Americans are gone. They took what they could steal and left. Spetsnaz reports they are on the base and no Yankees can be found. Now, there will be booby-traps, so do not pick up a damned thing until EOD has finished sweeping the area."

"I am so glad they are gone. I was worried one of us might be killed." Olga replied in a low voice, almost a whisper, and gave him a weak smile.

"One of us could still be killed. Just because they are gone does not mean the place is safe. They are known as experts in booby-traps and they have a thousand ways to kill people."

"Do you think we will go to the base this evening?"

"We will now, for sure. Some Colonel will probably write up a report about how the brave Russian soldiers, under his leadership, regained control of the base without the loss of a single soldier. He will get a medal and we will get nothing. He will be promoted and move on up into the senior officer ranks. I have seen it often in the past."

"I do not care what they do. I am happy in my own little world, which consists of you and my squad. Most of Russia thinks we fight for our country, but that is not exactly true. I fight to protect myself and my brothers and sisters in my squad. I fight to live, so I can make love to you once more." Senior Sergeant Vova smiled and said, "Good. Now, let me get everyone awake and up. We need to be ready to go at any time. I know the Commanders all got the same call I did and they will be leaving as soon as possible. This way they can have a glorious return to the base we ran from. Hopefully Moscow will not start lopping off heads."

"Senior Sergeant, Colonel Yurievich wants to see you right now. He said it was urgent." a private said as he neared the Sergeant and Olga.

"Tell him, I will be right there." He bent over to pick up his gear and weapons. He was tired of war, fight or no fight. He wanted to rest in a rocking chair on the front porch of his beet farm and sip vodka. He had been in the army so long he felt he could sleep a year or more. Putting his heavy helmet on, he moved toward their temporary headquarters in the woods. Time to retake their base.

They walked into the base through the front gate, found the Spetsnaz team drinking, and the only warning they had was, "Touch nothing. There are many booby-traps in this base."

The young troops moved over the grasses as if they were on a picnic and just as Vova was about to warn them, a woman in another unit stepped on an antipersonnel mine. She went up in the a wall of white and red, with a loud explosion, followed by a shrieking scream of pain.

"Medic!" someone yelled and Vova watched the medic run to the woman and quickly stuck a syringe of morphine in her arm. Slowly her screaming began to stop. The medic saw one leg missing and the other was so mangled it would be removed too, but in a hospital. Hearing a helicopter nearing, the medic screamed, "Someone contact that aircraft and see if I can put my patent in the helicopter to return to a hospital. Without a doctor she will bleed out in 45 minutes. She needs more help than I can give her and the helicopter has the needed medical supplies on board."

Olga handed the handset to the Senior Sergeant who said, "Hello any Russian aircraft near the base, respond. This is Monsoon Two. I have need of a medical evacuation and need your help, over."

"Uh, Monsoon, this is Bumble Bee two. We are due at the base in two mikes, over."

"Roger that. Can you take a patient out for me that will die without fast medical treatment?"

"Can do and will unload my passengers at your location. I need you to pop smoke, so I can locate you and check the wind direction, over."

"Medic, I have a helicopter coming for her, so get her ready to leave. He will be here in a couple of minutes." the Senior Sergeant yelled, popped a purple smoke grenade, and then said, "Bumble Bee, what color do you see?"

"Purple, is that you?"

"Roger that. Do you have me in sight yet?"

"Roger, and I am coming down. Wait for the passengers to leave, then have her loaded in the cargo area. You will need to send a medic with her, because mine stayed behind to treat wounded."

"Medic! When she is placed on the aircraft, you go too. The aircraft has no medic on board and you will be needed on the flight back. Gather up your tools and supplies, he is coming down now."

The medic waved a bloody hand and stood holding one end of a poncho; another man was holding the front and they'd pack her to the aircraft.

The helicopter made a safe landing, soldiers ran from the cargo hold and then the medic ran for the open compartment and lifted the injured woman into the aircraft. Then the medic climbed in behind her. A few seconds later the helicopter rose, lowered the nose and applied power. In three minutes they were out of sight, but *whop-whop-whop* was still faintly heard.

"Watch where you step, people. The Americans were here 12 hours ago, so any mines should have damp dirt on top and that soil will be a different color. Avoid stepping on any discolored soil. Do not forget trip wires and do not touch any dead, ours or theirs. They love to booby-trap the dead."

Off in the distance there came a huge explosion and Petr knew the gasoline storage tank had gone up by the oily looking black smoke that was rising to meet the low gray cloud cover overhead. He knew the JP-4 and JP8 tanks had gone up during the battle. The only tank left now was a smaller tank of processed oil used by the motor pool and flight line. He wondered how many the blast had killed, because it obviously was booby-trapped. He shook his head. Now they would have a shortage of petroleum, oils, and liquids (POL) and that would make the base more difficult to protect. Helicopters need, like a truck, fuel and oil or they could not be used.

Before the repossession of the base was complete, ten troops died clearing booby-traps or for doing something dumb they shouldn't have done, with 12 slightly injured and 3 wounded severely. The booby-trap at the Mo Gas storage area killed another six men and women, and injured 23 others. The Colonel was very pleased with his kill ratio, because he killed over 516 Americans, or so he'd report to Moscow. He'd simply add the Americans that died in the original assault and the troops took hundreds of photos of the American bodies with him in the photo. He'd fax them to Moscow today and when the planes were flying again, he'd send the glossy images, 8X10 color images, out by special carrier. So, with a little over 60 troops killed and maimed, he had the bodies of over 500 Americans stacked like firewood near a taxiway on the airfield.

Colonel Ludomir Yurievich, the base Propaganda Commander, took over as the new base and wing Commander, until Lazarev and Isaak were found, if they were not killed in the battle. If they were not found alive, he'd continue to command until a replacement was sent by Moscow. He knew his 500 dead Americans would show he was aggressive enough, so he could be assigned as the permanent Commander. A lot depended on what the senior staff in Moscow knew of the Colonel and his reputation as an officer.

Two hours after they'd secured the base, Lieutenant Colonel Orya Shura reported to the Commander that Colonel Isaak had been found, along with Colonel Lazarev's secretary, dead in the Base Commanders office. Both died of two shots to the chest and it was unknown who'd killed them. The Colonel thought, *The Base Commander was probably mad because it would be his responsibility to keep the base in his hands and to win a victory over the Americans. Obviously, that did not happen, so he had every legal right to shoot Isaak, but why kill his secretary? I think she may have been his lover and knew too much. I understand she was a very attractive woman.*

"Have both bodies prepared with aluminum coffins for shipment back to the motherland. Write up something heroic about Isaak so he looks good when they present him a medal. You know, the usual hype that goes with medal writing, like he almost saved the base single-handedly. Make him much bigger than he was in life. Were any classified documents taken from the office that you can tell?"

"Sir, I have no idea yet, but we are inventorying his classified files and his messages, to see if the Americans read it or not. His safe had the tumbler missing and a thermite grenade was used to melt it off. All the classified papers were thrown on the floor and some were found in his fireplace. I am confused that a Colonel was found dead in the office with his pistol still in it's holster, sir."

"I suspect he was executed for allowing the base to fall. Colonel Lazarev had the legal right to shoot him."

"Sir, I do not understand, his secretary was found dead as well and when we found her, she was missing her underwear."

"All of her underwear?"

"Yes, sir, but she had a short dress on. Do you think the Americans raped her?"

"Shura, how in the hell did you make Lieutenant Colonel? Who would rape an attractive woman and then make her put a dress on so they could shoot her? I want her to have an autopsy and the Colonel too. I do not think she was touched by an American soldier. I think if she was touched by anyone it would have been Lazarev before the attack started. I am sure any sperm they find in or on her will match the Colonels DNA. So, if he was poking her, then there was no rape. Many Russian and American secretaries sleep with their bosses here." The Colonel laughed and said, "Do not repeat that to anyone, but I feel it is very true. Both Russians are far from home and lonely. The American women sleep with their bosses for favors or to gain information, but that makes them the same as whores to me. At any rate, get the classified documents cleaned up, provide me with a list of all classified material he had because all of it has been compromised, and find Colonel Lazarev, or his remains. Now, get out of here, because I am suddenly doing the job of three Colonels."

The Lieutenant Colonel left and Lazarev's male secretary stuck his head in the office and said, "Moscow on the phone for you, sir. It is a Lieutenant General Kozakov Rollakov."

"Thank you, Sergeant." Yurievich said, and then picking up the phone he said, "Colonel Ludomir Yurievich speaking, sir."

"Ludomir, it is I, General Rollakov. I am calling to congratulate you on your kills after you took command in the recent battle you fought. Right now we have no idea of when you will get a new Wing or Base Commander. I suggested you to the council, mainly because of the successful kills you had and the fact I know you personally. I think they will leave you as Base Commander and we will vote on it this afternoon. I think, no matter where you are assigned, you will make General now for sure."

"I'm not sure what to say, sir."

"Any man that can kill over 500 Americans and have less than 60 casualties is General material for sure. I cannot talk long, have another meeting, but I wanted to tell you all of Russia is talking about the Colonel that killed so many Americans. Just stay alive and the rank of General will soon be yours, maybe as early as today. I will have my aide contact you, when I know the results of our vote. I don't expect you to get a permanent position there, not with a promotion to General. Mainly because that position is for a full Colonel and not a General; enjoy your day, my friend."

"Thank you, sir."

"Goodbye, Ludomir. Congratulations on your soon to be promotion."

"T . . . Thank you, sir." He then hung up the phone. He reached into his drawer, pulled out a quart of vodka and thought, *Me a General; hell, I was happy when I made full Colonel.*

He poured the glass half full and then thought, *General Ludomir Yurievich. I think it has a nice ring to the name. Boy, will Sarah be surprised.* He then chuckled. *Looks like my false report of the American losses was a smart thing to do. If they question me about the number of American dead when they took this place over, I can claim they took all their dead and wounded with them when they were ran off the base.*

His phone rang and he saw it was his female secretary, and she was right on time. The male administration assistant left each day at 1700, but the female worked at night. He usually let her go at midnight, but on other nights, they spent the night together.

"Sir, it is Lieutenant Colonel Shura on the line for you."

"Thank you." He pushed the flashing green light and said, "Colonel Yurievich."

"Sir, Colonel Shura, and we found Colonel Lazarev."

He felt his stomach quiver. He asked, "Is he okay?"

"No, sir, he is not. His remains were discovered in the wreckage of a helicopter and he had a briefcase with documents with him. Apparently he was deserting the base when it began to fall to the Americans. He had his passport, money, and a little gold and silver. He was badly burned, but we were able to identify him by his dental records and that was assisted by part of his uniform rank we found on the jacket he was wearing."

"No doubt it is him?"

"None. The remains still had his wedding ring and a ring with a gold nugget on his right hand ring finger. I watched the autopsy and they took fingerprints, but his fingers were so badly burned we could not use them. I saw each of the teeth indicated by his dental records. He will be ready to ship out with Colonel Isaak in the morning. I need for you, sir, as the Base Commander to notify Moscow two senior officers have been killed, and I would leave off the fact Colonel Lazarev was leaving his post, if I were you."

"Oh, and why is that, Colonel?"

"Uh, then he will be determined to have been deserting his post, his widow would be denied a pension and he would not get a military funeral. I see no reason to announce to the world that he was a coward, sir. This way his wife can still get his pension and she will never know what really happened here."

"Was it not you that just said he was deserting his post? I do believe you said that twice."

"Yes, sir, I did. I just thought to save the man's wife and family the embarrassment of him being a coward, and I think that might be better. I mean, he is dead now, and cannot hurt you or I, sir."

"Yes, we will do as you suggest, Orya."

"Thank you, sir. I am sure God will deal with his running."

"I do not think Lazarev will be speaking to God, not once he answers Saint Peter's questions. I want you to submit him for three medals and have the paperwork to my desk by dawn tomorrow. Have him climbing into an attack helicopter in the final minutes of the fight, so he could try to turn the tide in the battle. I want him and I submitted for the Hero of the Russian Federation, then just him for an Order of Saint George and the Order of Suvorov. I will sign as a witness as well five other officers. Take it to them tonight and have each sign as witnesses and tell them they are to do so by my orders. I do not care if they like signing or not, and you may tell them that. By the way, you can called me Brigadier General Yurievich as of today."

CHAPTER 13

Back in his base camp near Rolla, Missouri, John was pleased with the way things were going in the war right now. He was sitting in his office tent with a German-speaking American and the news was on. They had people able to speak other languages available at most bases.

"So, it's to rain the rest of the week, and in world news, Russia exploded today with riots forming at three demonstrations in three different cities. Two of the three riots the Russian police put down quickly, but the army was called for a massive one in Moscow. The estimates go as high as a million demonstrators were there. When the people began to turn mean and riot, the Russian police pulled back and let the army go in.

Some of the civilians had old firearms and a number of policemen were shot, twelve, and seven of them died. The army estimated a million people were in the crowd when it turned violent. By orders of someone unknown, the army began shooting those destroying private property and they were shooting to kill. Privately owned cars and trucks were set on fire or destroyed, and the afternoon was full of exploding gas tanks as vehicles burned and gunshots rang out from both sides.

Regional hospitals stated to me that they are full, with no empty beds, since the riots were broken up. Sources close to the rioters say over 150 people were killed and 15,000 were injured. Of course we have no way to validate that information and all bodies were removed by the army. Once the dead are photographed and their identities logged into the computer, the next of kin will be notified to come pick up their loved one."

"Damn, sir, the civilians are really mad about the war. They're tired of having their kids sent home dead. The two they are interviewing now state they belong to a group called Students Against the War in America, or SAWA, as they call themselves. Both of them have had brothers or sisters killed in the American War, as they call our war with them. Both have been arrested in the past and then beaten by the police, or so they claim."

Major Fan Woo was sitting beside Major Joy Barnes and he said, "The Government will take a long time to pull from any war just because the general public dislikes their children coming home dead. The leaders of Russia only care about running the country and collecting more wealth, not the people."

"I'm not sure," Joy said. She thought for a second and then said, "I don't know Russian minds, because I'm half German. I know a bit about the English, due to living in London as a Marine on embassy duty, but not the Russians. I've never talked to one, but I've killed a few. Only those two they interviewed sounded determined."

"They are much different than us, for sure. They have no problem shooting rioters, none at all." Major Woo said.

"A mother is a mother," Wolfgang Hanish said. "Too many Russian mothers have given their last child for the nation to only have them come home in a box. They promise to protest until the last Russian soldier is brought home safely." Wolfgang had grown up in Germany, came to America to live at the age of 19, and served in the army for four years. He'd gotten his citizenship while in the service. He'd been a successful middleman and distributor for the wine industry, and was wealthy when America fell.

The Colonel walked to the television and turned it off.

He then looked around the room and said, "We need to pray the riots continue and the people make the Russian government withdraw their troops from America. We have fought well and done our duty, but all we can do is to continue the war because we don't have a government, and there is no way the Chinese will send troops to help us. They are concerned about public opinion and the cost in dollars. I think the cost in lives and money is more than they wish to pay."

"Forcing the government to leave can take years." Joy said.

"We can wait. But, our eyes in Russia say they are about to pull their troops out of here anyway. They will have been here 9 years in three more months and they are somewhat closer to ending the war now than they were on the first day they arrived. They continue to lose more troops than we do each month and no army can afford to do that and still win a war." John said and then realized Joy was a very attractive woman. Then a thought hit him, *I don't need any more women in my life. They died, each time I've loved someone they died, and I can't take the pain of death any longer.*

"Are you okay, Colonel?" Joy asked.

"I'm fine, why do you ask?"

"You had a painful look on your face."

"I was thinking of the good people I've known who have died in this war. I've lost friends, family, two wives, and a lover. War is not where people should go who are in love. But, in order to live free and to truly be Americans, by God we'll do what it takes. We are a very hardheaded people and me especially, because I will not allow anyone to lead our nation into chaos and ruin. I will fight to my very last breath to keep us free, and many friends I know have done just that."

"I see." Joy said, and she wondered about his wives and lovers.

Joy was pretty, but not what a man would call beautiful, with a small nose, plump lips, big eyes and a sassy attitude. She stood a whole five feet and three inches tall, and she was slim, like all the partisans. She was also intelligent, with an IQ of 140. She had large breasts, a firm rear, with a narrow waist. Her blond hair and blue eyes were attractive, and many men had fallen in love with her in the past. But, she was a very private person and never knew she was considered 'hot' by some men and women. To her, she was all professional all the time, except with the right man, but she'd not had a man in her life in years.

She discovered she enjoyed extremely intelligent men, with rugged good looks, and a sharp sense of humor. Most of the women she knew were attracted to the Colonel, enlisted and officers, but she was attracted to him because to her, an intelligent man was a turn on. Before the fall she'd been a successful business woman, running her own food production company, and she'd dated doctors, lawyers, and other professional men. She had no interest in Bill the auto mechanic at the corner repair shop. No, she didn't think she was better than him, and she would have dated a smart version of Bill, but the garage workers were programmed to work all day, go home and have a few beers and then have sex, followed by sleeping. They were good men in their own ways, but she loved intelligent conversations. She enjoyed friendly arguing, in a polite and fun manner, about history and the world in general.

Even she had to admit she lived a boring life since the fall of America. She'd had a boyfriend for a couple of years, but he'd been killed when the Chinese helicopter he was in crashed into the side of a mountain, killing all on board. She'd been celibate for four years, was tired of being alone, and now wanted a good man. She was no whore but she enjoyed sex as much as the next person, but she'd not sleep with just any man to satisfy her needs.

"Are you okay?" John asked her.

"I'm fine, just thinking of friends and lovers I've lost in this war too. I think all of us have experienced the pain of death."

"I agree." Wolfgang said. While he translated and usually ate supper with this group each day, he was not really much of a talker. John had known the man for years and you could spend all day with Wolfgang and maybe hear him say six words or so. He was, however, a close listener. He was assigned to the group because at times they sent coded messages in German, to confuse the Russians. While it looked and read to be nonsense when a German message was sent, if using the code book, only every few words meant something. The rest of the words on the message were ignored.

Recently promoted to Corporal, Green, the radio operator stuck his head in the room and said, "Headquarters on the horn for you, sir. When you're finished talking to them, let me have the handset, because we have classified orders to take in code."

Standing, John gave a smile and said, "Interesting conversation. We need to continue it one day soon."

He followed Green to the radio room, put on a set of headphones, and said, "Copperhead, this is Cobra Actual, over."

"Uh, go Cobra."

"I understand you wanted to speak with me."

"Affirmative, Cobra. Do you know both the Wing and Base Commanders at the Russian base you attacked are deceased? Our people intercepted Russian radio reports with that information, as well as over three thousand Russians died during the attack. Additionally, we lost over 500 partisans to take the base, but it has had excellent results in Russia and protesters are planning a demonstration with over a million people at four of Russia's largest cities."

"Sounds like it might turn rough." John said, and inside hoped the Russians would pay attention to the marchers and end the war.

"The protest march could get nasty, because the people are angry that no one is listening to them or the reasons for their anger. They claim the military is wasting Russian lives in a war they have proven with over nine years of battle that cannot be won."

"Copy."

"Cobra, your orders are being sent to you in a classified message in a couple of minutes. Give me your radio operator so I can send the message. Copy?"

"Copy and read you five by five. Here is my radio operator." He handed the handset to Private Green.

"Classified message. I'll be in my tent when you translate it into understandable English." he said as he walked away.

In his tent, John undressed, stepped into his flip-flops and headed for the showers. They had no hot water and to shave, water had to be heated on an open fire and then a shave took place in a sleeping area usually. John had started wearing a beard a few years back and he always kept it well trimmed. He tired of shaving out of a bowl or bucket of steaming water.

He showered in cold water, dried off quickly, but by the time he returned to his room he felt sweaty once more. *Cleaning up in the field is almost a waste of my time. By the time I have walked back to my quarters in this heat, the shower does me little good*, he thought as he slipped a pair of Jeans on, and picked up a blue tee. Both were a little large, because he lost weight each year. He'd been 210 just before the fall, but now was 160, and he actually felt much better.

There was a knock on his door frame, because like most partisans, he lived in a tent. He moved to the door, holding the blue tee in his hand and towel around his waist, cracked it open a little and looked outside. There stood Joy and Hanish.

"I just showered so give me a couple of minutes to finish getting dressed," he said and then let the door close.

Less than five minutes later he opened the door and invited both of them inside. Joy sat in an old lawn chair John had and Hanish sat on the corner of his bed.

"We wanted to see if you're okay after talking to Headquarters." Joy said

"Actually, you want to nose in and find out what our new orders are, right?" John asked and then laughed. Once he sobered he said, "I have no idea what they are because they were sent in code and when I left, Green was translating it into English. He'll bring it to me once he has the job finished."

"We're hoping it's something big, which will mean more Russian casualties, and that may be what will make the Russians leave America."

"I'm as much in the dark as you are right —"

"Colonel, are you in your quarters, sir?' Green asked just before he knocked.

"Come on in, Corporal. What do you have for me?"

"The orders you were expecting, sir."

"Anything unusual?"

"The orders are classified secret, sir. Do you want to discuss that with these other in the room?"

"Yes, they all have Top Secret clearances and they'll be with me where ever we are sent, so it's okay to speak in front of them. Again, are our orders unusual, because they rarely send orders in code?"

"Kind of. Tomorrow night you are to hit a dam the Russians are using for power. The minute the lights go out, Partisans will hit their base. The timing of our attack must be perfect to allow us to hit and maybe overrun the base. The base is Fort Leonard Wood. Most details are in the orders."

"What, another base? Oh, and a big one this time." Woo asked.

"I think they want to cause a lot of casualties so more riots will occur." Joy said and then met the eyes of John.

"Joy, that's some sound logic," John said, "if you ask me. Attacking any base will cause Russians to die or be injured."

"I guess Headquarters has decided to make the Russians pay for having bases on American soil and there are sure to be thousands of deaths on both sides." Woo said and then added, "The Russian deaths alone will bring a civilian outcry. They will demonstrate for sure, once the media releases the attacks."

The next night, they all prepared for the attack on the dam. John made sure even Major Woo had a part in the attack, and the Colonel felt that all of his men and women needed combat experience, because of the lives they lived. They were all always susceptible to attacks and could come under attack anytime because they had in the past. Woo had been in one train attack, but it had been a walk in the sun compared to what the attack on the dam might be. Intelligence, provided by Woo, showed 40 mm Anti-aircraft guns were located in three spots on or near the dam. A hundred men and women were assigned to the defenses of the dam, but they were only 40% manned due to the recent attacks on various Russian bases. The Russians were removing folks from other places to strengthen up their air bases.

John's plan was to have his troops move in close to the defensive positions and then when a truck crashed through the entry gate, while the Russians were still shocked, hit the 40 mm guns and any machine-gun nests. Once security was taken out, they'd rig the dam with explosives and then take the dam out of action. That would render Fort Leonard Wood without any power for days, if not for months.

"Now, we will take a company sized group with us and the bulk will be led by me, with Joy leading the group to take the dam out. Woo, you will take another group and defend everyone against any surprise visitors. I expect your group to not be busy. If that happens, release all but ten men to her. The ten will watch the roads until the mission is complete."

"Any questions?" John asked.

"How many people will each of us have?"

"I will have 40 to overpower the defenses, Woo will have 20 people and you will have 40 to blow the dam. You have two explosives experts assigned to you, Joy, so use them. I want that dam gone when we leave, or cracked seriously."

"Do the troops know which group they belong to or do we have to just pick people as they off load the trucks?"

"Every person going knows where they are assigned. They know us as me being team 1, Woo, you are team two, and Joy you are team three."

"Now, let's get the trucks loaded, we have a dam to attack."

CHAPTER 14

"**S**ir, wouldn't lying about a medal be perjury? I mean I cannot force them to sign anything, because we are asking them to lie. What do I say if they refuse? I mean they have to swear they are telling the truth on the submission form." Lieutenant Colonel Shura asked.

"If they refuse, shoot them. By the way, Colonel, that is not a suggestion but an order. If you shoot one, the rest will sign quickly enough. Go find your men at the Officers and NCO clubs."

"Yes sir." and he hung up the phone.

Shura was an officer with integrity, but there was nothing she could do except lie on an official form, and it bothered her greatly. She had known Russian commanders who shot those they felt needed removing and knowing Colonel Yurievich, she knew he would shoot her if she disagreed with him over the medal.

Damn me, what a mess! she thought as she had her driver take her to the officers club. She'd check there first and only get a Senior or Master Sergeant to recommend the Colonel be awarded the medal. Officer ranks would carry more weight but an enlisted man was needed to show all felt him deserving of the medals.

She entered, moved to an empty table to see if anyone she knew was at the bar or at another table. She felt very dishonest on what she was about to do. She quickly spotted Colonel Matvey Gennadieyvich, who was in charge of the security of the base. She approached him and said, "Colonel Yurievich has sent me to tell you he has selected you for a medal and wants you to do the same for him, except I just need a statement from you about how his leadership saved the base."

"He knows well how the old game is played, right?" The Colonel sounded about half drunk and he was known by others to be an alcoholic. Many Russians drank too much but this man before her was known to drink his breakfast, yet he was a man of honor and courage under fire.

"He knows, just as you do. You take care of him and he will take care of you."

"I heard he was going to be promoted to General and he will make a good one. Sure I will write something tonight and have it to you at stand-up in the morning. Is that early enough? Let him know there is no need to submit me, because I am retiring after this tour is completed, I have already submitted the paperwork."

"Thank you, Colonel. Let me buy you another drink."

"No, I have had three doubles and I am fine. I need to get home and have supper. I have a nice suite and a very pretty Russian woman, a regular Sergeant, that cares for all of my needs. No, I have had enough, but thank you."

"Thank you, sir."

"Tell Ludomir that I will play his game and I hope he makes a room full of stars." the Colonel said, stood and left the Lieutenant Colonel at the bar.

The next three were a bit harder, but by promising the Colonel's endorsement on their performance reports and medals, they all agreed to have something for her by Stand Up. Then she was off to the NCO club, but it was empty, except for one old Master Sergeant. Shura approached him.

"Good evening Sergeant, mind if I join you? I hate to drink alone."

"Not at all, Ma'am. Grab a stool and I will buy you a drink."

"Bartender, bring me a beer and with little foam." the Lieutenant Colonel ordered.

"Well, Colonel, what brings you to our humble NCO Open Mess?"

"I am looking for a witness for a heroic act that never happened."

The Sergeant laughed and asked, "Which Colonel wants another medal? I suspect it is Colonel Yurievich, because he just took over as the commander of the base and wing. Did he single-handedly counter attack and take our base back all on his own?"

"How did you guess?"

"Ma'am, no disrespect intended, but I have been in this man's army for 35 years, which is probably longer than you have been alive, and I have seen all types come and go. Wing or Base Commanders all try to leave their assignments with a medal and promotion if they can. What does Ludomir want, the Hero of the Russian Federation medal with an oak leaf cluster?"

"No cluster, but you seem to know all of this."

"He is just a different name, but the lies continue. I will handle this and have it to you by morning. I also know he does not need it, because he is leaving within a month and returning to Moscow where he will be promoted to Brigadier General. What they do with him after that is anyone's guess."

Gulping her beer down, the Lieutenant Colonel, said, "Thank you, Sergeant. I need to get to my quarters and grab a bite to eat and then get a shower. I appreciate your help and understanding. It is difficult for a person with integrity to ask people to lie about a medal."

"Those that truly earn those medals are less important as more and more men lie to get the medal they want. The medal our Colonel wants is equal to the Americans Medal of Honor and I almost turned you down, but then I realized, it is possible you would catch hell if the men in the unit did not offer to endorse his submission. I have seen you around a lot and you are a good officer. Enjoy your evening, Ma'am. I will track you down with my draft early in the morning."

She shook the Sergeant's hand and then left.

Two weeks after the Colonel's medal submissions arrived in Moscow, he was contacted in his office.

He picked up the phone, since his secretary was gone for the day and said, "Colonel Yurievich here. How may I help you?"

"Ludomir, this is General Urvan Olegovich and I have some good news for you. It seems all three of your medals were approved and we want you here next week to present them to you and to promote you to the rank of Brigadier General, in the Federation army."

"G . . . General, sir?"

"You need to be here on Thursday and we will present the medals and promote you at a special awards ceremony, along with a five division salute to you and to honor your career. The salute will take place in the Red Square with aircraft overhead. Once they pass in review, your new rank will be presented. We have already made excellent accommodations for you and your lovely wife in the top

Hotel here. Your orders will be sent by FAX and you are to leave tomorrow so you are here in plenty of time. Tonight at 1800, a Colonel Stena will arrive at your base and is to be your replacement. I am most proud to say we have a full time spot for you here in Moscow. Congratulations, my friend, and welcome to the command level of the army, the Generals."

"Why thank you, sir. I know my wife will be thrilled at the promotion and the medals. I wish to thank all of you for making this happen."

"You made it happen, General, and on the day you gallantly led your troops personally onto your overrun base. You are a true hero, sir. Well, I must leave and you have to meet Colonel Stena at your airport in about 30 minutes. Good evening to you, General, and goodbye."

When he hung up the phone, Ludomir opened his desk drawer, pulled out a bottle of whiskey and poured himself a double. Knocking it back, he poured another. He was so excited about the medal and promotion that he felt like screaming. Since he was to be promoted in a week, he'd have his podium in the Stand Up room changed so the name would read, Brigadier General-Select Ludomir Yurievich. Just the sound gave him a big thrill.

He called his driver, and had him take him to the airport to pickup his replacement. When he arrived, the flight was late and it would be another hour before the man arrived. He went to the designated smoking area and pulled out a cigar. He just put in in his mouth when a bullet ricocheted off the concrete patio blocks on the ground and zinged off into space. He immediately ran inside and yelled, "Security! There is a sniper out back covering the smoking area."

"Stay inside, sir, as we try to find him. We have never had this happen here before."

"Get the bastard, because he almost blew my head off." He pulled a flask from his coat pocket and removed the lid. After sniffing the drink, he took a healthy slug for his nerves. The shot just missed him and he had a lot to live for now.

He listened to the search, but they found nothing.

"Sir," A pretty young Sergeant working the counter said, "your guest is landing right now and he will be in the terminal within ten minutes. Do you want us to page him, or do you know what he looks like?"

"No, I have never seen the man before, so paging him is a good idea."

"I will do that, sir."

Many long minutes later folks began to flood into the terminal and the Sgt. said, "Would Colonel Nady Stena, please report to the information counter. I repeat, would Colonel Nady Stena, please report to the information counter. You have a guest waiting for you."

Soon a young looking Full Colonel neared and said, "I am Colonel Stena." Then seeing Yurievich standing at the counter he asked, "Are you General-Select Yurievich, sir?"

"Yes, I am. I will have my Sergeant fetch your bags and take them to your quarters. We can go to my office and discuss your new assignment."

"Sounds good, sir. We will not have much time together. All of Russia is talking about you and how brave and smart you are. I am honored to take your position, sir."

"Thank you Colonel, there are many opportunities here if a man is brave and willing to work hard."

The evening was spent over a bottle of vodka as the old commander gave the soon to be new one a rundown of what it took to do the job. He also covered his best commanders, those that needed pushing to do their jobs, and those that he felt needed shot. The new man asked few questions and he was motivated to do the job, because like most Colonels, he dreamed of making General. This position would give him the chance, just as it had Yurievich.

Finally, Stena asked, "I heard the base was overrun not long ago and due to your heroic effort you were successful in taking it back, but how much of a normal day to day problems are the partisans?"

"The first thing you need to keep in mind, at all times, is you are here to fight and not just to have a successful base operation. Moscow wants bodies, resistance bodies, and the more you have, the more your star shines in their eyes. I was able to claim well over 500 bodies just by taking the base back. Remember, 99% of the base population are now combat veterans and overall they are super troops. Listen to your more experienced officers and senior NCOs. Some of these old Sergeants were in the army before you and I were born."

Suddenly the base siren began to blare. Picking up his phone, Yurievich called base operations and asked, "What do you have? I hear the base is under attack."

A Sergeant said, "Sir, we have a sniper in the woods on the west side of the base and he has already shot a Colonel, a Master Sergeant attempting to save the Colonel, and two medics. The warning will remain on until a Mig drops napalm on that side of the base. The aircraft is lining up now."

"Continue the good work." He replied, then hung up. Turning to Stena he said, "Come outside with me and see how we deal with snipers that anger us."

They walked outside and while it was dark and the Mig could not be seen, the afterburners were clearly seen as he zoomed toward the trees. Nothing was seen as he passed over the trees, then, suddenly, a huge fireball lit the night as it exploded, showering the trees with sticky burning oil.

"Like using a nuclear bomb on a spider, is it not?" Stena asked.

"No, I do not think it is overkill, because a good sniper can kill hundreds of men, so we deal with them hard. This one seriously wounded a Full Colonel, Master Sergeant, and two medics. But now, I am fairly sure his days of shooting anyone are over."

"I guess if it works, keep doing it. I need to set up an appointment with your intelligence section to discuss our current threat level and to assess our efforts at combating the Partisans."

"You can spend all the time you wish with them after Stand-Up in the morning. It starts at 0700 hours and all my commanders will be there."

"Good, very good."

Olga lay beside Petr in their bed and was crying silently. She'd discovered she now loved the Sergeant and she was worried he'd be killed before they ever got back to Russia. He was always taking risks and often volunteered for missions she felt were too dangerous. So far, he'd come through all without a scratch, but she knew one day he'd be seriously injured, maimed for life, or killed. She also knew she could not bring it up, because he would be insulted. He was proud of his bravery and seemed to be trying to prove he was the bravest of them all.

It was 0500, according to the old clock beside the bed, so she got up, put a tea kettle on to boil and changed. Her uniform of the day was camouflage tops and bottom, with a matching cloth cap. She laid her other gear out and placed a 9 mm pistol Petr had given her, under her loose camo blouse. She placed it where he'd instructed her, in the small of her back, next to her spine. She slipped the two extra magazines in her cargo pockets on the left side. She poured a cup of coffee, turned the Russian station on the TV and watched the world news.

"Natasha, the protesters here today claim they will continue to protest and riot until all of the sons and daughters of Mother Russia are returned home from the American War. They state the government has had years to win the war, but things are worse now than the first day we invaded the country. The media is in a frenzy over Colonel Ludomir Yurievich's body count of more than 500 Americans killed when he counterattacked and recovered Fire Base Alpha in a classified section of America. The public has no faith in any reports from America by the media. The general population does not believe so few Russian soldiers died and the people are calling for a full investigation.

"I have with me General Urvan Olegovich, and sir, would you tell our viewers if we are winning the war in America or losing? The General is in charge of the overall operation in America."

"In any guerrilla war, it is hard to determine most of the time if you are winning or losing because of the nature of the war. Partisans tend to hit and run, taking their dead and wounded with them. We are killing more of them than they do us, but as you know we rarely see our enemies. They kill using crude, but effective, booby-traps, mines, and snipers. Each time we have met them in open combat, we have won."

"What about Fire Base Alpha, it was open combat and the partisans ran our troops from the base and the Americans controlled it for almost 24 hours."

"Your information, is incorrect, sir. The Commander at the time, Colonel Andrei Lazarev, chose to withdraw, regroup and then retake the base. Regrouping is common in combat and so are withdrawals. Unfortunately, he was killed when the helicopter he was using as a command post was shot down by a missile. His widow was awarded his Hero of the Russian Federation medal with oak leaf cluster. We were lucky that with both top commanders dead, General-Select Ludomir Yurievich stepped in and led the counterattack that recovered the base. He will be highly decorated for his actions."

"What other Commander was killed, besides Colonel Lazarev? I have only heard of one full Colonel being killed."

"Colonel Dimitri Isaak, the Wing Commander. He fell defending his headquarters building and he has also been submitted for an award for his valor. I will approve the submission for his Order of the Saint George medal today. Our Colonels died as heroes and I am damned proud of them, as I am of all Russians in America."

"Sir, do you seriously expect to win the war in America?"

"If I did not think we could win the war, I would suggest we leave. I would like to point out that since the American and Korean War, no nation has won a conflict against partisans. We are determined and will win, because we have the power and forces to insure success. No nation can stand against the power of Russia."

Seeing a wave by his camera man, the reporter said, "Thank you for the interview, General, and I find your comments interesting. I am afraid we are out of time."

"You are very welcome." the general replied.

"This is Pyotr Arseniy, for Russian Forces Network America, live from Moscow with General Urvan Olegovich, commander of Russian forces in America. Now back to you, Natasha."

A beautiful anchor woman, with long auburn hair and a bright smile, said, "That was our investigative reporter Pyotr Arseniy, reporting from Moscow with the Commander of all Russian Forces in America. In other news today, Russia accuses China of assisting Americans in their war by providing supplies, gear, food, munitions, and even aircraft support. The Chinese refused to comment except to say the accusations are untr—"

She turned the television off, showered and then started breakfast. At first she started to cook porridge, but changed her mind and decided on rye bread with butter and sliced sausages, along with scrambled eggs. The drink would be coffee, which was a rare treat, since most drank tea. At special times both coffee and eggs were eaten in most Russian homes, but they were cheap in the commissary here and they had both often. She also placed a few slices of cold cuts on the table.

She was still thinking about her love for Petr as she cooked, only now she wasn't close to crying. She was thinking of all of his positive traits. She heard the shower running and poured him a cup of strong coffee.

"My goodness, that cooking smells so good." Sergeant Vova said as he entered the kitchen fully dressed. He was wearing the same uniform Olga had on, except his shirt had the stripes of a Senior Sargent on the sleeves. He kissed her on the forehead, squeezed her butt cheeks, and then added, "I did not think I was hungry until the scent of your cooking woke me."

"Silly, you were sleeping so you do not know if you were hungry while asleep or not." she said and then broke out laughing.

He laughed and then took a sip of his coffee.

"I am not much of a coffee drinker, but I can see why some people are. This early in the morning it really hits the spot. Why did you not sleep well last night? I felt you rolling around and at one point you were talking in your sleep."

Smiling she said, "And, what did I say?" She placed two plates of food on the table.

"Something about me. You kept saying, 'Petr, don't go." Petr replied and then took a bite of his sausage.

Lowering her head, she said, "I kept dreaming something happened to you. In one dream you lost both legs, in another you were blind, and another you were killed. I even cried this morning as I relived my dreams. Petr, do you really need to volunteer for so many dangerous missions?"

"Sit, and let us talk."

"Olga, it is extremely important for all Senior NCOs to constantly act unafraid of anything because we are leaders. We set the standards for our troops. If I do not face danger at times, how can I expect my people to go into dangerous places? We must lead by example."

"I can understand the logic, but you volunteer for too many missions."

"I ask much of my troops and you know I do not volunteer as much now as I did before we started seeing each other. I am more selective now. Why all the concern over my missions?"

Olga lowered her head and said, "P . . . Petr, I, uh, love you. I do not want anything to happen to you."

"Love is a pretty strong word, do you not think?"

"Does love scare you?" she asked, her head still lowered.

"Well, I am not overly fond of the word. Seems every woman I have loved has died and that makes me cautious in relationships. I was married once, about 20 years ago, but she contracted an unknown fever and within 24 hours she was dead. That in itself is sad, but she was pregnant and I lost her and the baby. The doctors tried to save the baby, but he was too small and died the same day she did. I swore off love from that day forward."

"I can understand that, really. I think if we do not love those people that come into our lives, when they die we will be hurt forever. None of us know when we will die and for us in the army, death can visit any day or any hour."

"Perhaps you are correct, because your comments are logical. I just cannot afford emotionally to love right now. Can you understand me?"

"Yes, of course. My loving you has nothing to do with you loving me. I was simply stating I care about you."

CHAPTER 15

The night was cool, and a full moon made it almost as bright as a sunny day while John and his troops were surrounding the dam. It was 0230 and they would attack at 0300, on the dot. Two of the 40 mm guns were on the road side of the dam and another one was on the far side, near some trees. Most of the troops waited patiently for John's group to take out the Russian defenses; slowly one by one, the roaming guards were taken out by knife. Then three Americans quickly slipped on the Russian uniforms. Pulling grenades, they pulled the pins and kept the spoon down. Once it was thrown, the spoon would fly off and the grenade would be armed and go off five seconds later.

Two of the Americans in Russian uniforms neared the two 40 mm guns, which were surrounded with sandbags. The guards at both guns said something, but neither partisan spoke Russian, so they quickly threw their grenades. The crews from both guns tried to run, but the explosions were destructive. One gun was thrown into the air by the force of the explosion but it was only slightly damaged, and that was to a support leg. The other gun was completely undamaged, but the crew was dead. Moving to a gun, one man began shooting at the 40 mm gun on the other side of the dam. Then, another partisan moved to the damaged 40 mm and discovered it was still operational. A few short minutes later, the big weapons were both firing across the dam and hitting the last emplacement hard. Wounded and dead Russians were seen falling.

A partisan with a flamethrower came out of the woods and squirted his hot and sticky flames on the members of the gun's crew. *Horrendous* screams were heard as the men burned to death. Behind the relative safety of the sandbags the crew danced as they screamed, and finally partisans were shooting at them to stop the noise that was getting on everyone's nerves.

Burning, John thought, *is the most difficult way to die*. He then shivered.

"Joy, get your troops to the dam and set your explosives. I have no idea where the closest Russian troops are, but you can be sure they'll be alerted once they realize we have control of the dam."

There was a slight holdup as the group with Joy had to clear out some Russian positions, and she estimated they'd killed over 20 Russians. Her Captain appeared and said, "Major, we're clear here. What do you want done with the men and women who work the dam? Most seem to be engineers."

"When we leave, release them. Check to see if they are armed or have anyway of contacting the Russians before you let them go. Anyone armed will be taken as a POW. Let's move and get the explosives on the dam. I'm glad we have C4 because it's good stuff. The engineers at Headquarters said we needed to place the explosives half way down and then at the very bottom of the dam. If the two explode at the same time, the explosion and resulting force should crack it wide open."

"Sergeant Turner!" Captain Johnson yelled, "Get the explosives in place. I want this ready to blow in 30 minutes, now move!"

Joy shivered as she watched two men rappel down the front of the dam and began working, suspended only by the ropes. Twenty minutes later the explosives were in place and the two dangling men were pulled up. She then ordered everyone out of the area and she moved to the side where she would blow the dam.

"One, Three here, I'm ready to do my task." she said over a hand held radio.

"Do it now, Three, and then evacuate to the truck and we'll depart. I repeat, blow it now."

Joy grabbed the handle on the detonator and twisted it hard right. A huge explosion was heard, and looking up, she saw both explosions go off at the same time. For some reason, she expected the reinforced concrete to blow into the air, but that did not happen. She did watch as the dam cracked in the middle and then a larger crack showed at the base of the dam. Water began to leak and the cracks grew larger and then turned into hundreds of small cracks.

Suddenly the concrete began to fly out of the middle explosion site and water leaked from the holes. The water spurted out and the dam started making noises. She left the detonator and ran for safety at the top of the dam.

"Get in the truck now!" the Colonel screamed at her. "The dam is breaking up and within 30 minutes it'll be wide open." Then turning to Private Green, John said, "Tell Copperhead our mission is complete, without any wounded or killed. Hurry, we need to be moving."

Joy climbed in the passenger's door and said, "Let's go, the dam is breaking up!"

The engineers were running in all directions and the tails of their white coats were flapping in the wind. No one bothered them, and it was as if they weren't there.

Minutes later, three heavily loaded trucks made their way slowly back to the base camp. The night had been a success, if they could reach home without a fight. It was still dark, so John worried about attack helicopters that would for sure have infrared detection screens. If they spotted them, there was no way they could hide the trucks, so they'd have to jump and try to hide on their own. The odds, however, were great that they'd lose people.

The drivers and most of the troops had their NVGs on because no one liked to attack in the dark. The drivers could see almost as well as during the day, except everything was a shade of green.

"Colonel, I have Copperhead on the phone and he's informed me that the Russians have sent helicopters to the dam. They counted four aircraft on radar; it appears to be three Black Sharks and one transport chopper. They can't tell with 100% accuracy, but he said to move your ass and do the job now. Once they realize the dam is blown, they'll come for us."

"Tell them we copy and we'll contact them once we return to our FOB."

"Roger that, Colonel."

"I know of a cave near here and it's large enough to drive one truck in, but no more. I know all our people will fit in there with a lot of room to spare." Staff Sergeant Fillmore said from beside the Colonel.

"Captain Johnson?"

"Sir!"

"Come here, because we need to talk."

Moving through the men, the Captain was soon beside John, and a Staff Sergeant stood and gave the Captain his seat.

"We need to go to this cave Fillmore was telling me about and unload our troops until morning. That way we won't risk them on the way home. Ask for volunteers to go with the trucks, but the odds are good they'll be attacked. I need one man in the back of each truck, also a volunteer, so he can warn the driver if a chopper gets on his ass and lines up to attack. Let them know this might be a suicide ride home."

"Yes sir."

"Fillmore, how much further to the cave you told me about?"

"Turn right on the next gravel road and go down a mile. Then turn right and it's on the side of a sandstone cliff, and it's a big mother too. I learned about it maybe two years ago when the Russians were on our ass and my Captain led us here. We lived in the place for over a week."

Sliding a window open to the cab, John said, "Driver, at the next gravel road take a right. When you go down about a mile, turn right and you'll see a cave on the side of a sandstone cliff. We'll get out there and then you drivers will return to base, but you will have a spotter in the back of the truck to warn you of helicopters. Both the spotter and driver will be volunteers. I pray you reach home safely. If you're attacked, jump from the trucks and try to hide. Don't be heroes. Good luck to all of you."

The men made ready to move and most in John's truck heard the full conversation. Six men volunteered to go with the trucks, and as they left in a cloud of dust, John wondered how many, if any, would be alive in the morning.

"Saddle up. Major Barnes, form on me. We need to talk."

As they moved, he explained his idea of hiding in the cave, maybe at the expense of three drivers and three spotters. She found the cost and advantage well worth the risk. Being a commander in combat was nothing like in peacetime, because human lives were often traded to gain a mile, to end a threat, or like in this situation, to save the majority.

If the men lived through the drive back to camp, of course everyone, including the Colonel would be happy, but if the men died, then John had the advantage he'd saved 94 lives instead of losing them. He felt commanders were investors of a sort and sometimes the cost in lives was worth the price.

"There's the cave." someone said.

"Fillmore, I want you and Private Smith to check the cave out and make sure it doesn't already have visitors."

"Will do, sir. Come on Smith, we get to see the view first." Fillmore said with a cackle and grin. John knew the man was relieved they were no long on the trucks.

The two men were as quiet as they could be getting to the cave and, once there, they moved near the entrance to the cavern. Not a sound was heard. Then, they both heard scratching or clawing in the dirt. Fillmore, suspecting it was the wind, moved to the front of the cave just as momma skunk ran out with her babies. Before he could even scream a warning, the skunk's tail came up and he was squirted in the chest. He began to dry heave and his eyes watered. Bending over, he began to puke.

Smith, not able to take the smell, moved into the cave and then returned a few minute later. He pulled out a handheld radio and said, "Cobra Two, Tiger One."

"Go One."

"The man with me has been sprayed by a skunk. The cave is empty, but the skunk was not happy leaving. Over."

"Copy. Have him undress down to his underwear and we'll give him a new uniform. He'll need to bathe first and he can used the river that runs along side the gravel road down here to wash. Wait for us or until his eyes clear enough to see. Copy? Over."

"Copy. Tiger One, out."

"Take all your clothes off except your undershorts. That will take most of the smell away and then, when you can see well enough, go the river and wash. You'll still smell after the bath, only not as much."

"I know this is funny to you, but by God, it's not funny to me in the least. Russians I expected, but never a polecat. Damn me, I can't hardly stand my own smell now."

Giving a low chuckle, Smith said, "You'll be okay in a couple of days, but I'm sure they'll not want you in the cave. I'll make camp outside with you, my friend, because no one should have to camp alone, especially with Russians out looking for us. Now, get un-dressed."

When he returned much later after scrubbing with river sand, he was still smelling foul so he remained outside the cave. He moved to the very top of the cave and discovered he could see great distances. Sending Smith in to borrow a pair of binoculars, he volunteered to keep watch during the day.

"How far can you see?" Smith asked.

"A good twenty miles or so. Can't you see that far?"

"I need glasses, but I've not had any since my last pair was bro-ken in a firefight. They fell off and I accidentally stepped on them."

"You don't act like you need glasses."

"I can see okay within fifty feet, but further than that and my vi-sion gets blurry."

"I never knew you wore glasses, until today."

"Do you see anything moving out there now?"

"Not yet, but I will if anyone comes looking for us."

"Good, because I think if someone shot into the cave, the ricochets would tear a man up. We definitely do not want to be caught and trapped in that hole."

"If you help, we can stand guard all day and night. Nothing can move down there and not be seen by us. Wow, I just picked up a small herd of deer heading to the river to drink."

The rest of the evening was uneventful as the partisans rested and ate. Most were eating out of habit and not because they were starving. Food was no longer the center of most peoples lives and they were forced to eat what they had, or like in this case, they ate the rations they had. People were seen trading side dishes from their ration packages, so everyone got pretty much what they wanted.

It was 0200 when Smith, using the binoculars, spotted lights moving in the valley below. He woke Fillmore and had him take a look.

"I'm not sure where they're headed, so we'll keep a close watch on them. If they get within a half a mile, I'll wake the Colonel." Fillmore said.

Twenty minutes later, the Sergeant said, "Wake the Colonel, I'm sure they're heading here or damned close."

Smith went to wake the Colonel and just a few minutes later he returned with John. John looking into the valley, spotted some lights moving toward them and said, "Wake everyone and have them ready to leave in a moments notice."

"How would they know we're here?"

"I have no idea, but someone may have seen us go in the cave. It was still daylight when we entered."

Suddenly a number of attack helicopters were heard and one lowered to the mouth of the cave and the door gunner began shooting into it. Screams were heard as John flattened himself against the dirt and aimed at the pilot's head, which was slightly below him to his right. He took a deep breathe and as he released it, he squeezed the trigger.

His bullet struck the side window on the pilot's door, entered the cabin and stuck the metal headrest mounting. It then bounced off with a loud zing and struck the co-pilot in his left wrist. The man screamed and grabbed his injury. Smith and Fillmore were shooting as well, but they were aiming at the aircraft engine. Holes were seen in the aluminum that covered the engine. Then a light gray smoke was seen and the chopper moved away from the cave. Now flames in front of the intake cowling were seen.

The light from the burning engine was still seen from the hill after the chopper had moved miles away. Fillmore wondered if the aircraft would make it safely to his base, but then put the concern out of his mind. They'd just killed many of his friends and if they crashed and burned it would have filled his soul full of joy. The other three helicopters were circling the cave high overhead now. They must have gained altitude after the first aircraft was shot at.

John stood in the cave and his mind was not prepared for what he saw. Some of his people were blown apart by the machine-gun and blood dripped down the walls. He yelled for all of the survivors to help him separate the dead from the wounded. They were about half done when John realized he'd lost close to half of his troops to that one single chopper. He finally found Major Barnes and she'd taken a round to her head, but the bullet had burned a path on her skull. It didn't kill her, but it had knocked her out. Looking her over closely, John was surprised to find her head was her only wound.

"Colonel, get everyone out of here and now! The attack helicopters are lining up on the cave. Hurry!" Smith yelled from outside the cavern.

Picking up Joy, he carried her to the entrance and helped four more troops leave the cave. They then moved to the left, on the cliff, and made their weapons ready. The three helicopters that had been circling, were close now, flying in an attack formation toward the cave.

There came a puff of smoke from under the armament rails on the lead chopper and two missiles were coming for the cave. One hit to the left of the hole in the ground, but the other flew into the opening of the cave, where it exploded, throwing huge boulders out the front. John knew anyone inside was dead.

"Not good." John said as the second chopper sent a missile to the side of the cave and the last one entered the cave, mimicking the last helicopter's shots. Big rocks and boulders were blown out of the mouth of the cavern again.

All the partisans fired at the choppers, but they seemed to have no impact on the big birds. John had no missiles or RPGs, so small arms fire was all they had. Finally as a chopper banked in a turn, the engine must have been struck, because gray smoke began to pour out of the engine housing. The helicopters left the area quickly, with two escorting the damaged aircraft. Again, John hoped the damaged chopper would crash on the way home.

"Cease fire! Cease fire! They are leaving!" John yelled and the firing slowly came to a stop.

"How many wounded were left in there or do you know?" John asked once it was quiet again.

"I have no real count, sir. We were busy treating the injured, but from the looks of things, we have about half of the company left."

"I wonder how they knew we were here?"

"I suspect our night fire gave our position away. If we can see down into the valley, it only makes sense they can see up here. They knew we're on the run, so it was simple to conclude we were here if the fire was seen." Major Woo said and then gasped.

"You okay?" John asked.

"No, I'm not okay. I have an injury to my back and I don't think it's a bullet, or it would have gone all the way through me."

"Private Toms, look Major Woo over when you finish with the more seriously wounded."

"Yes sir." she replied.

"Smith, run to Fillmore and tell him to keep watch as we treat the wounded. Also tell him to be ready to move with a minutes notice. I want us gone before the Russian army comes to look this place over, and they will come."

"Will do, sir. Then I'll come back and help with the wounded."

"Scat, and now."

Twenty minutes later, when they attempted to get the walking wounded on their feet, Smith walked to the Colonel and said, "Sir, the Russians have landed in the valley below by helicopter and they're forming up now to come here."

"Plant some booby-traps! Private Nelson, since you're my sniper, find you a good place to ply your trade. I want Smith to stay behind to be your spotter and extra eyes. Once they reach the cave, if you can, I want the two of you to meet up with us. We're taking the fastest way home. God bless and good luck. Lieutenant Jones, you will be my point and come to a heading of 146 degrees."

"Yes, sir." the Lieutenant said and started walking.

"We're very lucky we have enough people unhurt that they can carry the liters of the injured, or we'd be leaving them behind." Major. Woo said.

"Yes, and I'll be able to save the bulk of my people. I've had to make some serious choices like that over the years. In the first year or two, I'd kill any wounded we couldn't take with us, and that still haunts me. I had no choice because the Russians are nasty when they do an interrogation. They turn sadistic and I was not about to let my men or women be put through torture. Everyone ended up telling them what they wanted to know in the end, just before they killed them or threw them in a Gulag. I killed out of compassion, not anger or hatred." John said, his voice just above a whisper as he spoke. The tone of his voice was filled with pain.

Joy raised up on a stretcher and asked, "Colonel, are you okay?"

He moved to her side, took her hand in his and said, "I'm fine, but for a while there I thought my executive officer wasn't going to live. Never scare me like that."

"My head hurts. It feels like my head is sewed together." She laid back down and her right hand went to her bandage.

"Your scalp was cut by the bullet, and if it had hit your skull we'd not be having this conversation right now. The medic had to sew your scalp back together, so that is part of what you're feeling. Let me get the medic to get rid of your pain."

"Thank you. My head is pounding."

Toms neared, looked at her watch, and said, "Okay, I can give you morphine. Does the medication work on you? Some patients break out sweating or they itch like crazy when given the drug."

"I handle it very well, but it makes me sleepy."

Opening her medical supplies she began working on giving Joy a shot of the pain killer. "I can't give you anymore of this until 6 hours pass. If you wake up in pain later, I'll have to give you codeine pills."

"Please give me something that works because my head feels horrible."

"Feels like you have a hangover, doesn't it?"

"Maybe a hangover on steroids. My head has never felt this bad before, never."

When Toms administered the shot, Joy could have sworn she felt the medication moving in her veins, because there was a slight burning sensation. Seconds later, she drifted off to sleep.

"I hope I have enough pain killer for my patients. I may end up having all of you give me the medication from your individual first aid kits just to make it home."

"We can do that and if you must, just start asking and if they give you any lip, tell them I gave the order, okay?"

"Sure, Colonel, I can do that, and thanks."

John gave her a smile and wink and said, "Not a problem. I want my folks taken good care of and I'll help you in anyway I can."

CHAPTER 16

General-Select Yurievich was in his office, his bags at the airport and already on the aircraft, placed there by Americans working for the Russians. The American workers discovered the pay was good, the hours nice, and they had access to the flight-line and the surrounding buildings, except for a few that were classified. Unknown to anyone on the base, the partisans knew of the Colonel's leaving and they had plans to blow the plane up in the sky. Their employees even knew his flight number and they worked on the individual plane that was to permanently remove him from America.

A bomb had been smuggled inside the base, with great risk to the carriers. An American had crawled through the sewer drains under the base to hand the explosive device to a fellow partisan. That partisan placed the explosives in his tool box and then headed for the aircraft. He moved into the cargo area and began working on some hydraulic lines. When left alone, he found the General's bag and opened it. He activated the timer and stuck the bomb deep inside the man's clothing. It was timed to go off when the aircraft would be over the Atlantic ocean and hopefully kill all the crew and passengers.

This bomb has the newest in powerful explosives, so it should blow this airplane to hell and back, he thought as he pulled the aircraft records and indicated he'd worked on the hydraulic lines and all was okay now. The bomb, about the size of a soft drink can, was armed now, so he needed to leave the aircraft.

As he moved, a security guard asked, "Why were you on that airplane? Everyone else is finished and has been for hours. What is your name?"

"My name is Sam Burns and I had to check the hydraulic lines and pressure. The crew wrote a red X on the system, meaning it cannot fly until the hydraulic lines are checked and working well. They're fine now."

"Come with me." The guard motioned to another guard who walked to him.

When they were a couple of feet away, the guard holding the maintenance man said in Russian, "This one claims he was ordered to fix the hydraulic lines on the General's airplane. You and I will check the records, Posvich."

"I will hold him here, while you check. He will go no place until you return."

"Good, keep him here as I look at the aircraft records."

The partisan maintenance man was getting spooked and knew if they brought an explosive sniffing dog, he would be taken in to interrogate. The longer the security guard was gone, the more nervous he became. *I don't think he'll find anything, but damn me if they bring a dog. I need to kill this man and make a run for it. Perhaps I can hit the point of his nose and drive the cartilage and bone into his brain. I don't want to attract attention, but I can't take much more of this*, he thought.

Then the man was seen walking from the aircraft and he looked relaxed. He smiled and said, "The pilot put a red x in the box on the hydraulic lines and he requested they be checked before the aircraft's next takeoff. This man, named Burns, did the check. I am sorry to have detained you, my friend, but we live in troubled times. You may go now and enjoy your evening."

He picked up his tool box and moved away from the two guards at a normal walk. He knew if he walked too fast, they'd wonder why. He wanted to run because his fear was almost overwhelming, but forced himself to move like a tired man nearing the end of his shift. He made his way out the gate and then moved for his home. He would gather all his belongings and leave to join the partisans. He knew after the plane exploded, he'd be a suspect right off because the guards had checked him out.

Once at home, he quickly packed a backpack, moved to his barn where he dug up an old AK47 and a Smith and Wesson .38 snub-nose pistol. Pulling a complete Russian field uniform he dressed and tied a yellow towel around his left arm. He was upstairs in the house when he heard a large truck pull into his driveway. He looked out the window and saw a squad of Russian troops forming up to take his house. He knew his front door was booby-trapped with a grenade that had a zero wait timer, so that was protected. He had two large German Shepherds he let run loose in the house and he could hear them barking already.

He raised his AK and fired a short burst at the Russians and smiled when three of them dropped. The return fire was awesome and the entire window and frame was torn to pieces with machine-gun fire. He ran downstairs and heard them pounding on the door with something, so he opened the door to the kitchen and let his dogs out.

Suddenly the front door dropped inward and fell to the floor. As the Russians moved to the entrance, the grenade exploded with a big blast. Screams were heard and men dropped, then rifle fire began to hit the house. The loud noise of the rounds striking the house was frightening because the simple wooden framed house didn't even slow the bullets down. Dropping to the floor, Burns crawled to the fireplace, removed the third brick on the second row and pushed a button.

I need to get out of here, and soon too. The house will blow in five minutes. He moved to the throw rug in the middle of his living room, moved the rug, and taking his pack and weapons, he dropped down into a tunnel. He flipped a switch and lights came on the length of the hole and he began to crawl as he pulled his pack and guns, toward the ending. The tunnel ended beside a slow moving stream. He crawled from the tunnel, stood and then wiped as much dirt off his clothing as possible. Looking back at his home, he watched the soldiers entering through the front door.

He was looking at his watch when the house went up in bright crimson flames and black oily smoke. The six sticks of dynamite did the job well, and he could hear one Russian shouting orders. Obviously an officer, but Burns didn't bother the man. He'd just killed about 15 Russians and that was good enough on this day. He knew if he shot anyone from where he was it would compromise his position, so he began moving south toward the closest group of partisans. He took his time and stopped frequently to check for booby-traps.

The big jet was paused at the end of the runway, waiting for permission from the tower to take off. The airplane was number two in a line of five waiting for clearance to get into the air.

The pilot watched the aircraft in front of him get airborne.

"Uh, Whiskey One, this is the tower, you now have permission to take off. Have a great flight and be sure to come back and visit us another day." a male voice said in English.

"Roger that, Tower, this is aircraft Whiskey One, Niner, Niner, Zero, Three, Zero starting our take off roll now. Uh, be advised Tower, we will be doing a maximum climb once in the air to avoid any ground fire. Do you copy?" the pilot said as he stood on the brakes and increased the four throttles of his engines.

"Copy Whiskey One, you will be doing a maximum take off. Have a safe flight."

With the power almost to the max, the pilot suddenly released the brakes and the heavy aircraft lunged forward and down the runway. On and on it moved, until it struck takeoff speed and then the pilots pulled the yoke back gently.

"Uh, Tower, Whiskey One. I am in the air."

"Copy Whiskey. Contact flight control in Saint Louis in approximately one hour, over."

"Copy, Tower. Will contact Saint Louis in about an hour."

The trip was soon going well as the passengers and crew settled into their flight routine as they leveled off at 22 thousand feet. Most of the passengers tried to sleep, but some, like General-Select Ludomir Yurievich, started drinking.

A beautiful stewardess moved to the Colonel and asked, "Would you like a drink, sir?"

He glanced up into the bluest eyes he'd ever seen. Her lips were full with just a touch of lip gloss which accented their shape, and her eyes were an endless pool of blue. She had a perfect body and her narrow waist just made her large top and shapely bottom that much more attractive.

"Yes, I do. Bring me a double Kentucky whiskey with no ice, please."

"Any particular brand, sir?"

"It matters little, because Kentucky and Tennessee don't make a bad whiskey. Some of their drink is better than others, but they sell only excellent drink."

"I have to admit I like it, and keep a few bottles in my home. I can buy it in the tax free shops and the price is lower than a quart of vodka. I will be right back with your drink, sir." she said and then moved to the galley to prepare his drink.

When she returned, he asked, "Are you based in Russia or America?"

"Russia for right now." she said, "The airlines is concerned the war will soon end, so they sent all of us girls back home. I do not see any hint that the war will end myself, but I do not get the same news as the company does. I think we should leave, because it has cost us thousands and thousands of men and women and we are still where we were when the war started. No, we all need to come home for good."

They were now over the ocean and within an hour the bomb would explode. The mechanical aspect of the bomb was having problems, because with one hour left, the clock should have been showing the number of minutes until detonation, but it did not. An hour went by and nothing happened at all; the bomb was alive but could go off any second, or would it?

"Ladies and gentlemen, this is your captain speaking and we are descending 18,000 feet for the rest of our flight to Moscow. At that altitude, we will experience some turbulence and the crew recommends you keep your seat-belt on at all times. I have seen these rain squalls turn pretty rough. Please contact your stewardess if you have any questions. I want to also thank you for choosing Russian Blue Air as the airline for your flight. I hope you fly with us again."

Hot meals were being handed out and of course he was hungry. The Colonel took a warm tray from his stewardess and began to eat.

The aircraft was flying smoothly when he stopped eating and ordered another double whiskey. His courage up, thanks to the drinks, he told the stewardess, "Here is my card. If you would like to go out for supper some night, give me a call."

"Are you single?" she asked.

"No, I am married, but not happily. I need a woman on the side that knows how to please a man and to keep him happy. I am sure a General could open a lot of doors for a beautiful woman who would also be given some financial assistance on a regular basis. Do you know a woman like that?"

"I think I know one, but the relationship must be discreet, or the whole thing is off. Where does one apply for this wonderful job?"

Yurievich pulled out a card and pen, where he wrote down the hotel and room he would be staying tonight. Tomorrow he'd meet with the other Generals and learn about his new job. Since his wife would be at home, he'd have two nights to enjoy this beauty in the city and then he'd have to start working. She was invited but stated she was ill. He knew she didn't want anything to do with the current government. He'd return home later, spend a few days, and then back to the city. His wife, a plump country girl, had no urge to visit Moscow, so he could get an apartment for this woman and himself. Just the thought made his heart beat faster. He then said, "Be there tonight at 1930 hours. It is there you will be tested and I am sure you will do fine."

Looking at the card she smiled and said, "My hotel here is at the same place, so I will just walk up a flight to be on your floor. I may show early, especially if I think about the test very long. Would that be a problem?"

"No, come and visit when the urge hits, but keep in mind I will want to shower, eat and then get a little sleep."

"I will do the same, so I will be there on time. I look forward to this test, very much."

"Now I must sleep a little."

The aircraft suddenly dropped a good 500 feet and everyone screamed until the pilot finally leveled the flight out.

"This is your Captain again, we just had a little disturbance and I warned you about it before. Now you can see why we suggest you keep your seat-belt on. You can expect more, but I do not think we will have another one that severe. Stewardesses, to your assigned positions."

The stewardess handed the General a card and he noticed her name was Lena Stepanovna. He found her address and phone number.

He said, "Thank you for the card. I must say, if you need me, call me during the day and I will get you on my cell phone. Never call my home number, or if it is a serious emergency, call and leave a message that you are Colonel somebody and ask me to call you back."

"I understand. I will see you this evening."

"Yes, my dear, and I look forward to your test." He pulled a blue eye mask down over his eyes, reclined his seat and wrapped up in the blanket the stewardess had given him. After the meal and drinks, he was asleep in no time.

The bomb in the hold was affected by the drop of the aircraft and sudden stop. The timer reset and it would be another 6 hours before it exploded. That meant the plane would be on the ground and suitcase in the holding area. The face of the clock showed the time remaining.

Four hours later, the pilot came on the intercom again and said, "Ladies and gentlemen, we have begun our descent into Moscow and have been given approval for a straight in approach and landing. Please fasten all seat-belts and stewardesses, to your assigned seats, please. I want to remind everyone, remain seated until the aircraft comes to a complete stop." A series of bells were suddenly heard on the speaker.

It was right at sunrise and looking out the window Yurievich saw parts of Moscow, and he immediately grew homesick. He thought of good foods, alcohol, and the beautiful woman that wanted to visit his room this night. He had a lot to live for now, and all the years of hard work were finally paying off. He stretched in his seat and yawned. *I am so glad to be home. I am almost as happy with the Mistress I have found. All Generals have a woman on the side, only I never thought I would ever make Major, much less General. I am moving up in the world*, he thought as he prepared for landing.

He heard the whirling noise of a small engine as the pilot adjusted the flaps for a landing. The aircraft seemed to be moving so slowly when he looked out the window, seeing hangers, aircraft, and some workers moving with tool-bags in their hands.

He heard a loud screech as the rear wheels struck the pavement of the runway and then a slight bump that jarred his folded up table. Looking out the window, he could see they were moving past the Moscow terminal. The flaps were raised and the brakes were pushed as the aircraft engines were switched to reverse. Gradually they began to slow down.

In the storage bay the bomb still showed another 6 hours before detonation. If Sam Burns had known the bomb they'd risked so much with was a victim of a poor quality watch and right now was unstable, he would have cursed a stream. All that risk for a faulty timing device.

"Ladies and Gentlemen, we are currently in Moscow, Russia, and the local time is 0613. The weather is 8 degrees Celsius with winds out of the west at 16 kilometers per hour. The forecast for today is rain and storms moving in later this evening. Those of you going on to Penza, Russia will stay in the holding area and will depart as soon as the aircraft has been refueled. Do not leave the terminal and keep your boarding pass to return to your seat. Everyone with tickets to Moscow you may disembark now. I want to thank all of you for flying Russian Blue Air Ways and I enjoyed being your pilot on this flight. Remember us for your future travels. Please enjoy your day."

As soon as Yurievich left the aircraft he was met in the terminal by a Major holding a sign that read, "General Ludomir Yurievich, I am your assistant."

When Yurievich neared the Major, he said, "I am General-Select Yurievich."

The major snapped to attention, saluted him, and then said, "Sir, if you will come with me, I have orders to get you to your hotel room so you may rest. I have a Senior Sergeant getting your bags now. I have a limousine waiting for you outside. I trust you had a good flight."

"It was fine."

"Sir, your driver has a tray of fruit and cheese for you, along with some German wines and Russian vodka, if you wish to partake of either. Please follow me and we will get you comfortable for the short ride to your hotel."

"Yes, let us wait in the car where I can nibble on some cheese and have a glass of wine. I do not think my stomach can take vodka this time of the morning." he said and then moved toward a black stretch limousine parked in a no parking zone.

Wow, all of this is for me! I never dreamed a General was treated like this. I have my own limousine and driver. I will bet my room is a beautiful suite too, he thought and then unknowingly smiled.

He looked out the window and saw a Russian Infantry Senior Sergeant packing his two bags. They were placed in the trunk and then the Sergeant and the Major got in the car. The Sergeant sat in the front seat with a loaded Bison and four hand-grenades within easy reach. The Major seated across from the General-Select asked, "Do you wish to listen to some soft music, sir?"

"Yes, that would be nice, thank you."

The Major turned on what he called elevator music and then said, "The Senior Sergeant, his name is Rollan Ruslanovich, is your enlisted assistant. He will make sure your uniform is correct, your medals are lined up properly and take care of shining your boots. He is well suited for the job and volunteered when he discovered you were a combat veteran because he is, as well."

The car only went a couple of blocks when they neared a lighted building and in seconds they were underground, where VIPs were taken. The basement was used because it kept the individual from prying eyes. Not everyone in Russia loved Generals. And after the thousands killed in America, more than one threat had been made on the lives of Russian officers.

The engine was turned off and the driver was suddenly beside Yurievich's door. He opened the door and gestured for him to move toward an elevator.

Ludomir watched the Sergeant take his two bags and then followed everyone to the elevator. A few short minutes later, the door opened on the lift and everyone walked inside. The Major pushed floor 3 and then grinned. Turning to the soon to be General he said, "Sir, you will find your suite more than comfortable, with a beautiful floral arrangement, a fruit basket, and a quart of Russia's best vodka. If you have any problems with the room, just let me know. I am in room 215, one floor lower than yours. I am here to make your introduction into the General Assembly as smooth as it can be."

"I will remember that." He replied, but he'd already forgotten the man's room number. If he had a problem, he'd call the front desk, and not some Major.

The elevator stopped, the door opened and the Major said, "Take a left, sir, and we will soon be in room 317. I hope you enjoy your room."

Once in the room, Yurievich was shocked at how beautiful it was. Original oil paintings lined the walls and a crystal chandelier hung over his bed. The bathroom had a whirlpool as well as a heart shaped tub with shower. Never had he seen a place as nice as his room, and he knew he could get used to being a General officer.

The Sergeant tossed Yurievich's suitcases on the bed and then said, "If you have need of me sir, I am in room 103 on the ground floor. In the closet of your bedroom, you will find a Brigadier General's uniform and it is your size. Tomorrow a tailor will come and measure you, then make any adjustments needed for a proper fit. I have heard when you meet with the Generals tomorrow you will be promoted at that time."

"Very well, Sergeant. I will have no need for you today, because I intend to relax, drink a little and go to bed early. I need to quickly get used to the time change. You have a good day and relax, as well."

As soon as the Sergeant left, Yurievich laid on the king size mattress, never dreaming there was a bomb in his suitcase right beside him large enough to destroy a commercial airliner. He dozed off minutes later.

He'd been asleep for less than three hours, but he got up, showered, shaved and then dressed in civilian clothes for a walk on the streets of Moscow. He carried his pistol in his jacket pocket and thought nothing of going out in the middle of the day to walk. He strolled and window shopped, knowing he could now afford anything he really wanted, but his needs were simple. He liked good food, strong drink and hot women.

Suddenly from behind him there was an astronomical explosion that blew part of his hotel high into the air, and it was followed by a huge fireball. The top two floors were missing when the debris and smoke cleared the air, and the bottom floor was on fire. People were staggering out, with some of them leaking blood. One young man came out the door and his left arm was missing right at the elbow and blood spurted each time his heart beat. Ludomir ran to the injured and grabbed the boy with the spurting arm. Removing his belt, he quickly used it as a tourniquet to control the bleeding.

"It is too tight!" the boy screamed.

"It is supposed to be tight. Now leave the damned thing alone or you will bleed to death."

The wounded were getting outside and then collapsing on the lawn. Seeing two healthy civilian men watching, he ran to them and said, "Help the injured or get the hell out of here. We do not need an audience. Do you hear me!"

"Yes, sir. Ivan, you take the left and I will go right."

Yurievich then move to a young woman in her late teens and she was bleeding to death internally, only she didn't know it. She had a sharpened piece of wood through her chest and the injury was right between her breasts.

"You are going to be fine. There is an ambulance coming soon and they will take you to a doctor. Hang on now and do not go to sleep on me." he said to her.

"I . . . need . . . sleep."

"Stay awake! Do you hear me! Keep your eyes open!"

"I will try, but my eyes are so tired."

An emergency medical technician in uniform ran to the General and asked, "Will she live, General?"

With tears in his eyed, Ludomir met the technician's eyes as he said in a tone just above a whisper, "No, she is de . . . dead. I told her to keep her eyes open, but she closed them!" Then in a broken voice he asked no one in particular, "Who would do this horrible thing?"

He stood, seeing medics on the job now and even policemen were treating the less injured ones. Then he saw the stewardess. She was laying on her back in a large pink puddle that was growing larger because the fire hoses used by the firemen were leaking water. The water ran under her form and turned red where it pooled. Her eyes were open but they were no longer seeing. She had a long deep gash on her bloody neck and another on her head. She must have just died, because she was still bleeding. While he didn't really know her, she was just someone he'd met, they'd made plans to get together in the future. She'd been so alive and now she was dead. Her life was over, snuffed out by a terrorist bomb.

CHAPTER 17

Private Toms was giving most of the injured morphine for their pain, and they still had hours of walking to do before they'd reach safety. By her guess, she had just enough medication to keep them in good shape if they reached the base within six hours.

It was growing dark and they had stopped for a break and to care for the injured. One man, a Sergeant, had died, and John ordered his body be left behind. It almost caused a mutiny.

A corporal said, "Colonel, you don't know how good a man Sergeant Thomas was. He was the best of the best, and he saved many lives over his years in the partisans. Can his unit carry his body back for a decent burial?"

"How many are there of you now?" John asked.

"Nine, we lost Patton but that's all. Please, Colonel. Not many men are respected like he was. We can carry him."

"Okay, but if you slow down the group the body goes to the side of the trail, fair enough?"

Smiling big, the man said, "Yes, sir. Very fair in my eyes. Come on guys, put a man on each pole handle and we'll take Bill home with us."

A few short minutes later, the group along with Bill were moving toward their base. John dropped back and walked beside Joy for a while. She was awake and while they made every effort to be quiet, he asked, "How are you feeling?"

"The medic said I'm fine, except for my headache, and that I may have to be on morphine for a day or two longer. Once back at the base, they can check me over with the medical equipment the Chinese doctors use. We've come a long way from killing Russians to get their food and gear. I can remember starving times and times of extreme cold. We're almost like a conventional army now, except we lack uniforms. I need to sleep some more, because I'm so tired."

A few moments later, Joy was in a deep sleep. John moved to Toms, his medic, and said, "How is Joy doing, Mariann, and give me the truth."

"She may have a fractured skull or a concussion. The bullet that hit her was moving fast and at just the right angle for the bullet to ricochet off her head, but the thing hit with a lot of force. I suspect a fractured skull and with that some brain injury or swelling at the least."

"I was just talking to her and she seemed normal."

"Yep, and then again, she could die, and in just a wink of the eye. There are many things we don't know about a human brain. The odds are good they'll force her into a coma and then drill holes in her head if her brain is swelling. If any of this is done, it will mean weeks and maybe months to heal."

"The time it takes is not a problem, but I want her taken good care of. She's a damn fine leader and has contributed a great deal to the resistance."

"She'll be out of my hands by then but our doctors are good, real good, and the Chinese doctors are even better. I think it's only a matter of time before she's back to normal, if I can get her home safe and sound."

Suddenly the air was filled with *whop-whop-whop* and John yelled, "Chopper! Into the trees on the right, now!"

Clumps of grass and dirt were thrown high into the air as a Gatling gun opened up on the group. John saw bullets strike people and tear them apart as they exited. Sergeant Prings took a round to his neck and his head flew off and landed near the trees.

Once in the trees John said, "Scatter and make your way back to camp. They were looking for us."

"What about our wounded?" Msgt. Dias asked.

"Take them if you can, if not shoot them."

"I *will not* shoot them, Colonel. That is not a lawful order."

"No, it's not lawful, Dias, but do you want them to suffer hours of terrible, painful interrogation? No matter how they respond, they'll just be shot in the end."

"He's making another run!" Someone yelled and when John looked up two missiles fired and they were coming right toward him. He fell to the ground and then heard two explosions, followed by screams.

"Scatter! We don't want to be here if he calls a fast mover with napalm. Move, and that's an order! Make your way back home!"

People scattered into the four winds. John noticed they left as couples mostly with a few groups of three.

"What about Joy?" Master Sergeant Dias asked.

"I can pack her, hell she doesn't weight more than 90 pounds soaking wet and it ain't raining."

Dias said, "No, no rain yet. Grab the far end of the stretcher and we'll take her home together, Colonel. She's too good a woman to leave out here and besides, no one else left anyone. Hurry, sir."

Picking up the litter, they began to move almost at a run and John said, "Thank you Mary, Joy is a good officer."

"How long have you liked her, sir?" Dias asked, and then smiled.

"Liked? Oh no, you have this all wrong. She's my executive officer and no more."

"I've never called a senior officer a liar before, but I'm not buying your line at all, sir."

Silence as John gave thought to the Master Sergeants words. *I do like her, and yes I'd date her if things were different. Hell, right now I don't even know if she'll live or not. Okay, so I like her and I'm interested, but I for sure don't love her*, he thought.

"There is no love or affair between us, Sergeant. I've never been alone with her, never held her hand or kissed her. You can stop your match making right there. She is like you, just one of my troops that I like. You know as well as I do, if you and her were to change places I'd pack you out of danger too. I honestly care about everyone that works for me, male or female."

"I know that, sir. I was teasing, but I think I hit a raw nerve. I suspect there is nothing between you two, not that it's any of my business, only there could be if you allowed it. I've spent a lot of time with Joy, who like me, is fluent in Spanish. We discussed many things, and she deeply respects you. I would pack this woman on my own back out of here if you weren't here. But, I saw your face when you learned she'd been hurt and just a few minutes ago I saw your eyes when we discussed packing her out. Relax with her and see what happens, sir."

"Respect and love are different critters. I find her an attractive professional, with a good sense of humor and dependable. Now, let's stop discussing my lack of a love life and make tracks. I suspect napalm to hit these woods just minutes from now."

They moved as quickly as they could holding the end of a stretcher. After covering about half a mile, they stopped for a breather and John suddenly said, "Look to the east. See that flash of light in the sun? That is a MiG jet. I'll bet ten dollars he is carrying napalm."

"I'd be crazy to take your bet, sir."

The fast mover lined up for a pass and seconds later he was zooming toward the woods. Two containers released from the bird and they contacted the trees, where they burst into flames. A huge wave, part of every napalm run, came up and then fell on those too slow or lazy to move earlier.

Screams were heard in the fire, but there was nothing John could do to help them, because the victims were in a raging inferno.

Suddenly, Dias screamed and, looking at her, he noticed a couple of small globs of the sticky napalm on her arm. Removing his jacket, he moved to her and smothered the flames. Pulling his knife he scraped the jell from her arm. He then pulled his first aid kit and applied a burn ointment on her wound. Both burns were about the size of an old silver dollar.

"Feel any better?" he asked.

"It still hurts, but nothing like it did. Where did you learn to treat burns like that?"

"I've been a partisan for over 8 years, so this is not my first rodeo. It will hurt until later in the day and then it will only ache when you touch it or roll on it in your sleep. It will blister too. We're lucky. If we'd been closer we might have suffocated because the fire sucks all the air into the flames. I've seen bodies with no injuries following napalm drops."

"We need to move, he's lining up again and I expect missiles this time." Dias said as she moved with the stretcher and the Colonel.

"Let's move as quickly as we did earlier. In about a mile we can slow down a great deal. We need to stop talking too, because the Russians will have troops out looking for us."

"Let's go."

They moved as quickly as they could, and in about a mile, John had them slow down. It was then he heard a noise in the brush beside where they'd stopped. Lowering the litter he pulled his Bison around and the moved toward the noise.

Parting the bushes, he looked down and spotted two partisans, one of which was wounded in the neck. The wound had been bandaged.

"Both of you get out of the brush. You're lucky we're with the resistance and not Russians."

Once they were out of the brush, John saw one was a woman and the other a man. The woman had the neck injury.

"What are your names?"

The man gave a slight grin and said, "I'm Nathan Gomez and she is Sara Brown. We were with you, Colonel, until you told everyone to scatter. She took the injury when the attack choppers struck us. A bullet struck a rock or something and that is what struck her neck. It's not as bad an injury as it appears."

"I need you two to pack the stretcher for a while. We've been running with it and we just barely got out of the napalm run alive. In a few miles we'll take over."

"And, as we move no talking unless you see a threat, and then whisper a warning." Dias added.

Hours later, John said, "We're nearing the base, so keep your eyes open for booby-traps and our troops. Both can kill us if we're not alert."

"Off to our left, I see an entrance gate, or so it looks like to me. Maybe 100 yards to the left."

The Colonel moved them to the edge of the woods and then walked out in the open. He waited to be challenged by the guard.

"Hold it right there and don't move. Who are you?" the guard asked.

"I'm Colonel Williamson, assigned here. You can call and make a security check if needed."

"I'll make the check, but we've been expecting you and your people. Seems the Russians forced y'all to break up and return on your own. I've already had six two and three person groups approach me on this shift alone."

"I have four others with me and three of them are wounded. I need an ambulance or something to take them to the base hospital."

"Get your people as I check you out with my desk Sergeant."

"I'll do that. Don't forget the ambulance."

The guard waved, because he already had the phone in his hand.

The next morning John learned he'd lost about 60% of his people and as far as he knew, all were killed. He was depressed by the number, and after his staff meeting went to his tent for a cup of hot coffee and some rest. His whole body hurt and ached from the litter carrying.

He'd just taken his first sip of the bitter brew when he heard a knock on his entrance door, which was made of wood.

"Come in."

In a minute, a cleaned up Joy Barnes stood in front of him and asked, "Do you have an empty cup, that is, if you want to share that great smelling coffee?"

"How are you out of the hospital? I would have thought they'd keep you in for weeks."

"The x-rays showed I'd suffered a mild concussion from the bullet, which hurt like a bitch, but they decided I would heal as quickly if I returned to work as I would taking up a hospital bed."

"Well, that is good news, Major. I want you to spend the day sleeping and resting. I was worried about you, because head injuries can easily kill a person."

"Colonel, I want to thank you and Master Sergeant Dias for saving my life. I think by all rights I should have been left, but if I had been, I'd be dead right now. Thank you. I will never forget what the two of you did for me and I owe you both my life."

"Good executive officers are hard to find." John teased and saw her smile.

"I also want you to know I see you as one hell of a fine man, and wondered, uh, well, if we could share supper this evening?"

John started to say no, but he was lonely and tired of being alone, so he said, "Sure, if you don't mind eating Russian rations."

She laughed and then said, "What we eat is not as important as having someone to talk with. I get so tired of being by myself at times I want to scream. I have women I can talk to anytime, but there are times a woman needs a man's company and I don't mean for sex either."

"Please, sit down. Take the chair by my folding desk. Sex, hummm, I've heard that word, but forget the meaning."

Joy broke out laughing.

Once she was seated, John said, "I'd be glad to share this evening with you. I know how you feel, and I think all of us that fight for the liberty of our nation are lonely most of the time. Oh, I have a few married couples fighting with me, but 95% of my troops have no one. I know all of us, at one time or another, just need a member of the opposite sex to talk to and spend time with. You can be comfortable with me, because I was raised a Southern gentleman. I believe in chivalry and treating all women like ladies."

"I'm not worried about you, sir. I've discovered over time that you are a good man and an even better commander. For years I didn't want a man in my life, knowing one, or both, of us might die at any time. Fear of death keeps most folks from forming relationships. Finally, after about four years of being alone, I found a Sergeant I loved. I was so happy for almost two years and then he was killed in an attack on a train, after the mission his chopper flew into a mountain. It broke my heart and sent me into a phase of depression that lasted a good year.

I then met another man, a Captain, and we got along very well. He wanted to get married and I didn't. Finally, after a couple of years, he gave me a choice, marry or leave his life. I left. I discovered this year he died leading an attack on a radio station. I was shocked when I heard, but not overwhelmed, because death is so common with partisans. How about you, sir?" As Joy spoke, John saw her eyes water and then silent tears ran down her cheeks.

"I've lost every person I ever loved serving the partisans, except my first wife. She was raped and then killed one day, early following the fall of America. It was at a time when nothing was to be found to eat and folks were killing each other for a slice of bread. Her death almost killed me. If not for my dog, Dolly, I would have died a drunk. I have a German Shepherd that I left with a friend when I moved here. I'm expecting her and him any day now. Dallas/Fort Worth is a long way from the Missouri Ozarks. See, I've, like you, been moving around a great deal from Missouri to Texas, and even all the way to New York state once. My dog didn't need to do all that traveling with me. I love her, but she was safer with my buddy."

"Really? I love dogs."

John and Joy talked for over an hour and then he said, "You need to get some sleep and rest. If anyone asks you have bed rest, and will not participate in any missions of any kind for the next ten days by order of me, the commander."

Standing, Joy said, "Thank you, Colonel, and I'll see you near 1700 for supper."

"Please call me John."

"John it is, then. I'll bring the rations and a bottle of bourbon I have saved."

Looking at her in ways he had not in the past, John realized she was a beautiful woman with deep intelligence. Women with sharp minds always attracted him. He began to daydream about her.

"Well? Cat got your tongue?" she said a few long minutes later.

Grinning, he replied, "No, no cat. I was just thinking, but what isn't important. 1700 would be a great time to eat. I'll see you then."

John stood, moved to her and gave her a hug. She gave a surprised look and said, "Well, I could come to like being hugged."

They both laughed and then she said, "I'll be back later. And, I thank all of you that packed me out of those woods."

"You're very welcome. Now go and get some rest, and that's an order."

She saluted him and said, "Yes, sir. See you later." She then left the tent.

John noticed after she left the tent felt empty again and a sadder place. He grinned and knew he'd enjoy any time spent with Joy. He was tired too, so he stretched out on his bunk and was asleep in minutes. He woke hours later. He shaved, showered and changed into jeans, a cowboy shirt, and wore his old brown Stetson and cowboy boots.

Right at 1700 Joy returned with a bottle of excellent bourbon and two Green Frog Russian rations. John had a small propane gas stove, where he let her warm the rations. They ate as they made small talk. He didn't know it, but every minute he spent with her enriched his life to the point he'd soon be in love.

They'd just sat on the edge of his bed when there was a knock on his door.

"Who is it?" John asked.

"It's me, Richard, Colonel, and I have a useless mutt by the name of Dolly here with me. She keeps asking to see her daddy."

John jumped from the bed, opened the door. He and Richard shook hands. It was then Dolly saw him and lunged for the Colonel. She was a big dog at 100 pounds, so she almost knocked him over as she tried to kiss him. Finally John squatted and took her into his arms. She was giving a whimpering sound as she tried to climb all over him.

"Please sit down, Richard. Joy, I want you to meet an old friend, Richard Carson. We grew up together and he's Dolly's second daddy. Richard, meet Major Joy Barnes, my executive officer. Richard is a Lieutenant Colonel in the partisans."

As soon as the introductions were made and John sat beside Joy, Dolly jumped on the bed, stretched out and put her head in John's lap. He absentmindedly scratched her ears and neck.

Richard said, "I'm not here as a courier, I've been assigned here."

"Oh, and doing what here?"

"I'm to be part of your intelligence section. I'm to be the Officer in Charge, (OIC) and will take over Major Woo's spot. It's a Lieutenant Colonel position, anyway."

"Your assignment will disappoint him. He'd hoped to make Colonel while working the position and I know he's worked hard enough."

"Well, don't say anything, but he will be promoted, first time up, and he's to stay with me here and work Intel."

"Great news, but how do you know about his promotion?"

Smiling, Richard said, "I saw the promotion list for here and two names were on it for promotions from Major to Lieutenant Colonel, Fan Woo and Joy Barnes, both will be notified officially next week."

"Oh, John, I don't believe it. Me, a Lieutenant Colonel!"

"You've earned the promotion, Joy."

Placing a bottle of rye whiskey beside the bourbon, Richard said, "This promotion stuff calls for a celebration drink, my friends."

"It would be nice if the job came with pay." John said and then laughed.

"We have all the comforts of home and you want money too?" Joy asked.

"Actually," John said, "I'd love to have all our dead and maimed back with us and living well, but that can't be changed."

It suddenly grew quiet as everyone thought of those they knew who'd made the ultimate sacrifice. Some were friends, some were lovers, some were family, and some were comrades that had lived and faced the same dangers day after day. They'd perished or were seriously wounded trying to reclaim a country that no longer existed. They were all American partisans, determined to return their nation to its former glory in the world. These people valued America, their flag, their national anthem, and their way of life. They'd died as Americans, fighting for all the things that made Americans special. Joy felt a tear slide down her left cheek as she remembered her dead sister.

CHAPTER 18

J ohn opened the bourbon and poured about three fingers worth of booze in three glasses and then passed them out.

Raising his glass, John said, "To our soon to be new Lieutenant Colonel, Joy!"

All three knocked their drinks back and Joy began gasping for breath and coughing. Richard laughed and said, "Smooth batch, huh, Joy?"

"The drink took my breath away. My God, it's so strong!"

"Lets keep the discussion about promotions and not any more death or dying. This is an occasion where we should be happy and proud of our new Colonels." John said.

Joy wiped her tear stained cheek and nodded in agreement.

"You're just not used to drinking whiskey is all. I found it normal, but I keep a bottle in this tent for nights I can't sleep. I have a shot or two and I go right to sleep." John said and then laughed.

"A bottle is rare these days, and all we have was stolen from the Russians." Richard said.

John replied, "When I was in Texas we knew the Russians had a convoy with booze every month, so most months we hit the trucks. The only thing I have that my troops do not have is a bottle of alcohol. I eat the same foods, sleep in a tent, clean my own weapons, and dress no differently than anyone else. I figure as a full Colonel I have the right to a bottle once in a while. Most booze we find goes to the medics."

"Can I have another drink, please?" Joy asked.

Richard said, "I can have one more, then I'm going to bed. While it's early, I traveled on about four hours of sleep a night for a week. I have some catching up to do."

Looking down at his lap, John saw Dolly was asleep. He scratched her ears and said, "Richard, I'm so glad you brought my baby home to me, and I'm glad you'll be working with us."

Richard said, "I'm going to skip the second drink and get some sleep. I'm sure I need the rest more than the booze."

He stood, offered his hand to John who shook it. Then he shook hands with Joy. He reached down and scratched Dolly on the head. She opened her eyes and smiled at him.

"Stay safe." Richard said as he left the tent.

"My, that was a pleasant surprise. I'll bet you're glad to have Dolly and Richard back in your life." Joy said. She had been standing, but now sat beside John on the edge of the bed.

"Oh, I am happy, but happier you've entered my life. Today when you left, this place no longer felt good and the whole tent made me depressed. There was magic in this place, but only as long as you were here."

"Well, that's a nice confession. I felt alone too, but we need to move forward cautiously. We're no longer teenage kids, so with a relationship also comes responsibilities."

"I think we're both aware of what a relationship involves."

John found his head next to hers and when she started to speak, he kissed her.

When the kiss broke, Joy quickly kissed him again. When this kiss broke, John said, "Slow down a bit." and laughed.

"Maybe I don't want to slow down."

"Really? That's great news." He then kissed her on the tip of her nose.

"You kissing my nose made me quiver." she said and then laughed.

Slowly, Joy lowered both of them to bed and then whispered, "I want you, John."

Early the next morning John woke with Joy in his bed and both were naked. He put a towel around his waist and moved to the shower, with Dolly on his heels. After showering and shaving he returned to the tent to find Joy gone, but Major Woo waiting for him.

"What can I do for you, Fan?"

"I discovered last night I had a roommate." He gave a light laugh.

"I have known Richard since before the fall of America. He's a sharp man with a level head on his shoulders. He's been assigned as the new OIC of Intelligence. Since you're making Lieutenant-Colonel next week, you will work for him."

"Me? A Lieutenant Colonel? How do you know this?"

"Richard saw the promotions listing and your name and Joy's is on the paper. He said it will be released one day this week."

"Wow, I never dreamed of being promoted to that rank!"

"Well, you will be, and in a few days. Richard is a good man to work with and he takes good care of his people. He's got hundreds of hours of combat experience, so he knows what he's talking about. He's also worked as an intelligence officer for at least five years. I suspect both of you can learn from each other. He's a fair man, too."

"Don't misunderstand me, but why would Headquarters send him here if I was doing a good job?"

John gave a light laugh and then said, "I think he's an overage and they sent him here because at times we run out of folks in certain positions. If they didn't think you were doing a good job, I can assure you, you would not have been promoted. They know your section is busy, right?"

"Sure we're busy. I was just wondering, and he never said where he'd be working last night. He walked in, introduced himself and then crawled in the spare bunk and went to sleep. When I left a few minutes ago, he was still sleeping."

"Let him sleep. He brought my dog with him, too. I've missed her like some people miss a child or a lover. She's all I have to remind me of the old days. She's getting old now, because she was three when this fight started eight years ago." Dolly looked up at him and grinned, as if she knew what the conversation was all about.

"Nice to meet you, Dolly." Fan said and then reached over and scratched her ears. Dolly took an immediate liking to the small Asian. She sat up and then stepped from the bed and made her way to Woo.

When she reached him, she laid down with her body over his boot covered feet.

"Well, now this is unusual with her. She likes you a great deal, but you did scratch her ears." John said and then chuckled.

"I had a dog as a boy and his name was Tigger."

"Every child needs a pet, because it teaches responsibilities. You can't ignore a live animal, because they need feeding, potty time, and cleaning at times."

"Oh, I found that out and sometimes he had used the toilet outdoors in the middle of the night. My dad took him out the first time, but then over breakfast the next day he said it was my job and he'd not do it again. He was true to his word. One night I didn't wake up and I had to clean the poop from his kennel and from that time on, I took him out."

"I need to get to the communications tent. Joe has a message from Headquarters that they want to speak with me about at 0800 and that gives me five minutes to get there. Relax with Richard, he's a laid back nice guy that knows a great deal. If either of you have any problems with the other, come and see me."

Standing, Woo said, "I'll keep that in mind, sir. I appreciate you talking with me this morning and know you're pretty busy at times."

Glancing at his watch, John said, "We'll talk again after you two work together for a while, okay? I need to rush now."

They both left the tent at the same time and Dolly was hot on John's heels.

When he walked into the tent Green was holding a headset and said, "Here, sir. Copperhead is on the horn for you."

He handed the handset to John.

"Cobra Actual, go Copperhead."

"Cobra, this is Copperhead Actual and we will be sending you orders in German and in code. The mission is of grave importance and if you have any questions, send them in German code. Additionally, I wanted to personally tell you two of your people have been promoted to the rank of Lieutenant Colonel, effective today. Joy Barnes and Fan Woo. Please congratulate both of them for me, please. Tell them we appreciate their hard work. Over."

"Uh, copy Copperhead Actual." John knew the General was personally passing this information so it would be believed. He was glad he got to tell his people that as of today, they were Lieutenant (Light) Colonels. It wasn't often John shared good news.

Green received the classified message and began translating it from code to readable German text. It was a slow process, but it was the only way it could be done. The codes changed every week or two, which only made things more difficult for the radio operators.

John walked to the dining room tent, got a cup of coffee and then returned to Green who said, "I have the message, but I don't believe what they want us to do. They want us to attack power stations, all of them in Missouri, and in a month."

"That's a lot, but the order is legal."

"I know it's legal, but the Russians will figure out what we're up to within a couple of days, especially if we hit them night after night. If they have a German speaker on their staff, they might know right now. It's a suicide attack, is what it is."

"It may be, but let me read the orders." John held his hand out and Green handed the papers to him.

"When he finished, he said, "I don't like it much either, but they don't say when we are to attack anything, and if needed we can vary one attack from another hundreds of miles away. I for sure will not attack any within 50 miles of each other except on the same night. If we started hitting all the ones down in the Southern part of the state first, they'd quickly figure out the ones we would attack next. We'll hit one in the north, then the south, finally west, then back to south. We can confuse them, because they'll expect us to have a pattern. Hell, we may hit the same place twice and cause twice the damages."

"I think that would work. Like most people I thought we'd use a system. I like your idea though. They can't put guards at all the power plants, now can they?"

"If they do, they'll have to pull them from the field and they'll not do that at first. I'm not sure what they'll do later in the game, once they figure out we don't even know which power plant we're attacking next."

"Okay, I think your idea will work at least for a while, sir."

"When are the attacks to start?" John asked as he moved to the coffee pot hanging on a small fire just outside the door.

Green spoke a little louder since the boss was outside, "I called in a coded message for verification that the attacks are to start tonight."

"Tonight?" John asked as he entered the tent again.

"That's what the orders said, sir."

"When you hear from them, let me know."

"I will for sure."

Hours passed and finally, a little after 1039, a reply was sent.

Green went looking for the Colonel and found him in a meeting with his company commanders. Green let him finish and then handed him a handwritten note that said, "The raids are a go, starting tonight. Where to attack is your choice."

After reading the note, John said, "Ladies and gentlemen, I was just handed a note that we are on for a mission tonight. I want all the troops ready to go by 2200 hours. Our mission is to strike power plants in Missouri and there are ten major ones. Tonight we will hit two of them. The two I'm thinking about are on I-44 and very close. I will hold a mission briefing here in four hours. As of right now, this meeting is over. I need to see the company commander and his assistant."

The day passed quickly with weapons checked and then double checked. Gear and packs were arranged for no noise and comfort. Extra ammo and grenades were stored and two shoulder fired missiles were packed away as well. They were attacking armed to the teeth because they had no idea how the Russians would respond. If the Russians attacked with choppers, the missiles would be needed. Their mission on the dam had been a big success, but they'd not packed any air defense and it was a mistake paid for with blood. He had lost half his attacking force in the cave.

Live and learn, John thought.

Exactly at 2200 hours a small convoy of three deuce and half trucks left the base and headed west on highway I-44. John had twenty men, ten in each truck, and the third truck carried heavy weapons like the shoulder launched missiles, flamethrower, munitions of all sizes, claymore mines, and other explosives. Ten RPGs were in the truck as well. They would attack the power stations at the exact same time and coordinate the attacks by radio.

John and his men, in the first truck, turned off the highway and stopped, followed by the gear truck who provided them with all they needed to complete their mission. The gear truck then started up and followed the second truck to their power station.

About a half a mile from the station, the truck stopped, the troops emptied out of the back and the heavy gear was handed out. They were traveling light compared to normal infantry missions, where they usually carried over 60 pounds on their backs. With this mission, they had less than ten pounds of gear and most of that was ammo and grenades. The M-60 machine gun, Flamethrower, RPG's and other heavy weapons including a mortar were handed out until everyone was carrying something heavy. John carried two cans of M-60 ammunition and two Claymore mines.

"Drop your NVGs and let's move toward the stations. When Luke and Mark drove by here this afternoon, they saw only one guard. That doesn't mean there aren't two or more there now. I want me and Corporal Brown to cross the fence and take out any guards with knives. Any questions?"

Silence.

A minute later, John said, "Let's move, and Carrier, you're my point man. Stop about a hundred yards from the station building."

"Yes, sir." Carrier said and then started down the well worn macadam road.

The walk was uneventful and no mines or booby-traps were discovered. John found it strange there were no booby-traps, but then realized they'd not attacked power plants before. They'd knocked out radio and television stations, but no power plants of any kind.

When Carrier stopped, John and Brown moved to the fence. The fence was away from most lights, so they cut the metal with a pair of bolt cutters and then pulled the fence open. Remaining still for a few minutes, they only saw one guard. John motioned that he would silence the man. He then moved toward him and stayed in the shadows as much as possible. Brown stood, his rifle sights on the guard as John crept toward him.

When about twenty feet behind the man, he pulled his big Bowie knife and held it cutting edge up. He moved forward, expecting the man to turn any second, but he remained watching the road.

Once he was near the man, John threw this left arm over his head and pulled his neck back. As the man jerked and fought against him, John ran the sharp blade over the man's throat. Blood, warm and smelling of copper, spurted high into the air with each beat of the guard's heart. He stopped struggling as much, so John stuck his fourteen inch blade into his right kidney, slicing it to pieces.

The man tried desperately to cry out, but all he did was choke on his blood with each attempt. Two minutes later, he shivered violently, his bowels released, and he urinated in his trousers. Then, all movement ceased because the guard was dead.

John tossed the dead man to the grasses and then motioned for Brown to come to him.

Once Brown was beside him, he gave an excellent call of a hoot owl. Soon, he had nine other men with him. John whispered, "Okay, five with me and five with Brown out here. Keep us inside safe as we set our explosives. You can also set some explosives on the tall towers that carry the power to other smaller power plants. Set the timers for ten minutes. Ours will be programmed to explode in ten minutes as well. Now, let's move."

John moved to the door of the building and was surprised when he found it unlocked. Holding his Bison at the ready, he entered the building and noticed a second guard sleeping, his chair tilted back, and his loud snores were heard. John removed the guard's .38 revolver and then removed his handcuffs. He then tapped the man in the forehead with his finger.

The man opened his eyes and said, "What 'n the hell are ya doin' in here?" He grabbed for his pistol but found only air.

"This is a partisan raid and you are our prisoner. Make any noise and I'll do the same to you that I did to your buddy outside. I cut his throat."

"No, please mister, I have a wife and four kids. I took this job to feed them and I need the money or they'll die like so many others."

"Stick your arm out." Once the guard's arm was extended, John handcuffed his right arm to the man's left leg. He then added, "Where are the keys to the cuffs?"

"My left shirt pocket."

John removed the keys and seeing a drain in the center of the concrete floor, he removed the grate and dropped the keys inside.

Turning to his men, he said, "Let's go inside. Kill no one, unless they raise a gun."

When they entered the console room they found three men; one was reading a western novel, the other was sleeping with his head on his desk, and the last man was using his laptop computer. The man at the computer was shocked when they entered, but he quickly recovered and raised a .45 1911 pistol.

John fired, as did all of the others, and the man was almost blown apart by all the rounds striking him. Finally his head exploded and John knew he was dead. Of the others, the man with the book dropped it and filled his hand with a .38 snub nose. He got off four shots, before he too was blown apart by gunfire. John heard at least two of his men screaming in pain.

Looking at the survivor, John asked, "Aren't you going to reach for a gun too?"

"No, I'm not stupid." he said and then raised his hands. "I surrender."

"Anyone else in this building?" John asked.

"Just Frank, and he's in the bathroom. Said his stomach was bothering him."

"Duffy, I want you and Lee to check it out. Green, put hand-cuffs on this man and cuffed him to the console. Private Smith, what is the status of our wounded?"

Green looked up from the two men he was working on. "Hanish has an arm wound, through the flesh, Irving is dead. He took a round to the face."

"Prepare both to be moved. I want the explosives placed now and —"

The sound of two shots rang out.

Lee was heard saying, "Drop the pistol or I'll kill you. Drop it and I mean now!"

Then came a pistol shot.

CHAPTER 19

Colonel Yurievich was promoted in front of about 40 Generals and then awarded Russia's highest medal for bravery, the Hero of the Russian Federation, followed by two lesser awards, the Order of Saint George, first class, and the Order of Suvorov. By the medals alone he was one to the most decorated Russians still alive. Some who had died were awarded the same medals, but at the time, he was the only officer alive to hold the Hero of the Russian Federation medal. He didn't care much about the medals, but his promotion made him happy.

He no longer than finished his meeting with the Generals and was in his room relaxing when he heard a knock on his door. He'd changed hotels since his first one had exploded, and now opened all doors with a pistol in his hand.

"Who is there?" he asked as he stood by the wall, pistol ready.

"Russian Secret Police."

"P . . . Police? What do you want?"

"Just to talk, General."

He opened the door a crack and saw a man dressed in a dark gray overcoat.

He kept the pistol in his hand as he opened the door wide and said, "Come in, but no sudden moves."

Once inside the man said, "Here is my identification and badge." He held them up for Yurievich to see.

"What brings you here, Major?"

"Our investigation indicates the location of the bomb was in the bedroom of your suite. Do you know anyone out to kill you?"

"Uh, yes, I do. I suspect every American in America would like me dead. I am a very popular man there right now. In my bedroom, you say?"

"Yes, sir. Security gave all the rooms a good going over the day of the blast and it had to be a bomb in your luggage."

"My luggage? Why did it not go off in the air while I was on the plane?"

"We found the timer, and it was a cheap watch. Apparently it was set to go off within 24 hours, which is the maximum time they can be programmed, so we think it was jarred or dropped and the alarm reset itself to 24 hours. That had to happen or it would have gone off the first 24 hours it was in your baggage."

Feeling a shiver go through his body, the General said, "I shudder to think of that bomb going off while over the sea. They may have never found our bodies. I know my luggage was in the baggage hold for almost 24 hours. What now?"

"The base you just left said an aircraft repairman has not reported for work since he worked on your aircraft the day you left. Our background check on him did not indicate any involvement with the partisans, but his running away more or less proves his guilt. When the army went to his home to ask him about the aircraft maintenance forms book, he started shooting at us. We had two squads of men who had just completed another mission were being returned to base. Of the twenty soldiers only three were not killed or injured. Seventeen died taking the house. We now have a wanted poster up for him offering 50,000 American dollars for sabotage."

"How can I help you?"

Pulling a photo from his trench coat, the agent said, "Do you recognize this man?"

"I may have, he looks familiar, but I cannot think when or where. Why?"

"He is the man we think planted the bomb in your suitcase."

"I opened one bag to change so I could go for a walk. I never saw a bomb."

"How many bags did you have?"

"Two."

"I think the bomb must have been in the bag you did not open, then. Which bag held the bomb is not important. Can you think of anything that might help us?"

"Only as the Wing and Base Commander, the partisans must have put me on their hit list and that is not unusual at all. I was their enemy."

"Yes, we see that, but we have to also weed out that no one in baggage receiving here placed the bomb too. The fact a maintenance worker is missing in America may or may not be tied to your case. I know we found the fingerprints of someone on part of the bomb and the prints have been sent to America to match the prints on file of the missing man. If they match, then we know we have the right man."

"Complicated, is it not?"

"Not really, General, it is just a slow process is all."

"Anything else I can do for you?"

"Uh, no sir. If I have other questions can I contact you?"

"Yes by all means. I do not like being a target of a crazy man."

Quickly glancing at his watch, the Major said, "I must leave now, sir. I appreciate your help. I am sure you are safe here, and the partisans took a gamble but lost. Oh, they killed 58 Russians, but the man they wanted is still very much alive. Good day, sir."

The General walked to his door and opened it wide for the agent. After the man walked from his room, Yurievich shut and locked the door, and stood shaking his head. He'd come so close to being killed but wasn't, all because of a cheap watch.

He walked to his bar, poured a triple vodka and then moved to the sofa, where he sat and closed his eyes. *I hate the damned secret police because even a priest or nun feels guilty around them when they have done nothing wrong*, he thought.

He dozed off minutes later.

Meanwhile, back in America and on the Russian base, Colonel Stena was in a staff meeting in the middle of the night as he had his units searching for the partisans. He'd kept the manning at the base at a minimum as he tried hard to locate the source of his problems, but he was having no luck. He finally, out of frustration, sent his two teams of Spetsnaz out looking. He knew it was an abuse of the highly trained soldiers, but he felt if anyone could find their base camps it would be them. So far all of his available man power in the field had found nothing, except booby-traps.

"I am giving our troops two more days and if nothing is found, I am bringing them back to the base. I feel very uncomfortable having the bulk of our troops in the woods. We are vulnerable this way, or so I think. But, since General Yurievich had them out in the field already, he must have had faith that something would be found."

"Maybe, sir, he just hoped they would find something."

"He took a big risk sending that many into the field. I think a company of Americans could take this base over as lightly manned as we are. Who is my operations officer?"

"I am, sir. I am Lieutenant Colonel Golov Petr Borisovich," the man said as he stood.

"Arrange a pick up of all assets in the field over the next three days. I want almost half pulled out this evening and the rest by Friday. Do you understand your orders?"

"Uh, yes, sir. I fully understand. When I contact the units, they are sure to ask me why they are coming in early. What am I to tell them, sir?"

"Hell, that is easy. Tell them their commander wants them to return. They are Russian soldiers and I will not justify my orders when I want them to go someplace. Remind them, if needed, they are to follow orders and ask very few questions. By God, they are my subordinates."

"Yes, sir."

"Tomorrow at Stand Up, I want to know which units were returned to the base and your plan to remove the rest. Make it a point paper that I can read when I get the time. Now, I want my other commanders to have your people up and working to support the men coming in from the field. They will need new uniforms, showers, hot water to shave, some good hot food, and some rest. I expect all of you to support their needs. I want each man or woman given a double shot of vodka when they return. Thank them for a job well done."

"Sir," a young Lieutenant from supply said, "We are not open after 1700, sir."

"Lieutenant, you will be open 24 hours for the rest of this week as will all others, without exception."

"Sir, I cannot work my civilians that long or they will get time and half, which needs approval from Moscow."

"It is not real hard, Lieutenant; keep your civilians on duty during the day and use your military for the night shifts. You have at least two men on each shift and I am sure you have 4 men in an organization as large as supply, right?"

"Uh, yes sir. I will do what you suggested, sir."

"Anyone else have any manning or shift problems?"

Not a sound was heard.

The Colonel then said, "That is it for Stand Up today. I want all of you to return to your sections and start planning your 24 hours shifts, which start immediately." Stena then moved for the door.

As he walked pass a Master Sergeant, the big man stood and grunted, "Tinnnnn-huuut."

Everyone in the room stood at attention until the Colonel was out of the room.

There was the normal moaning and groaning that folk who usually had an 8-5 job would now have to be open 24 hours a day 7 days a week. Senior Sergeant Vova laughed internally. The folks in the rear would work 12 hour shifts, and it still beat the 24 hours a day the men and women put in while in the field. Most of the returning troops would want a shower, hot food, and then a few drinks. He knew that the package store sold beer to the young troops and hard stuff to Sergeants and above. Each man had a ration card that he needed to hand to the cashier anytime they bought anything in the store. A sergeant was allowed two quarts of hard alcohol a month and two cases of beer, or 48 cans. He was allowed to buy cigarettes too, but only 3 cartons a month.

He left the headquarters building and made his way back to his room where Olga was sleeping when he left. He opened the door quietly and when he looked, she was still sleeping in the bedroom. He then switched on the TV and watched a documentary in Russian about Custer's Last Stand, which interested him greatly.

He put a pot of coffee on to boil. He liked tea better, but they were running low on green tea, so he would try coffee this morning. He had about an hour, then he needed to be at work. He'd just poured a cup when Olga entered the room and asked, "Any new missions coming down?"

"No, nothing this week. I think the new commander is worried because about 80% of our manpower is in the bushes looking for partisans. If the base is hit again, well, we could very well lose the whole place and not get it back anytime soon. An attack by the partisans would ruin his career."

"Who sent so many people to the bush country?"

"General Yurievich did, and he had them all looking for partisans. They have found nothing so far. I think they would be smarter to let recognizance aircraft look for the partisans and call the troops back in for now."

"Well, if their calling folks to come back, we will not go on any missions anytime soon."

"That is really not true. A mission could come up and we could be tasked to do the job, only it would have to be a special mission. Of course, they are all special missions to me," Petr said, "because I can get my ass shot off on an easy mission too."

Olga laughed and said, "Relax some. I do not think we will go anywhere, not with them expecting an attack on the base. I cannot help but wonder if they are not getting paranoid. I mean the partisans held this base for 24 hours and yet, when the counterattack came, all of them except for maybe a dozen snipers were gone. All of us went out looking for them and they were gone, and there were what, two firefights? Thousands of them attacked here and we found less than thirty later. They do not hold on to country, they attack to kill and run up our death and injury rates. They know the people back home are angery getting their young men and women back in boxes."

"All guerrillas fight the same way. They hit and run, to wear an opponent down and drain his resources."

"We are not even close to being worn out."

"No, the army is not worn out, but our people are. When we leave America, it will be because of our citizens back home, not an army decision."

"Do you really think that?" She asked, surprised he would say that.

"It happened before, years ago in Afghanistan. My father was there when we left the country and he said it was a war they could not win." Petr said and then remembered his father as a kind but firm man who loved his family.

"I think this is another war we cannot win."

There was a knock on his door. Getting up, he pulled his pistol, cocked the hammer back and asked, "Who is at my door?"

"Private Pushkin, Senior Sergeant Vova. I have a message for you from the Base Commander."

Petr unlocked the door, opened it partially and seeing a frightened young man, he slipped his pistol into the shoulder holster he was wearing.

Opening the door wide, he said, "Come in and tell me what I can do for the Commander."

The young man entered, looked at Olga and said, "I am only to tell you the orders. Can we speak in another room, Sergeant?"

"I have things to do in the bedroom." Olga said, stood and moved into the bedroom, where she made the bed and began cleaning things up.

"Now, what are my orders?"

"You are to report to the Wing Commander for a classified mission against the Americans. You will take your squad, no one else, and you will sneak on their main bases and add something to their water supply. I know this war is going poorly when they openly have bases in places we have no control over. Three years ago those partisan bases would have been destroyed, but with Moscow cutting manpower here and the public raising hell, we have to make due with what they send us. I would do it on their field locations too, but I have no idea where the forward operating bases (FOB) are. Other than that, I can tell you no more, Sergeant. I have no idea what they want you to put in the water."

Poison most likely, Vova thought and then said, "It does not matter what it is, an order is an order. When and where am I to meet with the commander?"

"Today, 1700 hours, in his office. Only you alone are to come to the meeting."

"That is all he instructed you to tell me?"

"Yes, sir. He said he did not want the meat of the mission out for people to hear. He said it was a very important mission. That is all I was told, Sergeant."

At 1700 hours, Wing Commanders Office, Senior Sergeant Vova was surprised to see a large group of officers enter the room as he waited. Finally he and the officers were called in and Colonel Stena had everyone seated. He then called Vova to the front and, in a surprise move, promoted him on the spot to Master Sergeant a good three days early.

When he finished, the Colonel said, "Let us have a big warm congratulations to our newest Master Sergeant, and it is very well deserved. Now, I want all of you to line up and shake this man's hand. It is rare for a man to make Master Sergeant, with only 2% of the enlisted force reaching his new rank."

After the normal base stuff and a report on the number of troops returned to base, the officers were released and the Colonel invited Vova into his office for a drink and discussion.

Entering the office, the Colonel had Vova sit as he moved behind his desk and pulled out a bottle of American whiskey. "Care for a drink as I discuss your mission?"

"Uh, yes, sir. Give me about three fingers worth."

Drink in hand a minute later, Colonel Stena said, "Master Sergeant, I am about to send you on a very dangerous but necessary mission. We have orders from Moscow to take drastic steps to kill Americans."

"Oh, and what kind of steps, sir?"

"Chemical Biological warfare."

"Sir, that can be sent with artillery shells, bombs or other ways to disperse the agent or chemical." Vova gulped about half his drink down.

"In order not to attract attention, we want to deliver it to their drinking water."

"So, I am to place something in the drinking water of the Americans?"

Taking a sip of his whiskey, Stena said, "Exactly. So it will appear the poison was natural and to catch the enemy off guard. They must not catch you or discover you during your mission."

"Okay, I can understand that, but this sounds like something Spetsnaz is better suited for than my people."

"Spetsnaz is not available right now. They are in the field looking for partisans. I need my people to do this, and I think my airborne troops can complete this mission."

"I thank you for the confidence in us, sir, but the mission will be difficult if we are to add it to their water supply and never be seen. What poison am I to place in their water?"

"You will have the poison Botulinum. It is one of the, if not the most poisonous toxins in the world. Your nervous system fails and you die in extreme pain. You need to add very little to the water to kill the whole base. Our experts tell us as little as a tablespoon will be enough to kill everyone twice, but we are giving you two tablespoons of the poison to add to each drinking tank. The chemical will be in a water soluble container inside a water proof container, which means you have to keep it dry or you will die packing it. It will be given to you in a hard steel container with a screw on lid. The steel container is waterproof and you will have to intentionally open the container to add the chemical pouch to the water supply. The water will eat through the clear pouch in seconds, allowing the poison to mix with the water. Do not get the poison on your hands or clothing."

"If the UN hears of this, there will be hell to pay." Vova said.

"That is why you must not be caught. If it looks like you are about to be captured or overran, get rid of the poison. If you are caught with it, things will turn rough because the Americans will torture you to learn more about our deadly plans. Each of the stainless steel containers is equipped with a destruct button that will ignite a thermite lining around the toxin. It is destroyed within a minute. During the destruction process the container will become too hot to hold. So, push the button and then toss the container to the ground."

"How many bases will we attack?" Vova asked, not liking the mission at all.

"Two, but only one first, until we hear of how world opinion goes after we kill thousands of them. If you are not caught, then they cannot prove we had anything to do with the deaths."

"I understand, sir." Vova said and then thought, *I do not like this, because we are not trained to do jobs like this. I cannot refuse, because it is a legal order. Now, using the poison is against the UN but we did not sign any UN agreements on armed conflicts, only on the treatment of civilians in war zones. So, as a Russian soldier, the order is perfectly legal.*

"I want your people to land by parachute near the partisan base in Dallas/Fort Worth and poison their water first. If you can get in and out, we will know then the system is a go. This mission must be completed at all costs, *all costs*. Do you understand?"

"Yes sir, I understand, and the classification of this mission?"

"Top Secret, Eyes Only." That meant only two or three people in the world knew of the mission. He suspected a General in Moscow knew, the Colonel knew, and then him. His people would not be told of the mission other than they needed to gain access to the bases water supply. He'd have to tell his second in charge, in case he was killed, but no one else would know.

"When do we leave on this mission, sir?"

"Tonight, at 2300 hundred you will be inserted by parachute, and it will be a HALO jump (High Altitude Low Opening) with your parachutes set to open at 500 feet. Your jump altitude will be at 23,000 feet. It will be too late for you to move onto the base, but tomorrow you can look the place over and plan your attack on the water supply."

"Your mission needs to be done within 48 hours because at some time following that, a very important individual will be visiting the base. A man named Bo Turner is due there to speak with them about establishing a nation again, once we are gone. This Bo man is wanting to be their first President after we leave, if we leave. I think he is a bit premature, but it is not my call. If we can kill him with the water, then that is another feather in our cap. We do not have his *itinerary* or we would have a sniper take him out. Hell, we are not even sure of the date he will arrive."

"Sounds like this is well thought out, but I will give it more thought, sir."

"Your mission is called, *'Operation Instant Fury'*."

CHAPTER 20

At the power station, a shot was heard and then a much deeper boom followed. Then Brown yelled, "All clear, now."

The two men entered as the last of the explosives were being placed.

"You two take this man and the guard in the hall to the main fence and handcuff this one to it. The other man will go no place, so lay him close to this one. Once you're done we'll scatter. Hurry, because we don't have much time."

Ten minutes later, as they waited in the truck, the main building went up in a ball of red flames with black edges. As the fireball rolled inside of itself, the explosives on four tall towers went up as well. Immediately the lights around the facility went off, but emergency generators kicked on a minute or so later, lighting the place once more.

"Let's go, now! Head home by the shortest route too." John ordered as his men clapped and cheered at their success. John looked at the body of Private Irving on the floor, wrapped in a poncho, and knew the cost was too high.

The other group ran into resistance and it cost them three lives to blow the power plant. The group with John had seen the explosion as they rode back to base. There was a huge rolling ball of flames on the horizon to the southwest and the skies lit up in white. They knew it was the power plant going up and they wondered about casualties, because all of them had friends in the group. There was nothing they could do; deaths and maiming happened in their line of work.

It wasn't long until the radio said, "Cobra two, this is Cobra Three. We have 3 KIA and two WIA. The enemy has seven KIA. We are returning to base with our dead. Do you copy?"

"Uh, copy three. You have 3 KIA. Great job, Three, we see your flames. Return to base."

"Copy, we are returning now."

"Roger that. Cobra Two, over and out."

An hour later, as they sat in the mission debriefing, John said, "Both teams did an excellent job of taking out the power plants, but our losses were high, I think. It will be months before the facilities will be operational again. Well done, gentlemen and ladies."

"So, do we get a couple of days off now, or do we hit a new place tonight?"

"We are to hit one place and we will do so, unless the facility is highly guarded. Sergeant Gomez, I want you and Captain Braun to change into civilian clothes and check the next power station to see what the Russians have done since our attacks. You will both use motorcycles and move in close on foot, after obviously parking the bikes. Count the guards and do a target evaluation, like we normally do before we strike."

Gomez nodded and Braun said, "Yes sir, and when do we leave?"

"How about right now? If you two will come to the map, I'll show you where we intend to hit next. The rest of you are dismissed for the time being, but be back here at 1700 so we can do a mission plan."

Ten minutes after the briefing and looking the map over, the two partisans were changed into civilian clothing, jeans and tees, and mounted on two dirt bikes. They were handy for observation and spying on the enemy, or even as get away vehicles after a sniper had done their dirty work. They were fast enough, could be ridden in the woods, and very little stopped or slowed them down. This day they'd drive close to the plant, park in the woods, and sneak up on the place to look it over. If all went well, they'd be home in two hours. If things turned rough, they might never be home again. As partisans, both accepted the risk.

Thirty minutes later they rode by the power plant and spotted no one outside, but that meant little. They continued to the next section road and turned left. In a matter of a few short minutes they were back on the gravel road that ran beside the plant. They rode about a half a mile from the building and then parked the bikes in the brush. Pulling their weapons, they slipped the safety off and moved toward the power plant.

They both circled the plant and moved in close to the fence surrounding three buildings. Two guards left a building and moved to a deuce and a half truck where they climbed in the back, along with four men from inside the plant itself.

Writing on a thigh mounted pad of paper, Gomez said, "Shift change. But we know 6 are there at least."

"We'll watch for another hour, then report back."

Over the next hour nothing new was seen after the truck left, until two new guards walked out into the sunlight. They moved around and finally, they sat on a porch of one building and looked to be making small talk. One smoked, as the other pulled out a paperback book, so Braun tapped Gomez on the shoulder and they melted back into the trees.

Once at the bikes, Braun said, "Looks like a normal setup for me except they've doubled the guards. From the looks of things, they're bored and will be easily taken out. I do worry about the two buildings beside the power plant, because they could have men inside."

Gomez thought a minute and then said, "We could blow those structures up at the same time we blow the door to the plant."

"We'll bring it up to the Colonel, but he may want to handle them differently; who knows? We'll report just what we saw and then if he asks we'll tell him our concerns."

"Okay, let's ride."

Once back with the partisans they reported what they'd seen to John and he wondered what the three outer building were, and both could see they concerned him.

"They could hold more troops, but we only saw civilians guarding the outside. No one entered either building while we were there. Both buildings can be blown at the same time, right after you blow the main door to the plant. But, there were no machine-gun nests or tanks indicating they took the security seriously."

"Good, the attack will go on as planned and with just ten of us on the team. I want both of you along and we'll hit them at 0100, when everyone will be sleepy. Go rest and grab more ammo if you feel you need it."

At 2400 hours the ten men and women loaded on a deuce and a half for the short ride to the power plant. They were armed for bear, with two RPGs to take out the plant if they could not gain access. They were determined, but three of them wondered about the two other buildings. No one spoke of them, but they would be taken out quickly.

A half mile from the plant, they unloaded the truck and fell in behind the Colonel.

They found the power plant still guarded by what looked like two civilians. John had Lee and Carrier cut the fence and then they moved in behind the two buildings that Braun prayed were empty, and set two C-4 bricks against the back walls. The detonator was held by the Colonel. Msgt. Dias took a .22 pistol with a homemade silencer made back at camp that gave the gun a very low, *poot* sound when fired. The small caliber weapon would kill, if shot correctly.

She then moved around behind the guards, who were still sitting on the porch, and she fired once, seeing the small bullet strike the smoker in the back of the head. He simply slumped over and that caused the other man to stand. Aiming once more, she placed her second bullet almost between the man's eyes. The bullet struck him hard, but did not kill him. Instead the bullet ricocheted from his skull and zinged off into the woods. He remained standing and, while he looked confused, she put four more shots into his body. Finally, he gave a horrible scream and then fell to his knees.

Knowing the party was over, Mary fired a burst from her Bison, which stitched the man down the middle and he fell to his back, dying. The door to the building on the left flew open and out ran three Russian soldiers, but they were cut down just outside the door. Russians were heard screaming with more attempting to climb over the bodies. John detonated the C-4 right as four Russians ran into the courtyard of the plant. In a matter of seconds the soldiers were dead and a thermite grenade was placed against the locked plant door. It hissed as it began melting the steel lock.

Then the other building went up in flames, throwing books, papers, and desks high into the air. No one ran from that building. Both buildings were burning now and anyone inside either structure was dead. The lock on the door of the power plant fell off and when the door was opened, an automatic rifle hit two partisans and knocked them to the ground. Gomez tossed a grenade down the hall, where it exploded with a loud boom. Two partisans entered and they began to clear the building. When they tried to enter the control room, heavy weapons fire stopped them. Gomez tossed in a *white phosphorus* grenade and then slammed the door shut. With the explosion, there came a series of horrible screams as the metal struck people and the pain of the burning became real. Gomez kicked the door in and entered shooting. One man went down instantly, his shirt on fire, and a second was struck in the head. He did manage to fire twice as he fell to the floor, the top of his skull missing. Gomez took the last two bullets in the chest and collapsed on the floor screaming.

Then, Gomez was pulled to the hallway and relative safety. Braun entered, along with Carrier and Smith, and they moved up and down the room, killing those who resisted. Finally, Braun called out, "All clear. Now, set the charges for five minutes, move!"

The charges were placed next to the computers and consoles, and the explosives were armed. Everyone ran from the building. Moving to the gate, they sent two men back to bring the truck forward so they could load on the road beside the place. John raised his arm to see how much more time was needed when the place went up in a big explosion that turned off the lights instantly, but back up generators flipped the light back on. The fire ball was twice the size of the other two power plants, but the damage was complete, as debris and computer parts fell all around.

Watching the huge flames rolling skyward, John yelled, "Everyone to the truck. Bring any injured or dead. Now! Let's move, people! I suspect air cover in a few minutes. Once someone on this grid notifies the Russians the power is out, they'll come looking. I don't want to be here!"

The governors on the truck engines had all been removed and the truck they had was soon doing 60 MPH as the driver drove without his lights on, and depended on his NVGs.

They were soon back home, but as they unloaded, John knew any strikes after this would not be as easy as this night. They'd hit the Russians hard and a good quarter of the state was without power, but he wondered if the remainder of the power plants wouldn't be suicide to attack. He gave the idea a few hours of thought and then contacted Headquarters at dawn with his idea.

"Cobra, we see the merit of waiting a month and while we'd like to do that, there is a reason we want to kill all of the power, over."

"Can I ask that reason, since my people will be the ones to die in the next few attempts?"

"Uh, wait one."

"What'd they say?" Joy asked.

"Nothing yet. He's talking to the General."

"Cobra two, Copperhead."

"Go."

"Copperhead actual said you do not have a need to know. He will provide you with a little additional instructions in a classified message he'll send you in the hour. Confirm you copy, over."

"Copy, Copperhead. Cobra Two, out."

"Well, there is a reason, but I'm not to know what it is, or so the General said."

"Looks like if the danger is to us, we'd be told something." Joy said.

"You would think so, but maybe not. He's sending me a message within the hour so in the meantime, let's visit Gomez and see how he's feeling. I was by his room in the tent earlier and he was out of it and on morphine. I spoke to the doctor who said he'd survive easily and the bullet was more to his shoulder than chest."

"Good, he's a brave man. He kicked the door open, stormed in and killed at least three of them. Then a female Russian soldier shot him as he killed her. At first we thought it was a man, because of her short hair. She took two bullets, one to the chest, right between her boobs, and one to the head. No one could have saved her even if she'd been in a hospital, because she was dead in seconds."

"Gomez is a good troop and he needs promoted. He's demonstrated some great leadership traits this last year, and I think he should be at least a Staff Sergeant and a squad leader."

They walked to the hospital only to be turned away, because Gomez was sleeping. They went back to John's tent, where they opened two Green Frogs.

They were sitting on his bed eating when Private Green knocked and entered. He said, "Decoded message from the General, sir."

John opened the envelope and pulled out a message that read, 'Top Secret, not to be disclosed to non military personnel at any time.'

"I knew it would be classified, but Top Secret?"

He then read aloud, "Your timing in cutting the power to the state of Missouri is crucial to our planned mass attack on all Russian bases at the end of this month. I will tell you no more, but figured you needed to know that much. Without power, they will not have much working in their command post. We have mortars to use on their generators. Enough said."

"Well, damn it, I should have known he had a serious reason, but I never dreamed we'd be hitting the Russians so soon after we overran the base."

"Sir, must I remind you that this conversation never took place? If you hand the message to me, I'll lock it in the safe with the rest of our classified."

John handed the message to Green and said, "Here, this is good news, especially with Bo Turner coming to visit us. It looks to me like the end of the war may be closer than I thought."

Taking the classified, Green said, "Huh? You lost me, sir. I for sure didn't read that in the message you just read."

"Never mind, I was more or less thinking out loud. Gather all the troop leaders and have them in the meeting tent in an hour. We need to go over some things before our next power station attack, but nothing Top Secret. I just need to motivate them a little."

Near midnight John and his men bunched up near a power plant and for some reason John had a real bad feeling about the mission but wrote it off as just mission jitters. It was not unusual for him to feel like he did on most assignments, only this was stronger than most. Two men cut through the fence, entered and moved to silence the guards. The two partisans were Bill Love and David Sidwell, both experienced long time partisans. They were good at their jobs, but had to be to have survived eight years of almost constant contact with the Russians.

As Love moved toward the guard near the plant building door, David moved for the man reading a magazine. When both were about four feet from their targets, there were two shots and both men fell. David began screaming in pain, but Bill dropped, instantly dead. A bullet had burned a hole through his chest, striking his heart.

"Now, everyone, charge the place!" John screamed.

Seconds later, a machine-gun opened up. The *rat-tat-rat-tat* sound of the gun indicated the gunner had plenty of targets. Men and women fell as the gun fired. Dias toss a grenade and the gun when up in a flash of fire and screams.

"Brown, come with me!" She yelled and when the man joined her, they moved to the machine-gun and found it in good shape, with the Russian crew dead. The two of them dusted off the gun, loaded it with bullets and began firing at the Russians. Her night vision goggles assisted her in spotting her enemies.

Brown screamed as he fell, his left arm missing and Lee soon joined him, having take a bullet in the groin which was so painful he passed out, never knowing his penis and balls were gone. Blood soaked both men.

Hanish, seeing the two wounded screamed to be heard over the firefight, "Medic!"

Toms ran to the two downed men, placed a tourniquet on Brown and applied a dressing between the legs of Lee. Both were given shots of morphine and then the medic moved forward with the fight.

"Copperhead, this is Cobra Two, over."

"Go, Cobra."

"Any Chinese aircraft in my area? Over."

"Negative. All have been buttoned up for the night."

"Artillery available?"

"Wait one."

Joy screamed, "Must have been a company size force in the plant compound. They were waiting for us."

John nodded, but didn't speak, he was waiting on Copperhead's reply.

"Cobra, Copperhead and I do have two 105 artillery guns for your use. The call sign for them is Gun Fighter, over."

John quickly gave his map location and said, "I need two rounds as soon as possible (ASAP) on my location." Then blowing his whistle, he recalled his troops to the fence line.

Soon the cracking, whistling sound of a big artillery shell was heard. It exploded just inside the compound and on the west side.

"Excellent, shooting Gun Fighter, move your rounds up 50 meters and give me six rounds of White Phosphorus (WP)."

"Copy, get your heads down. WP is nasty." the gunner replied. "On the way!"

The first shell hit the center of the compound and exploded in a beautiful white explosion that reminded John, for some reason, of a peacock tail. He knew the shells were deadly and while they looked pretty, those struck would be in horrible pain, as the shrapnel would burn as long as it was exposed to air. The only way to keep it from burning was to cut off the air supply and mud worked well, but it was too dry for mud to be around. John had been taught to pee in the dirt and make his own mud, but right now, any Russians in the compound were doomed, or so it looked.

When the shells stopped falling, an eerie silence followed, except for screams of Russian wounded. John blew his whistle twice and the partisans moved toward the power plants control room. Like the other power plants, the structure was made of reinforced concrete, so it sustained little serious damage during the bombardment from the 105 mm guns. A few surviving Russians took pot shots at the resistance members, but after a few Russians were killed the shots stopped.

A thermite grenade was attached to the lock and door handle and the pin pulled. The grenade sputtered and spit as it burned through the steel lock. When the grenade quit, Corporal Tomkins kicked the door open and tossed two grenades down the long hall.

The explosions were loud, and screams were heard a few seconds later. A small group of three entered, shooting at anything that moved. Once in the control room, they encountered rough resistance, so John sent a man with a flamethrower inside.

At the control room door, Brown kicked the door in and the flamethrower spurted a long strand of burning jelly at any movement. The interior was now a room of flames. Horrible screams were heard as the men inside the room burned to death. Prings threw two grenades inside and with the explosion, the screams stopped.

Brown set the explosives at the control room door, with the timer to go up in five minutes. The small group ran out of the building and yelled, "Five minutes."

"Cobra, this is Copperhead."

"Go, Copperhead."

"Radar indicates four aircraft which they believe are attack helicopters, moving in your direction. We suggest you get out of there now."

"How much time do I have, Copperhead? Over."

"At the most, fifteen minutes. Your orders are to leave now, copy?"

"Copy. We'll leave in about three minutes. Need to see the control room go up first, over."

"Roger, your choice. Over and out."

"Joy!" John yelled.

"Yo!"

"Take everyone but me and Carrier and leave now. Move back toward base, but be aware we have company that flies due here in about 12 minutes. They think the threat is attack helicopters so watch your ass."

CHAPTER 21

Master Sergeant Vova and his troops were sitting on red troop seats as the aircraft they were on flew at 20,000 feet toward Dallas/Fort Worth, and all were antsy to get out the door and on the ground. They were all dressed for HALO, with oxygen masks on so they could breathe 100% oxygen before and during their jumps. All were experienced jumpers, but most got a little restless before any jump.

They had communications set up with each person, and that assisted them in landing and locating each other after they landed.

The load master neared and said, "I am going to lower the back ramp. When the pilot tells me, I will have you jump. When I say go, leave immediately because if you wait too long, you will miss the drop zone."

"Understood. Monsoon to the pilot, how long before we drop?"

"You have about seven minutes. All of you move to the back ramp. When you hear the load master say go, glance at the now red light to see it if is green. If it is not green, do not jump."

"I understand. Come on, let us all move to the ramp." It was easier said than done, because each jumper carried about a hundred pounds of gear, counting their parachute.

They did not carry reserve chutes because if the thing didn't open at 152.4 meters, they'd be dead before they could deploy a reserve parachute. They would be falling at almost 54 kilometers an hour, or terminal velocity. As the Master Sergeant knew, by the time you realized your chute didn't open you'd already be 153 millimeters in the ground.

"Get ready, you are four minutes out." the load master said.

The remaining minutes passed quickly now.

Then, "Go, go, go!" from the load master, and the light turned green.

Master Sergeant Vova was the last jumper off the aircraft ramp because he waited to make sure all his troops jumped. He stepped off the ramp and once clear of the aircraft, he went into a spread eagle position with his arms and legs extended to stabilize him as he fell. He kept his eyes on his altimeter, so he knew when to expect opening shock.

He was growing concerned when he passed through one thousand feet, and then was suddenly pulled up into the air and he heard a loud uuummmppp. He knew the noise came from him. He looked up and saw his parachute was in good condition with no blown panels. He grabbed a quick release on his right side, pulled it, and about 80 pounds of gear packed in a nylon bag dropped 5 meters below him.

Before he had time to assume a good landing position, he struck the ground hard, and quickly pulled his parachute releases. He unknowingly smiled that he was able to disconnect the chute from his harness, because he'd seen many paratroopers get dragged over rough ground, and it was hard on anybody. Some had even required a hospital trip, and a jumper had to be pretty hurt to agree to seeing a doctor.

Using the radio mic, he quickly made contact with his men and women.

"Private Leonid, do you read me, over?"

"Master Sergeant, one of our people did not get a chute and Selidov is the only one not answering. I am sure now it was him. Should we look for him?"

"Yes, but keep the noise down and don your NVGs."

Ten minutes later, Mara Sabitova said, "I have found him. He is dead and hit a tree when he landed. He has been speared by a broken limb and is on the ground. I get no pulse and his eyes are fixated."

"Everyone, form on me." Vova said, and waited for his squad of nine.

Twenty minutes later, the chutes and jump gear buried by collapsing an overhang of dirt on the equipment, the Russians moved north by west, in the general direction of Dallas/Fort Worth.

It was near noon before Vova called for a break to eat and rest a little.

Green Frogs were opened and the meals eaten cold. The Sergeant found he had rice with chicken and vegetables, along with Goulash with potatoes. He also discovered canned bread, crackers, chocolates, and a wet wipe to clean up after the meal. There were matches, ketchup and other condiments, but he didn't eat them. He placed the chocolates, fruit energy bars, and candy in his shirt pocket to eat as he walked. He pulled out a small bottle of hot sauce and sprinkled some of it on his meal. Once his meal was complete, he took a long swig of vodka from his canteen and then wipe his face clean.

He glanced at his watch and said, "We leave in 8 minutes. If you need to relieve yourselves do it now or hold it until our next break in about three hours." He saw two of his people heading to the woods.

They were soon walking again and Sergei was on point, and he was a good point man because he was fast and spotted all mines and booby-traps on the trail. Finally, after looking at a map and deciding they were within two miles of the base, Vova said, "Let us call it a day. We will sleep sitting up, our backs together. I want a 50% watch overnight. If I catch you sleeping as you guard, I will cut your throat. No more talking either. We are close to our objective."

Moving slowly now, each moved to the trees and brush where they opened another ration and took their time eating. There was something about packing a pack that weighed between 27 and 31 Kilos that wore everyone out, completely. Once they spent time in the bush or in combat, the weight of their packs went down quickly. This time the Master Sergeant got canned portions of stewed beef, two meat-with-vegetables porridges, and a tin of canned fish. He had the usual dried tea, dried coffee, candy, fruit energy bars, and dehydrated soft drinks. He saved the soft drinks to have later in the mission. He ate all in his pouch but was still hungry. The entrees were small servings of about 250 grams and while the meals provided 3570 calories a day for all three meals combined, they never filled him. He started to open another meal but knew if they poisoned the water system or were seen, they might have need of the two extra meals then. He leaned back against a tree and relaxed.

"Olga, call this position in for the night. Also check and see if our orders have changed or not."

"Okay, will do."

A few short minutes later, she said, "Nothing has changed, and they now know where we will be sleeping too."

"Good. Now we can rest easier. If you must use the bathroom, go now because when it becomes full dark, we will be back to back and will stay that way all night. Sergei, put out three of our command detonated mines, and sprinkle some butterfly mines around us."

Ten minutes later Sergei said, "The mines are in place and here are the clackers."

Vova took the two squeeze clackers and placed them on the ground beside him. Once squeezed, hundreds of ball bearings would leave the mine at the speed of a bullet, killing or maiming anyone they struck. The mines and guards would help make the evening safer for all of them.

Less than an hour later, Vova said, "Everyone get into your back to back positions and I want the folks not on guard duty to try and sleep. Remember, if you are a guard, I want no sleeping. A sleeping guard is useless, and dead if I catch you."

It was near 0200 when the new Master Sergeant heard a noise and he gave it thought. It sounded like someone walking in the leaves, but no one sneaking up on them would make that much noise, or would they? He elbowed his people to wake all of them. Then he heard it once more. Finally, he spotted quick movement against the moon and knew they were in no danger.

Whispering he said, "Deer."

"Good," someone whispered in return.

"Hush, no noise."

By 0500, he had his people up and eating a cold meal. Most hated the stuff without heating because cold, it gave many of them heartburn, only it was all they had and he'd not allow a fire. Most ate in complete silence.

Right at sunrise, the Sergeant said, "Mount up, we need to be moving. Petrovna, you are my point person and Sabitova, you are my drag. Everyone in position, and let us move."

The morning passed quickly and uneventful. The noon break was relaxing; while they were close to the base now, they spotted fewer and fewer mines or booby-traps, which meant to Vova they were on trails used often by the Americans. He constantly warned his point people to move slowly and not to run into any Americans, because he felt they were near. It was near 1500 when Makarovich, who was on point, suddenly held a balled fist in the air and then motioned for everyone to hide beside the trail. Folks moved into the brush and a few squatted or like Sergeant Vova, they laid down completely. The brush along the trail was dense.

Five minutes later a point man walked by and he was camouflaged from head to toe. Many wondered how Makarovich had spotted the man, but the Sergeant knew the point man's movement was probably seen first, then his form was seen.

Then, after the point man moved by, the main body of Americans were seen. Joy counted over 100 of them and they scared her badly. She knew if they caught her, she'd be raped and beaten, or at least that is what the Russian army usually did to female captives. After the drag woman passed, the Master Sergeant ordered them back on the trail. Soon, about two hours before dark, they were near enough they could see the water tower on the base. The Sergeant had his people stop in a densely green spot that had a lot of dead trees on the ground and he knew they'd be hard to spot with their camouflage on so they would spend the day and part of the night there.

"Call in our sleeping spot." he said, looking at Olga.

She was heard on the radio and when finished she said, "They know where we are and no changes on the mission. Everything according to Hotel is in the green."

"Tonight, I will complete the mission and then we'll head back for a helicopter pickup. I will take Private Petrovna with me. The rest of you will remain here and cover us. I must drop something in their drinking water."

"I hope you are safe."

"I will be as safe as I can. I hope they do not see me, then all is well. My goal is to do what is ordered and then leave without being seen."

"You will be fine, because you are good, Master Sergeant."

"We shall soon see if I am good enough."

She shrugged and knew he'd survive or he would not. It was all out of their hands, and God would decide if anyone died this night or not. That didn't mean she'd not worry about him, but dying was best ignored.

"Now, everyone back to back and let us rest this afternoon."

The rest of the day was quiet with no one coming near them; Vova thought he heard people near the trail an hour before dusk, but if they were there they weren't looking for them.

At 2200 hours, the Sergeant and Private Petrovna were moving toward the water tower. He had the botulinum container ready, with the poison in a special plastic bag, and all he needed to do was drop it into the water. The skies were overcast and it looked like rain to the Sergeant, and that would make his task that much easier. They used bolt cutters to cut a hole in the fence, then they moved cautiously to the water tank. It was a round water storage container and he knew he had to climb to the very top to add the poison. He began to climb the ladder. He knew he'd be hard to see by anyone not wearing NVGs, so he climbed as quickly as he could. Suddenly there was a loud blaring siren, announcing the base was under attack. He wondered how that could be when a handful of bullets struck the tower about a foot above his head; they then ricocheted into the darkness. He ducked when he heard them strike and knew he was under fire now. Glancing up, he was about ten feet from the hatch to the water, when he felt a bullet take him low in the back. Using his upper arms, his legs suddenly useless, he pulled himself to the hatch and tossed the botulinum into the water.

Two more bullets struck him in the middle of his back and his world faded from view as he lost consciousness, and fell 61 meters to the ground. He was dead before he realized he'd been fatally injured.

By the time Master Sergeant Vova struck the ground, Private Petrovna was on his way to the hole in the fence. He quickly left the base and ran right to the group waiting for him.

"Where is Petr?" Olga asked.

He quickly explained what had happened.

"You didn't check his body for life?" Olga asked, her anger obvious.

"There was no time. If the bullets did not kill him, hitting the ground after falling from the tower surely killed him. He must have been 60 to 79 meters in the air when he fell. I am sorry, Olga, he was a good man."

"Hand me the radio." Olga said, and Leonid neared and handed the handset to her.

"Hotel, hotel, this Monsoon."

"Uh, go Monsoon."

"Monsoon One is KIA, I repeat, Monsoon One is Kilo, India, Alpha. Do you read, over? The package has been delivered. Do you read me Hotel?"

"Yes, I read you 5 by 5. Wait one."

"Copy, will do."

"Monsoon, you are to move to the pick up point, contact us, and we will send a helicopter after you, copy?"

"Roger, copy. We should be there by noon tomorrow, over."

"Over and out, Monsoon."

Handing the handset to the radio operator, Olga said, "I am going to confirm the death of Master Sergeant Vova and you, Private Petrovna, are going with me. You will show me his remains. If something happens to me, Private Ikovle, you are in charge until I get back and if I don't return, you get everyone to the pick up location. You can read a map as good as any of us."

"I will do that, but you return, okay?"

"Are you crazy? There will be Americans all over that place. No, I will not go with you and you cannot order me, because you are a Private too." Pvt. Petrovna protested.

"No, I cannot order you, but I can shoot your arse if you do not show me where his body is and right now. I will kill you. Let us move."

At the fence they both stopped, saw no one on the tower or near it and there was something laying near the ladder. They both ran to the spot and in the faint moonlight, Olga saw her worst nightmare was true; Petr was dead and gone. His head and body were bloody and when she reached to find a pulse, she felt his cold skin. Beyond any doubt, Master Sergeant Petr Vova was dead; he was growing cold and had no pulse. She broke out crying and Private Petrovna said, "We have no time to cry over him now. The Americans will soon be here to see if they killed anyone when they fired. Come, and now! Please, we will die too if we do not leave right now." Finally, seeing lights nearing, Private Petrovna fled to the fence.

Some short time later, Olga heard the Americans talking, so she slipped her Bison off safety and waited. Seeing a good half dozen forms moving in the darkness, she fired a long burst and heard three screams. She then moved to a steel leg supporting the water tower and let go another long burst. She was rewarded with more screams and then an American yelled "Grenade," but she had no idea what the man was saying. When the grenade exploded, she took most of the blast in her head and chest. She felt the shrapnel burning many holes through her body and the pain was intense, so intense she fell to the ground and began screaming in pain. She was still screaming in pain minutes later when an American Captain neared her and fired two rounds into her head. Olga Makarovich was dead.

Private Petrovna showed up and told the others that Olga had died fighting the Americans and they all stood, and within a couple of minutes began moving to the spot on the map that Sergeant Vova had circled in red. It was near 1100 hours the next morning when they neared the pick up point, and they were tired.

Ikovle took the radio and said, "Hotel, this is Monsoon Three, over."

"Go Monsoon Three."

"We are at the pickup point and need to get a ride home."

"Roger that Monsoon. I have sent a helicopter to pick all of you up and to retrieve your dead and wounded, over."

"I have no casualties, Hotel. Both of my KIAs died in battle and bodies were not recovered. Our Master Sergeant and our radio operator, Private Olga Makarovich were killed, but the area was too hot to reach their bodies."

"Copy Monsoon, the bodies could not be recovered. It has been noted. The Helicopter will be there in twenty minutes, copy?"

"Uh, yes. We will be here. Monsoon Three out."

"You sound stupid on the radio." Private Evelina said and then smirked.

"Think you can do any better?" he asked, because at least he was trying.

"No, Ikovle, you are doing fine. She is just mad because you know what to do to get us back home. I would not have any idea what to do. I trust you." Private Georgievna said and meant it all because he'd only been in country 34 days.

Many long minutes later, "Monsoon Three, this is Save One, and I am a rescue helicopter here to pick you up, over."

Ikovle said, "Our landing zone is cold and green, I repeat, our LZ is green." Then he quickly remembered something, "Anifisa, toss a smoke grenade so the helicopter can see the wind direction, hurry."

"Copy, Monsoon, I see bright green smoke."

"That is us, Save One."

"I will land in a minute and I want all of you run to my left door in single file. Climb in the helicopter and listen to what my men in the cargo area tell you to do. I expect you to mind them as you would me, copy?"

"Copy and out."

Five minutes later they were all on the helicopter and as they relaxed, most had tears in their eyes, knowing they'd just left two good people behind —both dead. As the helicopter lifted from the ground, the pilot was heard saying, "Mad Dog, this is Save One and I am taking ground fire from the trees on my left."

"Copy, Save, and I am lining up to take that problem out."

"Roger that, and hit them running north to south, over and out."

A minute later the entire tree line erupted in a hot rolling flame.

As the helicopter gained altitude, every one of Petr's troops changed into hard men and women. They'd been left on their own and survived, and combat no longer terrified them because they'd seen the elephant.

Ikovle said a prayer of thanks as he stared at the napalm flames burning below him.

CHAPTER 22

"Alright people, you heard our orders. Green, you are my point and Wilkins, you bring up the rear. Move fast, but no jogging or running. Point, keep your eyes out for booby-traps. Let's go, and now!" The group exited by the power plant main gate and were soon lost to sight. Joy was leading the group and John was sure they'd be fine. He hated giving the job of leading the group to Joy, but she was a Lieutenant Colonel and was qualified to do the job.

They'd no sooner left than the explosives went up and the resulting fireball was grand. It twisted and rolled as it moved for the sky. A few secondary explosions were heard before John said to Carrier, "Let's move, and we'll head in the opposite direction of camp. We'll move southeast for 12 hours and then loop around and return to camp. Keep in mind, any Russian helicopters we see are probably using IR, so keep your poncho handy. By covering our bodies with a poncho, we won't show on their infrared radar screen. Now that only works for five minutes or less, but keep it in mind."

"I've done it before, but it's hard to lose them once they pick you up on the screen."

"Move out at a jog, and do it now." They both began a slow jog they could keep up all day, but both knew that they could trip a booby-trap at any time. However, their survival right now meant distance from the power plant.

An hour later, John heard the loud *whop-whop-whop* of a helicopter and said, "Get your poncho ready, because they're looking for us."

When John saw movement against the sky, he said, "Cover, now!"

Both crawled under their ponchos.

The chopper hovered over their location for a couple of minutes and then moved on. For over an hour they stayed in the spot circling, suspecting or knowing the two men were there. Every few minutes John and Carrier would be forced to remove the poncho and have it ready if the chopper neared again. If they kept the poncho on too long, heat would be clearly seen on the infrared screen as the poncho leaked the heat from the ends and sides.

"They're moving away from us." Carrier said as the chopper moved to the left about a quarter of a mile.

"Move out at a jog and move due south."

It was just before sunrise when Carrier stopped and whispered, "Do you smell wood smoke?"

John sniffed the air and said, "Yes, move toward it and we'll see who it might be."

A few minutes later, both men watched as a tanker crew broke camp and began loading their gear on a big Russian T-90S battle tank. While the tank required a crew of three, there were at least a dozen soldiers with the crew, so John suspected they were the tanks night time security.

I'd love to take this baby out, but I'm not foolish enough to attack a tank and about fifteen men with just the two of us, John thought as he nudged Carrier to move again. They slowly went around the Russians and once past them, they began to run again.

About an hour later, John was on point when they entered a grove of oak and hickory trees. John suddenly tripped on something, fell and then saw movement overhead in his peripheral vision. During his fall he lost his cowboy hat. He looked up to see a tree branch with a row of sharpened stakes on the limb, and his cowboy hat was stuck through the crown by a sharpened stake. He realized he'd tripped and saved his life because the limb had been pulled back, and by tripping on the thin fishing line, he'd tripped the trap. He was lucky he fell below the limb.

He reached up and removed his cowboy hat, cursing at the new hole in his Stetson.

"Damn, John, are you okay? When I saw that limb swing out, I knew for sure you were a dead man. I think we need to slow down now, we're miles from the power plant." Carrier said.

Giving a dry chuckle, which he did out of nervousness, John said, "I agree. Slow it down some and I want you to take the point, until my heartbeat gets back to normal."

"I'll do that. Now, let's move."

The rest of the day was uneventful, but they did run into more traps, which they marked and went well around. It was near dark when John asked, "Do you smell that?"

"What do you smell? I don't smell anything at all."

A voice, followed by laughter was heard, but the man was too far away to make the words out. Moving forward, the two men squatted in the brush and watched nine partisans making camp. John was about to call out to them when the man on the left began speaking in Russian. Two other men quickly spoke and the man shut up instantly. One man, obviously the leader said in English, "You will only speak English and you will speak no more Russian until we return to the base, understand, Private Lukovich?"

"I understand, Major. I forgot to speak English, sir."

"Pay more attention, and now move out a bit and place our mines for the night."

John pulled his knife and moved to where he'd meet Private Lukovich. The Russian had two mines that looked like copies of the American Claymore mines and he was unraveling the cord to the detonators as he moved. Since he was placing mines, he was not watching around him, but concentrating on doing his job properly. John moved behind the man, grabbed him and pulled him close, as he stuck him near his kidneys with his big 14 inch Damascus steel hunting knife. He knew with each plunge of the blade he was slicing the man's kidney to pieces. He had his hand over the Russian's mouth, but when he bit his fingers, John let go.

The Russian screamed loudly.

The men and women in camp went to ground, just as Carrier tossed a grenade among them. Everyone was so shocked by the scream they failed to noticed the grenade.

The explosion was loud in the early evening air and screams were heard immediately. Raising up, Carrier fired his Bison on automatic as he sprayed the camp with lead. John then tossed a second grenade and it exploded, bringing more screams. Then he joined Carrier in shooting the camp to hell and back. When he stopping shooting, the evening was suddenly eerily quiet.

"Colonel, want me to move forward and check them? I'll use caution and if one twitches, I'll shoot 'em again."

"I can do that, I'm closer, but keep me covered." John moved slowly toward the Russian camp. He held his Bison at the ready, only he soon learned the Russians were all dead. He called Carrier into the camp.

"We didn't need these fools out in the bush causing problems for the partisans. I wonder how many other English speaking units are out here?"

John looked at the man the Private had called sir, and he had taken a grenade fragment in the face, which ripped about half his skull off the back of his head as it exited. His blue eyes were open, but they were unseeing. The woman beside him had taken a bullet to the chest and another low and in the gut. She'd bled out quickly. He was used to seeing dead, and the sight didn't bother him in the least.

"One is too many. I have no idea, but I see a radio over there, so let me see if I can reach Headquarters with the thing. I should be able to reach them, since this unit was masquerading as partisans. Surely they have the radio frequencies we use."

"Hell, I don't know, but check the radio out."

John moved to the radio and said, "Copperhead, Copperhead, this is Cobra Two. Do you read me, Copperhead?"

"Uh, go, Two."

"My group has broken down into small units to return to our base. Two of us just killed ten Russians, but they were masquerading as an American Partisan unit. I heard them speaking perfect English."

"Uh, understand they were spies then. If we send a chopper, can you see the bodies are loaded and then return with them?"

Looking at Carrier, John said, "They want the bodies at Headquarters and they offer to give us a free ride home. Do we take it?"

"Hell yes, I'm tired of walking."

John almost broke out laughing, but said, "Roger that, we'll have the bodies in a field near here, and have the bird contact me when they are five minutes out, over."

"Copy and I'll pass that on to the aircraft commander. Copperhead, over and out."

"Understand, Copperhead. Cobra Two, over and out."

He placed the handset on the radio and said, "We need to stack all the Russian bodies in the field to our left. They are sending us a taxi for the trip back to base. I imagine they'll be sending a Chinese pilot and let's hope this one can speak English."

Thirty minutes later the radio came alive, "Cobra Two, this is Ranch One, over."

John was wearing the radio because while moving the bodies he didn't want to miss any contact.

He pulled the handset and replied, "Ranch One, Cobra Two, how can I help you?"

"Do you have the bodies ready for pick up?"

"Roger that, and we're ready to leave as well. So far we have a green LZ."

"Copy and understand your LZ is cold, over."

"Affirmative, Ranch One."

"Pop smoke, I have you visual." Ranch One said, and then John could hear the *whop-whop-whop* of a number of helicopters. Scanning the skies, he spotted two rescue aircraft and two Black Hawk attack helicopters. The attack helicopters suddenly moved lower and then went wider in a circle.

John popped a smoke grenade and then said, "I have bright orange smoke. Do you see my smoke, Ranch One?"

"Copy, Cobra, but I have blue smoke to your west."

"That is not me, repeat, that is not me. I am orange smoke, over."

"Ranch One to Eagle One, hit the blue smoke, over."

The chopper soon lined up, and as he approached the blue smoke, his Gatling guns were heard to fire and to John they always sounded like a big zipper being pulled down. Just before he pulled up, the Black Hawked fired two missiles into the trees.

Minutes later the rescue chopper landed in the field and the Russian bodies were quickly loaded. The aircraft took off and Ranch Two landed to load the two partisans. Both climbed into the cabin and quickly buckled in the seat-belts. It was then ground fire was heard striking the bird.

"Eagle One, Ranch Two, and I'm taking fire from my right side and from the trees."

"Copy, Ranch Two, and I'm rolling in hot now."

As the rescue crew and passengers watched, the Black Hawks struck the woods hard with missiles and Gatling guns. The ground fire quickly stopped.

"Thank you, Eagle, I can breath better now. Over."

"No problem Two and we're to escort you home. Over."

"Well now, that's nice to know, over and out."

The trip back to the base was uneventful, but the cool air in the cargo hold, where the passengers were seated, was enjoyed by all. Less than 30 minutes later the pilot said, "We've been cleared for a straight in approach and landing, so we'll have no wait. I expect to be on the ground in less than five minutes. Crew, prepare for landing."

John saw them fly over the base fence and then he could see the runway under them. Minutes later they slowly lowered, he felt them land and taxi. He then heard the difference in pitch when the engines were shut down. When the crew started unbuckling seatbelts so did John and Carrier.

"Sir, there will be a car and driver to pick you up in a couple of minutes. You're to be taken to the Base and Wing Commander, so you can give a detailed report of the spies you killed." the aircraft Commander said as he stepped from his seat and moved to the cargo area.

"Thank you, Captain." John said and then stepped from the chopper. He was glad to be safely home again.

Seeing a staff car approaching, John said, "Leroy, our ride is here. The commanders want to talk to us."

"So I heard. I'm glad we got a ride and didn't have to walk home this time. I need a shower, some good food, and a shot or two of good whiskey. I'm beat."

"Me too."

They walked to the car and the bored looking Airman asked, "Are you two a Private and a Colonel? I'm to pick up two men, but they didn't give me any names, sirs."

"Yep, it's us you want." John said.

"Please get in then, sir, they're in a hurry to see both of you. All I heard was something about spies. Are you two spies?"

"No, son, we're not. We're just two airborne infantrymen going to speak with our commanders. When Colonels want to see you, well, you go see them, right?"

"Yes, of course, sir."

"So take us there, then." Carrier said, tired of the young man's talking.

Ten minutes later they pulled up to the headquarters building and the Airman asked, "Do you two know where the conference room is?"

"I know," John said, "but Carrier has never been to the room. Not many Privates go to conference rooms."

Carrier chuckled and said, "Let's get this over, sir, I'm tired."

John said, "Hell, I'm 20 years older than you and you don't think I'm tired?"

They entered the building, were passed by security and then moved down the hall to the conference room. John told a pretty Lieutenant that they were there and the Commanders wanted to speak with them. She left and soon returned with two Full Colonels following her.

They all shook hands and then entered the room.

"I am Colonel Richard Dye, Wing Commander, and that man is Colonel Joe Morris, Base Commander. We had the two of you brought here because we understand you were the two who killed the Russians dressed as Americans. I was also informed you two heard them speaking Russian and English. Is all of this true?"

"Yes, sir. English was spoken and Russian too. We heard a Russian officer chew out a Private for speaking Russian and then he told him to only speak English. Colonel, they spoke without accents, and sounded like they were from the mid-west."

"Not good. Tell us the complete story and start before you hit the power plant, and tell us about that too."

When John finished, he said, "That's it, sirs. We climbed on the chopper and here we are."

Colonel Dye said, "We are running their prints and DNA through the Chinese computers. They have software that will track most of these men down, I think. We should know something by morning. They ran the man identified as the officer and discovered he was a Senior Lieutenant in Spetsnaz. One other man has been identified as an airborne Master Sergeant. Other information about both will soon be sent to us. Because of the importance of your power plant missions, which have had a lot of impact on the Russians, and the ten bodies brought in, we feel the two of you should be given a medal."

"So, as of this date, both of you are entitled to wear the Silver Star and, John, I know this is your fifth oak leaf cluster, but it will look good beside your Medal of Honor." Colonel Morris said.

John just nodded, but he didn't care about medals and such things. He didn't even care about being a Colonel, except it allowed him power to usually plan his own attacks and to help his troops get the supplies, food, and weapons they needed.

"We thank you for the medals, and I feel we were just doing our jobs. We wanted the Russian squad dead, because they might have caused countless deaths among the partisans. We both felt, but never spoke of it, we also needed to report it. How many other partisan units in the field are not really made up of Americans?"

"All they would have to do is kill an American team of partisans, take their gear and equipment, then listen to the radio. Most Radio operators write their call sign with grease pencil on the radio itself. They sometimes used 15 different names in a month. There is no way they can remember the names, so they write them down."

"So, by killing an American unit, they can become that unit if their English is good enough. I can't speak for all Partisans, but the English we heard in our group was better than most Americans, which could mean serious trouble within the organization, sir."

"Then we start calling teams in and check them against the fingerprints we have on file. Years ago a man named Captain Willy Williams, a prior Green Beret, started fingerprinting our troops. We now have the prints of every member of the resistance. When the units come in, we check their prints in the computer and verify they are who they claim to be. Those caught lying will be hanged or shot."

John said, "I knew Williams personally. He was my commander when I joined the resistance. He was one hell of a fine man, and intelligent, too."

"Well, then you are aware we fingerprint everyone."

"John," Colonel Dye added, "I also have the extreme pleasure of telling you that you have been chosen for the rank of General officer, effective the first day of next month. Due to your new rank, you will no longer go out into the field with your troops and will be responsible for all partisans in Missouri, Arkansas, and Oklahoma. That means, sir, in ten days your active combat days are over. Congratulations, John, it's well deserved, and keep in mind when they pin the Medal of Honor on you, it comes with an automatic promotion in grade. So, within six months of the war ending, you will be a Major or Lieutenant General." Both Dye and Morris stood at rigid attention as Dye grinned.

"What if I turn it down?"

"Are you crazy? John, they want your expertise in the bush to help plan workable attacks on our enemies and when the war ends, that doesn't mean the fighting is over. It just means we won't fight Russians. There are many different political groups in this country that want the power of running this nation, and some are dangerous for our people. We do not want socialists or communists to get in power or this country will fall again before it ever gets close to healing."

"That is something I've not thought about at all. I figured when the Russians left, we'd hold elections and Democrat or Republican would take office."

"It would be nice if that happened, but it won't. We figure two years or more of civil unrest and maybe even a civil war. Everyone wants the power. Even the Conservative, Bo Turner, is running for the power he'll have. However, his first task, or so he claims, is to apply the Constitution to our nation once more and to live by it. He wants a small Federal government and larger state governments. He has plenty of good ideas, but if he doesn't get into office, his ideas will become useless."

"Someone must bring this nation back together and keep us that way. Turner might be the man, I really don't know." John knew little of politics now.

"Oh, one other thing for both of you," Colonel Dye said, "and this is important; avoid our water. Don't drink it or even shower in or it will kill you as dead as hell. The Russians managed to slip the poison botulinum into our water system. Botulinum is one of the worlds top five poisons and it killed 63 of our people and made 175 sick. Some just washed their hands or took a shower using our water. Avoid it, and we have community showers at the Gym, and most places have portable showers outside the various organizations. Drink nothing but bottled water and you'll find fifty pint bottles in each of your rooms."

"I understand." John said.

"You may leave now, Colonel, and in your room, sir, you will find a message with your line number to General, five new uniforms for a General Officer, and a copy of what your pay would be, if we were being paid to fight."

CHAPTER 23

J ohn woke up, showered and shaved. He then removed a uniform from the closet and, putting it on, he stared at the image in the mirror and could not believe he was a Brigadier General today. Eight short years ago he was a discharged Staff Sergeant and owned a security and alarm business. These days he was still running a squad like a Sergeant but he had orders now, and his days of combat were over. He also knew he wasn't able, physically, to keep up much longer. Carrying a 60 pound pack was hard enough on a youngster, but for him it was simply too much these days. He was happy over his promotion and relieved in many ways that his days of combat were finished. At least by making General he could avoid combat and save his personal honor. He knew if he continued, he'd either not be able to keep up or he'd cost them lives trying to fight like he was 19 again. Most men 10 years younger than him were working in non-combat jobs supporting the resistance, or they were senior officers. He smiled in the mirror and thought, *This promotion may have very well saved my life.*

There was a knock on his door and when he swung it open, Joy stood there, wearing a Full Colonel's uniform.

"My, my, don't you look handsome all decked out as a General. Congratulations, sir, and may I be the first person to salute and kiss you?"

He bowed and then said, "By all means, my beautiful Colonel, I'll enjoy saluting you first. But, hurry, I'm to be at a meeting in thirty minutes."

She snapped to attention, gave him a sharp salute and said, "You'll be on time, sir. Your driver is out front waiting for you." He quickly returned her salute and then grinned. She leaned forward and kissed him deeply, moaning at his touch.

John broke the kiss and said, "Come and ride with me. You can wait until the meeting is over, I'll go by the package store and get us some beer and we can return here and party. It will be a very small party, because I've only invited you."

"What will my boss say?"

"Tell him the General had need of you and you always obey orders. Hey, wait a minute, you work for me!" He then broke out laughing.

Taking his arm, she said, "Come, or you really might be late for your first public appearance as a General."

"To me that wouldn't be a big shame. I don't feel comfortable in a dress uniform and I discovered a General can't wear a cowboy hat with his utility uniform either. I may not have any real power at all, huh?"

"Come on, lets get this over with, so I can come back with you and relax some. I need a cold beer, and some sleep is what I really need. Maybe later we can go to the officers club and have a decent meal for a change."

John laughed as they left the building.

The end, fini

BE SURE TO WATCH FOR THE FINAL

CONCLUDING VOLUME OF THIS SERIES,

MISSION OF PEACE, BOOK #10

THE FALL OF AMERICA:
BOOKS 1-3

Now available as audiobooks at iTunes, or at Audible.com.

ABOUT THE AUTHOR

W.R. Benton is the pen name for Gary Benton. The author has previously authored over 60 books of, fiction, non-fiction, action and adventure, and Southern humor. Such notable authors as, Matt Braun, Stephen Lodge, Don Bedell, and many others have endorsed his work. His survival book, *"Simple Survival, a Family Outdoors Guide,"* is a Silver Award Winner from the Military Writers Society of America.

His hobbies include hunting, camping, fishing, hiking, web design, cartooning, and reading. When he's not working, you'll usually find him, along with his wife, Melanie, in their RV at some remote location in the south. Mister Benton has an Associates Degree in Search and Rescue, Survival Operations, a Bachelors Degree in Occupational Safety and Health, and a Masters Degree in Counseling Psychology completed except for his thesis.

Mister Benton lives in Mississippi, with his wife, dogs, and cats, on an imaginary ranch with thousands of make-believe cows and horses.

www.facebook.com/wrbenton01

"**Simple Survival -** A Family Outdoors Guide" is more than a book—it is an outdoor resource bible that every family should have a copy of. This is one of those books that you should have in your camping bag along with the tent and other equipment. However, reading it

at home before you go off on some outdoor adventure would be a great help when potential situations happen.

Available at Amazon and other online bookstores

Impending Disasters - This helpful and comprehensive book covers most major disasters and how to stay safe if you decide to evacuate or stay. It has a section on prolonged survival, which will assist keeping you alive after the natural disaster has done its damage. Many

people die following natural disasters, from one mishap or another, but you can learn to survive.

Learn to deal with Tornadoes, ice storms, hurricane, flooding, blackouts, riots, and much more. Contains easy to understand information, and critical gear/equipment lists you will need.

Available at Amazon and other online bookstores

On a trip to the Lake Clark area of the Alaskan bush, a sudden arctic weather system forces down the small plane of Dr. Jim Wade, and his son David. Both have survived the crash, but not unscathed. Food, fire and shelter are all a priority. Following the death of his father, now it is up to David to figure out what to do next, and how to survive, on a remote Alaskan mountain—in winter!

This is a fictional story of survival, resilience and of the spirit to live. It is both authentic and accurate, having been written by a former Air Force life support survival instructor. For ages 10 and up

Both are available at Amazon and other online bookstores

Set adrift, a family of three are cast out to sea in a rubber raft, where they must find a way to conquer one terrifying tragedy after another or die in the process.

In this gripping story of survival everyone will be tested to their limits. Christian faith and hope are hallmarks of this tale that will touch your heart..

The NEW WORLD ORDER series
'A political-thriller uncomfortably close to today's headlines'

As the rich and elite of the world move to put the new world order in place across the globe, they understand they must move quickly. At times just as rich and exciting in content as real American history — this is a series of heroism, valor, patriotism, greed, blackmail, sex, traitors, and death, as normal day-to-day Americans make a valiant stand against the takeover.

Available at Amazon in both ebook and paperback

Mark of the Beast, Vol. 1 - the rich and elite move quickly to take complete control of the world and all governments. They attempt to place the whole world under the control of one leader, unidentified, with a totalitarian world government. They hope to have one world bank, one currency, one government, and they promise comfortable lives for all citizens of the world. Countries are invaded by UN troops and martial law is declared, a few weapons are gathered, food is suddenly strictly rationed, no cars, no gas, and no utilities for anyone who is not wealthy and a part of the New World Order.

California Invasion, Vol. 2 - In Volume 2 of the New World Order series, the Order shows a new U.S. President what will happen if he doesn't do their bidding. These shadowy puppet-masters will sacrifice anyone, even elites in the upper circles of power, and they prove that to the new President in vivid detail. Individual lives mean nothing when their objective is so close they can taste it.

COWBOYS AND ZOMBIES

A bone gnawing tale of western horror

Exhausted from his long vision quest, a young warrior falls prey to the lies of the Sioux demon "Double Face". He is tricked into accepting the gift of eternal life, but immortality comes at a terrible price; he will need to feast on the flesh of the living to survive and his bite will turn all men into his army of unspeakable undead creatures.

Available for the Kindle
..and in Paperback

THE TEACHER
FROM BOSTON

A new *Nate Grisham Tale*

Sheriff Thomas Holder is on a mission, bounty-hunting a wanted man. A former teacher from Boston has been accused of the rape of one of his female students and ten thousand dollars is well worth tracking him to the edge of the western frontier.

Falsely accused, the man seeks to disappear into the wilds of the Rockies mountains with some trappers he meets along the trail, but he doesn't realize that he is being pursued by a worthy foe. What he doesn't know is that native tribes seeking to stop the trappers from poaching in their lands will be as much of a danger to him as the bounty hunter. And it will culminate with a showdown from which only one man will walk away alive. Nate, Deacon, Cotton and One-Eyed Jack are all here in the latest installment of the *Nate Grisham: Black Mountain Man* series.

Available in Paperback & ebook

America has Fallen: Book 1

James is a Sioux teenager living on a rural reservation, when the America he knew and loved collapses in a financial meltdown. Soon hyper-inflation and unemployment take their toll on every aspect of the national economy. The Federal government falters, then the state and then the local. Transportation networks grid to a halt and store shelves go empty. Things turned even uglier when there is no power for long parts of the day... then forever. Police, doctors, and trash collectors just stopped showing up for work when their paychecks were delayed too often, or stop being honored by banks.
Once friendly neighbors turn bitter rivals as vital resources vanish.

James takes it upon himself to look after his family, his disabled father, his mother and younger siblings, struggling everyday to provide something for them to eat. Later he take up the mission of protecting them from roving gangs of bandits looking to take what little his family has, or even to capture anyone young and strong so they can sell them to the highest bidder. James teams up with the remaining members of the reservations and together they lookout for their own, but late one night his neighbor appears at the door, his farm has fallen to outlaws. Now an army of thugs outfitted with state of the art weapons sits within striking distance of the James' home and he must choose, drive the invaders back at any cost, or take what they can carry and run?

Available in Paperback & ebook

TSUNAMI

Many will die, only a few will survive...the wrath of the waves are unstoppable.

When scientists discover that a large, previously unknown asteroid is on a collision course for Earth they immediately form a plan to intercept it and try to break it apart before it devastates the planet.

The mission is a long shot but unless they try something it's impact will surely kill millions by triggering super-tsunamis and mega-earthquakes on a massive scale. And weather disruptions afterwards may doom even more tens of thousands. Running may not be an option but getting farther inland from any coast could help your odds. This is the story of an ordinary family trying to survive an extraordinary world-changing event.

www.ModusOperandiPress.com

9 781944 476915